"Hello, Valetta.

She turned so slowly, her fear so palpable, that Lincoln was pained. He should have warned her, called ahead, not appeared so suddenly as to cause her the unpleasant shock of his unexpected arrival.

The way she stared, her long fingers curling on her daughter's shoulder… Was her recollection of him all that painful?

Lincoln. Valetta mouthed his name, but no sound came forth. The rush of years fell to the wayside, back to a time when she was young…and helplessly in love.

Not that he had ever known. So much older than she, Lincoln Cameron had never looked her way. He had been more brother than lover. Her heart had paid no attention then.

She prayed it would be more co-operative now.

Available in September 2008
from Mills & Boon®
Special Edition

Finding His Way Home

BARBARA GALE

MILLS & BOON®
Pure reading pleasure™

*First published in Great Britain 2008
by Harlequin Mills & Boon Limited,
Eton House, 18-24 Paradise Road, Richmond, Surrey TW9 1SR*

© Barbara Einstein 2007

ISBN: 978 0 263 86073 3

23-0908

*Harlequin Mills & Boon policy is to use papers that are
natural, renewable and recyclable products and made from
wood grown in sustainable forests. The logging and
manufacturing processes conform to the legal environmental
regulations of the country of origin.*

*Printed and bound in Spain
by Litografía Rosés S.A., Barcelona*

For Carly
Are we not like the two volumes of one book?
—Marceline Desbordes-Valmore

BARBARA GALE

is a native New Yorker. Married for thirty-five years, she and her husband divide their time between Brooklyn and Hobart, New York.

She loves to hear from readers and responds to all letters. Write to her at PO Box 150792, Brooklyn, NY 11215-0792, USA or visit her website at www.BarbaraGale.com.

Dear Reader,

Owning a cabin in rural New York, I spend many weekends walking country roads. From the dust of summer to the snowdrifts of winter, they never fail me with their beauty. I am often asked if I will ever move upstate permanently, a conversation I frequently have with my husband because the main focus of our lives is bounded by the concrete pavements of New York City. Talk about two ends of a spectrum!

I realise that people move all the time, that America is a Ferris wheel of change, our highways dotted with moving vans. But no matter the state, the city or town, moving from one place to another not only involves a change of venue, but can entail enormous sacrifice and loss. Writing about a wealthy, professional sophisticate who is asked to make this choice was the inevitable outcome of my own thoughtful walks in the woods.

Finding His Way Home is the story of one man's voyage of discovery. I hope the book gives you pause for thought, and helps in your own discovery that change can be painful, but not without its rewards.

Sincerely,

Barbara Gale

Prologue

Valetta emerged from the bathroom, swiping at her mouth with a terry cloth towel as she fell down onto the bed, not caring one jot if she woke her sleeping husband.

"Feeling better?" Jack asked with a drowsy smile, not bothering to open his eyes as he snaked a hand around his wife's thickened waist. Pulling Valetta close, he nuzzled her neck while she drew the covers to her chest and sighed.

"Do you think it's possible to be nauseous for the next nine months? I've heard that it happens."

"Val." He laughed, burrowing deeper into her side, his brown hair a shaggy swag across his handsome brow. "You're almost done with the second trimester, so it isn't going to be nine more months. Three more, actually, from what I remember learning in med school. Yeah, I'm pretty sure you only have three more months to go."

"What do you know?" she grumbled. "You're just a doctor."

"Yeah, but a good one." He smiled as he sent sleepy, warm kisses over her smooth, bare shoulder.

"And running late, Doctor Faraday," she said with a quick glance at the clock, "so don't get too involved."

"I already am *involved*," he murmured as he wrapped his legs around her thighs. "Feel that? *That's involved*."

Valetta smiled against his mouth as he tried to coax her to return his kisses. "Your patients will be lining up at the clinic in about an hour. Don't you think you should be there to greet them?"

"I can be a few minutes late. Everyone will understand if I say I got sidetracked!"

"You wouldn't!"

"Ten minutes should do it," he whispered wickedly against her ear.

"Ten minutes?" Valetta shrieked. "As in *slam, bam, thank you ma'am?*" But her hands were already sliding round his neck.

"Fifteen?" her husband asked, seeing how his mouthy kisses were beginning to take effect. "God, how I love you, Val," he breathed against her soft, downy cheek. "Shoot, honey, you can take twenty minutes, if you like."

The rest of Jack's words were lost as he tunneled his fingers through Valetta's copper curls and pressed his mouth to hers. The swish of linen sheets was the only sound in their bedroom for some time until the sighs of their mutual pleasure surfaced and they collapsed in a giggling heap. Too soon, Valetta felt her husband give her bottom a playful pat, felt cool air hit her as he pulled back the covers and scooted from bed.

"Mrs. Faraday, that was the best slam dunk I've had in…um…a day." Jack winked as he leaned across the bed to give his wife a quick kiss. "You can play basketball with me anytime."

"I'll file that invitation for future reference," she promised as she snuggled beneath the covers. "Meanwhile, should I make you some coffee?"

"Gee, would you?" he teased as he headed for the bathroom, knowing full well she wasn't going anywhere.

Valetta smiled as she heard the shower begin to run, knowing she would be in for a song. Moments later, she heard her husband begin to sing his favorite aria, "Il Pagliacci." Feeling the baby kick, she wondered whether it was a sign of enjoyment, or a complaint at the disturbance.

"Holy cow, look how late I am!" Jack laughed as he emerged minutes later, toweling his wet hair in a rush of steam.

Valetta peeked from the comfort of her toasty-warm blankets. It was pure theater to watch him rummage through the bureau drawer for a clean T-shirt, shove his long legs into a pair of gray cords, then knot a tie that had nothing to do with his outfit. Today he chose the one of Miss Piggy dancing with Kermit, because it was children's day at the clinic, and Jack knew it would make the kids laugh.

"Hey there, sleepyhead, are we still meeting the Carmichaels for dinner tonight?"

Sliding up against the pillows, Valetta stretched. "If you can manage it."

"I can manage it. I have a staff meeting around three, so unless there's an emergency, I should easily make it there by seven," he said, bending to give her a goodbye kiss.

The way her eyes twinkled, Jack knew that Valetta was thinking about the last time they made plans to meet. The night little Terry Muldrow interrupted their plans when he decided to sneak a ride on his dad's new chestnut, at the cost of a broken collarbone. "Kids do the darndest things." He grinned with a wiggle of his eyebrows.

"I can't wait to see."

"Well, at least you'll have a doctor in the house."

"What a relief to know! I would throw a pillow at you, but I'm too comfy to move."

"And I would crawl back into bed with you," Jack replied, his eyes warm as they lingered over his pretty wife, "but someone here has to put food on the table. You writers don't make all that much."

"You sound like a Neanderthal, Jack. *Marry me, sweetie, and I'll keep you in steak the rest of your life.*"

"Hey lady, that's a good deal these days, considering the economy." Shrugging into a well-worn tweed jacket, Jack checked his appearance one last time. "But since filet mignon is probably around twenty dollars a pound, princess, could we please stick to hamburgers until I pay off my student loans?"

"Better yet, how about tofu burgers? So much healthier, don't you think, Doc?"

"As a Neanderthal, I have my limitations," Jack protested as he grabbed his keys and wallet. "And a tofu burger is high on that list."

"About as high as your cholesterol?"

"There's nothing wrong with my cholesterol that would warrant a tofu burger!" he teased as he waved goodbye.

Jack's step was light as he took the stairs, his early-morning energy always astonishing to Valetta. She was the total opposite, in that way. She would much rather stay in bed the extra hour or two and linger late at the end of the day to finish her chores. Jack preferred to call it an early night and crawl into bed with a good murder mystery. It came as no surprise when he began reading Patricia Cornwall last summer, *for the second time.* Patiently, Jack had explained to his wife that not only was Cornwall a fabulous read, but that as a doctor, he was dying—no pun intended—to catch the heroine-doctor in a medical mistake. That he probably never would was unimportant. It was the journey that counted.

Oh, Jack, she sighed, a wifely, loving sigh of pained tolerance as she eyed the overflowing stack of books on the floor and made a mental note to buy him a bookcase for Father's Day.

"I love you!" she heard him call as he slammed shut the front door.

"Love you, too!"

Even though the bedroom windows were shut tight against the February cold, she could hear him start to warm up the car. The seven-year-old Ford needed the extra time. In her mind's eye, she saw him put the car into reverse and carefully back out of the driveway. He was meticulous about that, knowing that kids didn't always bother to watch as they raced down the road on their skateboards and bikes. Not that they'd be biking this cold April day, not after the snowstorm that had covered the area in four inches of white fluff, unexpected but not unheard of in the Adirondack region.

At seven in the morning, no one was about except the salt spreader. From the safety of her warm bed, she heard her husband shout out good morning to the driver, Ned Pickens, no doubt, the only person in Longacre who seemed to know how to attach the massive snowplow to the town pickup. Good old Ned Pickens, she thought as she fell back to sleep.

Valetta began her day pretty much as she had the last six months of a difficult pregnancy, but she hoped that since she'd made it this far, she and the baby could get through the rest without greater complications. One more month and they would be in the homestretch. It was her good fortune to be able to put her feet up, since Jack was a generous and caring husband. Not that they lived grandly or ever would. They had no aspirations that way. He was a country doctor, she was a country wife, and the arrangement suited them both. Even better, deeply in love, they were about to begin their family.

Valetta slept till almost ten and then enjoyed a leisurely bath. After a light breakfast, she booted up her PC. Unable to sit for long periods of time, but not wanting to feel a total slug, she had been determined to continue her freelance writing. Hence the article she had written the day before for a local newsy. Of necessity, she had cut down her hours drastically, but she was still proud of the money she was earning, even if it wasn't much. She thought, too, that Jack was secretly pleased to introduce his wife, *the writer,* as if she were on the verge of winning the Pulitzer prize. Darling Jack, she thought, with a rueful shake of her head.

Hey, Mrs. Faraday, how about a little less time mooning over Jack, and a little bit more for this article, she laughed to herself. No one was going to pay her to daydream about her husband.

The afternoon flew by and before Valetta knew, it was six-thirty and time to make the short drive into town. Longacre was one of the many small towns clustered along a narrow ridge of the Adirondack Mountains, a range once as high as the Himalayas. They lived on a dirt road just outside of town, so the trip wasn't all that far. Dragging on her boots, she slipped into her heavy sheepskin jacket and gathered up her belongings. The shiny new pickup parked on their driveway was Jack Faraday's one big splurge, his gift to Valetta. Safe as houses, Jack had insisted when he campaigned for the purchase, even though Valetta insisted they couldn't afford it. But Jack had argued—loudly—that she needed something trustworthy to drive. But what about him? He drove the mountains far more than she, on his rounds and during emergencies. But Jack had dug in his heels. This was one matter he wasn't going to negotiate. He didn't want to worry about his wife and child driving alone on the back roads. Valetta had capitulated, and given the way the roads were tonight, treacherous sheets of ice in spite of the morning's salting, she was glad of the heavy wheels beneath her.

She made the drive with ease, pulling up in front of Crater's Diner just in time to see her friends arrive. She slid from her truck and they entered the restaurant together, laughing and taking bets on how late Doc Jack would be.

Not tonight, Valetta grinned. *He'd promised.*

Oh, but hadn't she heard? There'd been a spinout on Route 10, a three-car pileup on some black ice, and serious injuries. *Very serious,* according to the radio announcer. Jack would have been called to attend, no question. He was the closest doctor available. Perhaps they'd better go ahead and order, Patty suggested as they settled into a booth. Valetta could order some hot soup for Jack, maybe the corn chowder, hot and sweet and creamy, just the way he liked it. It would be cold work out there on the road, patching up the injured, and he would appreciate the thought.

Jerome Crater's diner would have been a landmark restaurant in any other city. In Longacre, it was a combination restaurant, town hall and bully pulpit for anyone who had a mind to speak. Valetta enjoyed many dinners there, and many a conversation over a cup of coffee. Jerome Crater had a warm spot for the skinny redhead, as he liked to call Valetta, and treated her like the daughter he'd never had. The bottom line was Valetta was Phyla Imre's niece. Since Phyla had lived in Longacre her entire ninety years, right up until the day she died, Valetta had been gathered into the fold, no questions asked, even though she had only moved there a few years ago. The fact that she had stayed on after Phyla died, and chose to remain living in Phyla's house, also worked in her favor.

And then, marrying Jack Faraday, their favorite son! That was icing on the cake! The whole town had been invited to the wedding, and Jerome had even baked the cake, a frosted tower of lemon curd and vanilla icing that still had everyone talking. So, if the lady wanted to order an extra large serving of corn chowder for the absentee doctor, so be it. Jerome served it with nary a grumble in a covered tureen, to keep it warm until Jack arrived.

"Feeling the baby?" Jerome asked as he set the chowder down.

Valetta smiled patiently. Ever since Phyla died last

summer, Jerome had been acting like a mother hen, and the pregnancy had doubled his concern. "Everything's fine, Jerome," she promised.

"Just checking. Hey, I came up with a name you might be interested in. Sort of like a song."

Flicking his napkin onto his lap, Chuck Carmichael smiled. "You running a contest, Val?"

"Hush now, Chuck. Go on, Jerome, let's hear it. You've had some good ideas."

Sending Chuck a scornful look, Jerome made his announcement. "Mellie!" he said proudly.

"Mellie." Patty Carmichael ran the name around her tongue. "Mellie. Hmm, you know, Val, I kind of like it. It has a certain ring to it. Odd, though. Where'd you dig it up, Jerome?"

Valetta only half listened as Jerome and Chuck and Patty discussed this latest suggestion, busy as she was spreading a slice of Jerome's famous sourdough bread with half a pound of butter. These days, if she wasn't nauseous, she was hungry, but Jack said not to mind the calories, she was too skinny as it was, and she cheerfully took him at his word. She was buttering her second slice when the door swung wide, as wide as her radiant smile when she spotted a familiar man enter the diner, his black wool hat covered with new-fallen snow.

"Hey, Faraday," she called with a sigh of relief. "Over here."

Hood pulled low, his parka snow speckled, he looked like a veritable snowman. But standing at the diner door to shake free of the snow, he made no move to greet her. Something about the way his hands toyed with his hat…

Why, it wasn't Jack at all! It was Ned Pickens, his

eyes bloodshot and bleary. Carefully, quietly, Valetta placed her spoon on the table, cast her heavily lashed, gray eyes down and folded her hands. Ned's footsteps were heavy as he approached the booth, his long shadow enveloping her like a shroud. He was so close she could smell the wet wool of his parka, but steadfastly, she refused to meet his eyes. If she didn't, she would not have to listen to the terrible news she knew he had come to deliver. Something about an accident… black ice…Jack's car…

No, she thought, floating somewhere above the maelstrom, somewhere she would not have to listen to Ned's dreadful sobs, not have to measure a grief that would never know a yardstick, not hear the absolute silence of the diner, not hear the sound of time standing still.

Oh, Jack. This wasn't the way it was supposed to end. We had a story to tell, a child to raise, an old age to share.

Oh, Jack, she thought, the air suddenly stifling, her head whirling as the weight of her bleak future bore down on her, and bore her down.

Oh, Jack, I loved you so much!

Chapter One

Nine Years Later

He felt, as he turned the handle, that all things strange and wonderful lay behind the door. That by crossing the threshold, he would be leaving the familiar and true, begin marching down a road from which he would not return. So whimsical, and so unlike him, but he knew what he felt and it was uncomfortable, a faint prickling at the back of his neck that would not be ignored. Maybe it was the peremptory way he'd been summoned, but when he turned the brass handle, a thing he'd done a thousand times before, its carved impress seemed suddenly cold and oily beneath his palm.

The heavy, ornate mahogany door opened onto a blaze of sunlight that rendered him temporarily blind. He was used to that, too, and took a moment to adjust his eyes. He knew she did it on purpose, set her massive antique desk *just that way* against a bank of windows, to impress people, to send the not-so-subtle message that her visitor was entering holy ground. Hence her refusal to hang venetians, shades, or even a curtain, not even on the sunniest day, and it could be very sunny in Los Angeles. Even the air-conditioned penthouse floor of the Keane Tower, where the publisher of the world's largest newspaper, the *L.A. Connection,* presided, was not immune to the solar glare. But Alexis Keane was a stubborn woman.

When his eyes adjusted, he crossed the few yards to the desk where she was huddled, his footsteps muffled by the thick Aubusson carpet that spanned the room. Dwarfed by the huge stack of newspapers that were delivered every day, from every part of the country that counted, Alexis Keane appeared to be so involved in her reading that she didn't hear him enter. She liked to say that although she might not read every line, no one could fault her for not being on top of the news. But that was her job, the only thing she lived for, and she did it well, as everyone knew.

The sun blazing in through her huge picture window created the effect of a halo to enhance her even more. At least, he assumed, that's what she hoped. If only Alexis knew, he thought, as he coughed lightly, it made her look small and gnomelike. But damned if he was going to tell her. There were many things he would not tell her—had not told her—over the two decades they had worked together. And there were things she did not want him to tell her. There were moments when a person in her position needed to be able to say *I didn't know,* and he accommodated her.

Right now, though, the small, beady brown eyes he had tracked for twenty years suddenly seemed unfamiliar. They were wary when they had no reason to be. The world was quiet this morning—no battles, no earthquakes, no mysterious outbreak of disease—and everyone in the news business knew that sometimes no news really was good news, that sometimes it was all right for the newsroom to sit back and relax for a few hours. It wouldn't last. So he was surprised to detect the flash of worry on her face, fleeting and gone in an instant. But he was not mistaken. She paid him well not to make those sorts of mistakes.

"Lincoln."

Her greeting was curt, aimed at the chair he stood beside, rather than his face.

Lincoln Cameron sat, his legs hooked at the knees, his long body unsuited to even the largest leather conference chair.

"Alexis."

His salute was brief. He waited quietly while she shifted the newspapers into various sundry piles.

"You need a shave," she said, taking note of his heavy beard.

Lincoln rubbed his cheeks with his big, bony hand. "Then I guess it's five o'clock," he said with a faint smile.

She was buying time. Fine. He'd seen her do it before, when the news was bad. But her voice, gravelly and low, seemed to factor newly to his ears. He'd heard rumors…and had treated them as such. The office grapevine was a phenomenon to be scrupulously ignored, but suddenly he wondered if there wasn't some truth to the rumors. Now he was sitting there observing the sickly green hue of her skin, the sallow yellow tinge of her watery eyes as they avoided his, the simple fact that she did not rise to greet him when she was known for her impeccable manners.... He watched as she shook her head, amused as she looked him over.

"Another custom-made Armani?"

Lincoln glanced down at his dark blue suit, then back at his boss. "Did you really call me in to discuss my sartorial splendor?"

"Well, thank goodness you didn't tell me *I* was looking well," she snorted.

"Is something wrong, then?"

Alexis seemed to find his question amusing. "I'm one of the richest women in the world, and one of the most powerful. What could possibly be wrong?"

Hearing the telltale thread of anger beneath her words, he opted not to answer, but a chill foreboding traveled up his spine.

"And *you,*" she stabbed the air for emphasis with an exquisitely polished nail, "as my executive editor and one of the most powerful men in the newspaper industry, *you* would be the first to know, wouldn't you? I would hope so, in any case, since I'm the one who tutored you. Everything you are is because of me, isn't it, Lincoln? The White House reads every damned editorial you write, even the lousy ones, before we even go to press. And I damned well know you have the president's ear, since I myself gave him your private number."

Lincoln smiled—the deep lines carved along his gaunt cheeks *told* he was smiling—but his black eyes were cold. It was unusual for her to wave her flag. "I often wish you hadn't. That man calls me at the most ungodly hours."

Alexis smiled, knowing he was angry, and perversely pleased. "Puts pause to your private life, does he?" she chuckled, although Lincoln heard it transform into a cough.

"That I would not allow. But my sleep, now *that* is another matter. He is careless of such details," he replied with heavy irony.

"Perhaps, but enough of that. I called you in to talk about the rumors that are spreading." Alexis rose to her feet, or wished to, but unable to muster the strength, fell back in her chair. "The rumors are true. More than true."

Lincoln's black brow rose. "I don't listen to rumors. Why don't you tell me what I should know?"

"You don't listen to rumors?" Alexis mocked. "Aren't they your bread and butter?"

"Where people are concerned, rarely. And where the running of the paper is concerned, I look to the primary source."

"Good of you, but you're in the minority these days. In any case, it seems that cancer makes no distinctions," she announced with a harsh laugh.

"It's true, then?"

"Those rumors you never abide?" she smiled unevenly as a sharp stab of pain underscored her words. "Yes, well, they're true, all of them. All those wasted years exercising, eating all sorts of unspeakable green things, never smoking—not even breathing in second-hand smoke—and mortality laughs in my face. Ironic, don't you think?"

"Mortality?" Lincoln frowned, wishing she would not parry the question.

"It's pretty evident that when your doctor avoids

your eyes, the news isn't good. I had to force it from her. You don't seem surprised."

"You're wrong," Lincoln protested. "I'm shocked. I just don't know what to say. I'm not very good in this sort of situation but I'm sorry, Alexis, I really am."

"Lincoln Cameron, *sorry?* Now there's a rare moment," Alexis observed wryly. "Well, you may lose the pity, Mr. Cameron. I have no patience for that sort of thing."

Even at her most vulnerable, Alexis was insolent, but Lincoln simply nodded. "I'll do everything I can, of course. I'll go to Africa, in August, in your stead," he offered, stifling a sigh.

Alexis's laughter was dry. "Knowing how much you hate to travel, I appreciate the offer."

"A major drawback to this job."

"The only one?"

"I like to sleep in my own bed," Lincoln said with a shrug.

"Ah, yes, your nocturnal habits, again. Well, thanks, but I don't need you to go to take over my job, not just yet. What I do need is for you to run an errand of another sort that does mean giving up your fancy feather bed for a few days. Of course, it's up to you...."

"Just tell me what you want, and it will be done."

"I'm glad to hear that," she said, giving him a long look. "It's about my sister, Valetta."

Lincoln sat up quickly. The mention of Valetta Keane was one of the few things that could touch him. "Vallie? Is something wrong?"

"Absolutely not," she reassured him. "On the contrary, I want her to come home."

An imperceptible sigh of relief escaped Lincoln.

She was a runaway.

Alexis had immediately called in private detectives and soon made it known that her sister was safe. But as to the cause of their fight, she would not be specific. Lincoln figured—*of course*—there was a story to be had. Valetta had been a typical, melodramatic teenager, so there was *always* a story, and because of that, he had never listened closely to her complaints. Valetta's sudden departure was the price he paid for being inattentive.

Any further news of Valetta Keane was doled out by her sister grudgingly over the years, but he had missed the curly-haired beauty. Now, it seemed, he was being given the opportunity to make amends. "What happened to Vallie when Phyla died?"

"Oh, a little of this and a little of that," Alexis said vaguely. "She's fine, she's holding her own."

Alexis's sparse information was frustrating, but Lincoln didn't press the matter. The fact that he had never heard from Valetta was a cut that ran deeply. If he had been blindsided by the notion that the Keane sisters had thought of him as family, hadn't his heart been in the right place? How had they ignored that? The loss of their affection was a hard-won lesson he took to heart, and who could blame him? If his laughter died the night Valetta left, no one noticed. Now, a decade later, the idea of seeing Valetta was an awakening, a temptation that brought, if not quite a smile to his lips, certainly a faster beat to his heart. But mastering his feelings, Lincoln didn't ask any more questions. Instead, he unfolded his long legs and leaned forward, dangling his long hands between his knees. His five o'clock shadow made him seem even more threatening than his growl. "What happens if I persuade Val to return?"

Alexis's lips thinned with anger, but she framed her answer carefully. If Lincoln refused her, she would have nowhere else to turn. "There is no *if*. I intend to hand the reins of the *L.A. Connection* over to Valetta. As my sister, she is the logical choice."

Jolted, Lincoln jumped to his feet. "That's a ridiculous scheme, Alexis!"

The *L.A. Connection* was too influential for that to happen; he had given it too many years and won for it too many Pulitzers to idly stand by while it was managed—*mismanaged*—by an amateur. Even if Alexis was sick and probably not thinking straight, he couldn't help lashing out. Even if the woman sitting across from him had sacrificed as much blood and sweat as he had, he was so angry that his hands shook as he paced the room.

"I don't wonder you haven't called her. The *Connection* is a huge responsibility. Huge! But to hand it over to some fledgling girl! I am absolutely astonished! You have me at astonished, Alexis!"

Unused to being rebuffed, Alexis clenched her teeth. For goodness' sake, didn't the man understand that she had no choice? Apparently not, judging from his mocking, caustic words.

"And another thing. Has it never occurred to you that Valetta has her own life?"

"Oh, that she does," Alexis said quietly.

"Well, then, you understand my point. It's very likely that she won't take kindly to a disruption, not of this magnitude. She might even be married." Lincoln held his breath. "Is she?"

Alexis's answer was terse and to the point. "She is not."

Alexis said no more but it was enough for Linc, although he couldn't say why. Afraid to let her see the relief in his face, he crossed the room to stare across the city rooftops as he tried to regain his composure. Millions of people walking the streets below read the *L.A. Connection* every day, shared their coffee with *his* editorials, read columns written by reporters that *he* had personally groomed, traded their stock according to what *his* power brokers wrote. "What the bloody hell can she know about running a newspaper?" he muttered.

"Perhaps you should ask her. She may want your help."

"Such big plans!" he scoffed. "And supposing that Valetta does come home. Supposing she does take over the paper. What if she doesn't want my help? Have you considered that?"

"It will be up to you to see that she does. If she does, maybe we can talk about a partnership. What do you think? Would you be interested in a partnership with Valetta Keane?"

Lincoln's black brow was an angry furrow that matched the deep lines of his gaunt cheeks. "My, my, Alexis, you seem to have this all figured out very neatly."

"It's not that complicated when you think about it. I don't have that many options, but I won't allow the Keane *family* paper to die for the sake of a young girl's tantrum. Or perhaps you would prefer I did?" Alexis left off with a shrug, suddenly looking drained as she sank deeper into her leather chair.

Lincoln watched her implode but he was in no mood to be generous. Too much was at stake. "What about

Valetta?" he asked grimly. "You don't say what she's done with her life, but I'll bet the bank you've had her watched all these years."

Alexis smiled bitterly. "That's why you're my managing editor, Lincoln. Nothing escapes you. Well, guess what? Valetta started her own small-town paper about five years ago. She calls it *The Spectator.* Appropriate, don't you think? I suppose it's something in our genetic makeup. Printer's ink instead of blood, perhaps. Oh, her paper is nothing to speak of, call it a rough draft for the rest of her life, but she's been getting some very interesting notices lately, statewide. Not unimportant when the state happens to be New York. Still, it's given her enough practice for my purposes. I'm rather proud of her, actually."

"Then why don't you tell her? Why aren't you running this errand for yourself, Alexis? Why send me?"

Because she's ready for you.... And you're ready for her.

But Alexis didn't say that. Truth was a commodity, language her coin of choice, and she was not known for her generosity. She would say as much as she needed and not one word more. Her eyes fixed, she parried the truth. "To be honest, I'm too weak to travel, but she... she always had a soft spot for you."

Lincoln was unimpressed. "Come on, Alexis, she was just a baby last time I saw her, a boy-crazy high-school kid."

"Surely she's grown up in the last ten years. I would hope she's learned a few things on the way."

"About men?"

"About life, Lincoln." She sighed, although she

would have liked to scream for the fool Lincoln was being. For the fool he took her for, too, thinking she'd never known how he felt about Valetta. The truth was, he had been partially the cause of Valetta's abrupt departure ten years before, even if he didn't know it. Personally, she had always thought she had been more than generous, allowing Valetta to leave home. She could have stopped her, if she had really wanted. Found a way to force her to return home, if she had really wanted. Brought the brat home in bloody leg irons, if she had really wanted. *Except* for the one fly in the ointment: Valetta's colossal schoolgirl crush on Lincoln Cameron. It had blinded Valetta, consumed her as nothing Alexis had ever seen.

And Lincoln Cameron had been a potent mix, his handsome, scowling face in the news all the time—at a podium delivering a speech, at the helm of a sailboat, at a black-tie event with his arm around some starlet's shoulder. Valetta had kept an album full of Lincoln's exploits and pored over them, day and night. As a result of her infatuation her schoolwork began to falter, she moped around the house writing silly love letters to the one man on earth who didn't know she was alive. Lincoln Cameron's powerful figure loomed large on Valetta's limited horizon, and the fool hadn't even known it. Men!

Puppy love, Alexis had called it in a moment of acute frustration. Valetta hadn't appreciated that. Words were spoken. Unfortunate words that should not have been said by either sister. When Valetta bolted, Alexis had not stopped her, almost relieved to see the brat gone.

Valetta needed time to grow up; Alexis understood that. Recognizing that she wasn't going to be the one to help her sister, she gladly stepped aside for their aunt Phyla. Her mother's long-lost sister, the same aunt who, with her own two hands, had built herself a log cabin in the Adirondacks and had not left the mountains since. If Aunt Phyla could tame wild raccoons and live in the company of bears, surely she could tame a spirited teenager with raging hormones.

If Lincoln had had any opinions at the time, he had kept them to himself. Now, ten years later, watching him prowl her office like an elegant panther, rooting about her knickknacks, not understanding his discontent—or perhaps he did—perhaps she was reading him all wrong. Adjusting her sights, she allowed herself a mental shrug. If things hadn't turned out precisely as she had planned, there was still time. If Lincoln had been Valetta's first heartbreak, he was going to be her last love, if she, Alexis, had anything to say about it. And not a bad choice, she thought, as she watched him pace about. Yes, the time had come. Lucky you, Mr. Cameron.

Lucky Valetta.

Chapter Two

Lincoln had much to think about, flying out to Albany two days later. Mainly, that the unspoken subtext to his conversation with Alexis had been clear: *no Valetta, no partnership*. Oh, Alexis had been subtle, her touch light, but the message was in her jaundiced eyes, in her exhaustion, in her merciless request. She had no time to spare for the niceties. Her time was limited, her risk was great, and her revenge would be sweeping. No two ways about it. If he didn't bring home her recalcitrant sister, he would find himself out of a job, not a pleasant thought at his age. Forty was the witching season, and though his power was unconstrained, it would not be so again in his lifetime. There simply was no bigger newspaper in the country, and working anywhere else would be a step down. And what of the four thousand employees of Keane industries who depended on the paper for their livelihood? His responsibility was heavy. So when he landed at Albany International Airport, his first step was carefully—and firmly—placed on the tarmac.

Wisely, he opted to spend the night at an airport hotel and get a good night's sleep. He had a bit of a drive ahead of him along narrow mountain roads to a town so sleepy the hotel concierge had never heard of it. Well rested, he arrived in Longacre midafternoon, having only lost his way twice. Driving down Main Street, he noticed a winter's worth of snow had been bulldozed into a huge pile in the town square. Pristine and powdery, perfect for some serious sledding. No chance of pollution up here, he thought wryly, as he gazed at the mountains that towered in the distance.

Parking didn't seem to be a problem, either, he mused as he pulled up to Crater's Diner and the promise of a hot meal. As he opened the door, a bell jangled above his head to announce his arrival. The smell that greeted him was tantalizing. On the far side of the restaurant, an elderly man sat on a stool by the counter reading a paper, a walker parked behind him. His gray hair was a short frizzled crop, his weathered brown skin evidence of long years in the country. The rheumy glance he sent Lincoln from behind his wire-rimmed glasses was intelligent and alert.

"You've already missed breakfast, it's too early for dinner, and I don't usually serve lunch to passersby," he informed Lincoln crisply over the edge of his newspaper.

Lincoln was amused by the old man's sass. Vaguely, he wondered which paper he favored. Never more keenly did he feel how far he was from home than when the old man laid his paper on the counter and

Lincoln was able to read the banner. The *Schenectady Sun*. Oh, for the sweet smell of smog!

Beneath his thin, brown corduroy jacket, Lincoln beat back a shiver and shoved his cold hands into his pockets. Stupid, really, not to have taken the time to pack some warm clothes.

"Judging from your fancy clothes, I'd say you're not from Albany. They're great believers in L.L. Bean and Patagonia," he explained, staring hard at Lincoln's leather loafers. The old man smiled at Lincoln's clothes, from his silk tie down to his gabardine slacks, looking as if he doubted they even sold winter coats wherever this man came from.

Lincoln glanced down at his shoes and shrugged. "It was all I had. I just flew in from Los Angeles, a last-minute decision that didn't leave much time to pack." But Lincoln wasn't interested in talking fashion. "What *is* that wonderful aroma?"

"If it's Tuesday, it's Mulligan Stew," the old man explained as he gave Lincoln another quick going-over. "I follow a strict cooking schedule. Makes life easier, all around."

Lincoln savored the yeasty, warm smell of freshly baked bread as he glanced around the empty café. "Business must be good if you're turning away a customer."

The old man laughed—or cackled—Lincoln wasn't sure. "Ten customers a day, it's a windfall, hereabouts, son. But since these old bones don't let me move as fast as I used to, I cook according to the clock. *My clock*—and my customers respect that."

"All ten of them?" Lincoln asked with a smile.

"It's a small town," the old man snickered. "They

have no choice. Well, if you're really that hungry, I suppose I *could* scramble you up some eggs. That's my offer, take it or leave it, and don't go frowning at the idea of eggs, son. They're local, fresh laid."

"I wasn't frowning!" Lincoln said, but Jerome ignored his protest.

"I spent three years in France during the war. World War II. When I was young. That's where I learned to cook, so I know a lot about eggs. I even had me an *authentic* taste of *Hollandaisey* sauce—cooked by a real honest-to-goodness French mademoiselle, mind you. Way back when. When I was young. I can still recall the taste of it," he sighed. "My, but those French could cook."

"Well, then, if it's not too much trouble," Lincoln said, throwing a doubtful glance at the walker standing in the corner.

The old man followed his look and frowned. "That damned thing! I don't pay it no attention. It's just for show. I had a little back problem and they insisted I use that contraption."

"But you don't," Lincoln said, a statement that found grace with the old man.

"Got that right, sonny. I just keep it there to make the townsfolk happy."

"Well, then, eggs would be fine," Lincoln said politely. "Over easy, if you would."

But Lincoln was talking to the air. True to his word, the old man could walk just fine and had disappeared behind the kitchen's swinging door, leaving his sole customer to settle himself into a booth and be glad of eggs cooked any style.

The diner was straight from an Edward Hopper

painting, very fifties, long and narrow, its faded red-leather booths perpendicular to the long windows that looked out onto Main Street. But where the booths had seen better days, the walls were a freshly painted yellow. And while the diner's gray Formica counter was lined with old-fashioned chrome stools, scratched but still shiny, the linoleum that covered the floor had been worn thin by several decades' worth of footsteps. His chin settled on his fist, Lincoln gazed absently out onto Main Street, a hint of a smile in his eyes.

How could he help but smile, finding himself in a remote town glued to the side of a mountain? Who would have guessed that the editor in chief of the most prominent newspaper in the world would find himself stuck in a one-horse town in the middle of nowhere, looking for an heiress who didn't want to be found. It wasn't that he was a snob. No, not at all! It was just so out of character, so opposite to the way he normally did things. Any free time he had usually meant the rare opportunity for a quick sail on his catamaran. Shoveling snow was not what he did best, and when he skied, except for the occasional trip to Switzerland, he preferred to do it on water. And darned if it wasn't beginning to snow right that minute! Thank goodness he had rented a Jeep.

"So, you come looking for something?" the old man asked as he set a plate of bacon and eggs in front of Lincoln, moments later. "More likely *someone,*" he snorted. "Oh, don't look at me like that, sonny. One and one still makes two."

Too hungry to respond, Lincoln only nodded as he scooped up a forkful of eggs—cooked over lightly, just the way he liked them. Cautiously, he began to munch on a slice of bacon and found it so full of flavor, he wondered if it was home-smoked. And no supermarket ever sold such fresh sourdough bread as this.

The old man must have heard his stomach growl because he left Lincoln to eat in peace before he returned to refill Lincoln's coffee cup, gripping his own mug in his gnarled fist as he sat down in the cane chair he had occupied when Lincoln first entered the diner.

"Got to admit, you were looking a bit peckish when you walked in. A man your size shouldn't go so long between meals."

"Peckish?" Lincoln smiled. "I haven't heard that word in years."

The old man leaned back in his creaky chair and shrugged. "There's nothing like an honest-to-goodness, home-grown, American-as-apple-pie hot meal to satisfy a man's belly. And the name's Crater, Jerome Crater."

Lincoln nodded. "Glad to make your acquaintance, Mr. Crater."

"Jerome. Everyone round here calls me Jerome."

"Jerome, then. I'm Lincoln Cameron."

"Now there's a fine, strong name, if ever I heard. Can I call you Mr. Lincoln?" Jerome laughed.

"Why not?" Lincoln shrugged as he sipped his coffee. "Everyone else does. In any case, what makes you think I'm looking for someone?"

The old man scratched his grizzled head. "Being as how there hasn't been a stranger here since last summer, and it's February, and you're miles from the nearest ski resort, and you just flew in from California—on short notice, I think you said—"

"Whoa, okay, you got me! I guess I was an easy mark. When I—"

Whatever else Lincoln was going to say was inter-rupted as the diner door swung wide with a loud bang, and a tiny hurricane rushed in on a wave of frigid air. Stomping red boots free of snow, the little boy held the door open for a dog to follow, the nastiest, scruffiest-looking yellow-haired mutt Lincoln had ever had the misfortune to set eyes upon. The panting creature took three careful steps into the diner, halted and settled on his rump, his revolting wet, pink tongue dangling as he stared adoringly at his master. Watching the child's every move, the creature was apparently awaiting some private signal known only to them. Lincoln was thoroughly disgusted, and Jerome Crater seemed to be, also.

"Hell's bells, little one, do you always have to enter the place like a tornado?" he growled, shuffling to his feet.

"Oh, Jerome," the child sighed soulfully, "there are no tornadoes in the Adirondacks! Mrs. Gerard said so."

"I don't care what that blamed teacher of yours told you," Jerome retorted, his arthritic finger pointed at the miniature firebrand. "I know what I see, and what I see right this minute is a little pack rat racing around like a regular whirligig, I do! And make sure that infernal mongrel don't move one dratted inch from that mat or else out he goes, and no second chances like last time! If someone slips and breaks their neck, I don't want no lawsuit because that mutt brought in the snow!"

"He *is* on the mat, Jerome!" the child protested, righteously indignant.

His mistake, Lincoln realized, embarrassed by his error. For when the child removed her hat and he could see a face more clearly, Lincoln realized that she was a little girl, all of ten, maybe younger.

Her head a gleaming hood of copper curls, he was put in mind of a young Shirley Temple, although this child was not half so artful. Her hair was cut in such a choppy, careless way he wondered if it ever knew the hand of a professional hairdresser, but he admitted that he was used to the overly polished look of California. This was rural New York, very different territory. If he was in doubt where he was, her ragtag outfit was even more confirmation. Her blue jeans worked overtime with a purple blouse, red sweater, green socks and a lavender headband. Still, the quality of her sweater seemed fine, and her boots sported a logo that read L.L. Bean. Bachelor that he was, with no insight into children whatsoever, a sudden flash of intuition told him that the little minx probably picked out her own outfits and would balk at the idea of walking into a beauty parlor.

And the little minx was apparently familiar with Jerome's cranky temper because she ignored his threat for one of her own.

"Mom's coming, Jerome," Lincoln heard her whisper loudly, "and Castor wants you to know that if the cake isn't ready he's going to—" the little girl left off, apparently unable to recall the dire punishment that awaited Jerome, but it didn't seem to faze her one bit. Lincoln was taken by the radiant purity of her sudden smile and the mischievous delight in her wide brown eyes. "I forgot exactly what he said but I think it's going to be *terrible!*"

"Now you listen to me, young miss," Jerome snickered, "and don't go flashing those dimples at me. I said that cake would be ready on time and Castor has no call to threaten a poor, defenseless old man when it ain't gonna make me go no faster!"

Wincing, Lincoln sent a silent prayer of apology to the god of diction. And marveled at the *defenseless old man* part. No one he had met in ages seemed less defenseless than this old geezer!

"I was just setting it to cool when this gentleman here stumbled in, starving and in dire need of sustenance. I had already whipped up the frosting. Yes, yes, vanilla. That's what Pollux told me, wasn't it?"

Castor and Pollux? Lincoln was enchanted.

"Hell's bells, I never saw such a fuss about a birthday cake," Jerome grumbled as he stooped to retrieve the little girl's scarf.

"Oh, Jerome, I was just making sure," the little girl promised, planting a kiss on the old man's leathery cheek. "Vanilla is my favorite!"

"Sure it is," Jerome snorted. "And if I'd made chocolate you would say the same thing!"

Catching Lincoln's eye, he winked. "Meet the town princess," Jerome said to Lincoln by way of introduction.

"Royalty resides here?" Lincoln asked as he sent the child a smile.

"As near as," Jerome swore as he folded the girl's scarf and handed it to her. "This here is Mellie."

"Who are you?" Mellie asked bluntly, as she stuffed the scarf into the sleeve of her jacket. Just shy of four feet, her frown was more intimidating than her stance.

Lincoln was impressed with her feisty presence, and he was used to real royalty. "I'm just a traveler passing through. My name is Lincoln Cameron."

"Like President Lincoln?"

"Exactly, but no relation."

In silence, Mellie turned to Jerome.

"He's safe, sugar," Jerome assured her.

"Your grandfather's excellent coffee kept me linger-ing," Lincoln told the little girl.

"She's not my granddaughter," Jerome corrected him, but Lincoln could see that he was pleased with the mistake.

"But she might be?"

"Close enough," Jerome allowed, his adoring eyes fastened on the little girl. "As for the coffee, I don't know if *excellent* is the correct word, but I do make sure it's always fresh made and hot. Mellie's mama stops by for a cup every morning on her way to work."

How cooperative. Lincoln would have liked to ask more, but there was no time. The door had swung wide again and brought in a gust of cold air. He supposed the dinner hour was fast approaching, and a glance at his watch told him this was true. *The mother,* Lincoln guessed, as a tall, slender bundle of blue muffler, green parka and red gloves rushed in, her shoulders dusted with the fresh fall of snow. It was easy to see where Mellie got her fashion sense.

"Mellie, sweetie," she said, stomping her boots clean. "I asked you not to rush ahead. I was worried you would fall."

"Oh, Mom, I'm—"

"I know! I know! You're a big girl!" her mother finished with a light melodious laugh that made the hair on Lincoln's neck rise. As she tugged free her hat, her hair spilled forth, its short style falling across her brow. But whereas her daughter was blessed with red curls, this woman's hair was a sheet of white silk, a pure platinum white that looked so natural he felt sure it had never known a bottle.

Side by side, their resemblance was unmistakable. But whereas the little girl was adorable, the mother was breathtaking. Beyond her shocking white hair, her tall, lithe figure was a slender reed of colorful wools and scarves. Her gray eyes were so luminous they seemed to glow as they gazed fondly at her daughter, her smile so bewitching she put Lincoln in mind of an angel.

But she always had. Lincoln felt an ineffable sadness at the years that had come and gone.

"Hello, Valetta," he said softly.

The woman's hand, hovering over her young daughter's shoulder, was suddenly still. That voice…so familiar…no, beyond that… Unmistakable.

She turned slowly, her fear so palpable that Lincoln was pained. He should have warned her, called ahead, not appeared so suddenly as to cause her the unpleasant shock of his arrival. The way she stared, her long fingers curling on her daughter's thin shoulder… Was her recollection of him all that painful?

Linc. Valetta mouthed his name but no sound came forth. The rush of years turned back to a time when she was young…and helplessly in love with this man. Not that he had ever known. Linc Cameron had never looked her way. He had been more interested in playing her big brother than her lover. Not that her heart had ever paid any attention. It seemed that time had not, either. The lines of his craggy face were deeper; gray hair teased his temple, but the years had been kind to him. He was still an arresting figure. *She* was the one who had changed, and she was surprised he had recognized her.

Linc, why have you come here?

Her eyes filled with tears, Valetta was unable to ask

the question out loud but it was just as well, because she was absolutely sure he had no explanation that would suit her.

Go, Linc, leave now. You can see for yourself that you don't belong here.

She shouted the silent plea, sure he could hear if he wanted.

I've made my life. My salvation is here, wrapped in this tiny bundle of red wool. Valetta glanced down at her daughter, pulling her closer, almost as if to shield her from his sight.

It was Jerome, alert to the tempest brewing, who saved the moment. Curious, protective and polite all at the same time, he observed the guarded looks on the faces of both Lincoln and Valetta with amusement born of old age and experience.

"Guess you found what you were looking for," he said as he removed Lincoln's cup. Too bad the stranger didn't look too happy about it. Too bad Valetta didn't, either.

Chapter Three

At precisely five o'clock, on a brutally cold winter's night, in a small town perched on the edge of the Adirondack Mountains, Crater's Diner was suddenly a revolving door of hungry, weary customers all wanting the blue plate special. The diner became a low thrum of voices recapping the day, making plans for the weekend, arguing good-naturedly over who was going to drive the ski team to Plattsburg for the state finals, figuring out who was going to coach the soccer team next spring. While the adults sorted out their schedules, their kids sat quietly hunched over their schoolbooks, getting a start on their homework while they waited for their dinner.

In the midst of all this, Valetta and Lincoln stood suspended in time, unheeding while the world rushed past them. Ten years and a thousand *what-ifs* fell by the wayside as the past merged with the present. But there was no time to talk, to salute each other with meaningless words while they recovered their composure. Mellie's tug on her mother's sweater called them back to earth. "Come on, Mom, let's go sit down! I'm starved!"

Valetta forced a smile. "You're always hungry, sweetie. Go check on Yellow and then we'll see what Jerome has for dinner."

"It's Tuesday, Mom! It's Mulligan Stew!"

"Please, do as I say, Mellie." Valetta watched as her daughter skipped over to her dog and whispered in his ear. She heard Lincoln whisper, too.

"I'm sorry, Valetta, I didn't think to warn you I was coming. It was inconsiderate of me. I can see that my appearance has come as a shock."

"To say the least."

Lincoln could see that she was troubled, but so was he. "That little girl comes as a big shock to me. I'm talking about Mellie," he explained to her confused look. "She's adorable."

Valetta was surprised. "You mean, you didn't know? Alexis never told you?"

"Valetta, I had no idea you were even married," Lincoln said quietly. "Alexis never said a word."

"I…I'm…"

"Okay, I'm back," Mellie piped up as she returned from her errand. "Yellow promised to stay put," she announced over her shoulder as she marched down the aisle and flung her backpack in a booth.

"May I join you?" Lincoln asked politely.

Valetta hesitated, unsure what to do. He hadn't flown three thousand miles to sit down at a counter. Come to think of it, why had he come? "Is Alexis—"

"Alexis is fine," he assured her quickly.

Relieved, Valetta's reluctant nod was a forced concession. She led the way to the booth, glad that Mellie had chosen one at the back of the diner, just in case the conversation got out of hand. Not that she would ever allow that to happen, not with Mellie present. Not that the Lincoln Cameron she remembered would ever be so crass, but conversations had a way of getting out of control.

Judging from the way Valetta's eyes darted nervously about, Lincoln knew that she was upset. It was easy to read, too, in her stiff spine as he followed her down the narrow aisle, although she greeted everyone politely. He guessed that she and her daughter were regulars, that eating in the diner was a habit, maybe for the whole town, the way the booths had filled up. There wasn't even a seat available at the counter. Jerome Crater served more than ten customers! Judging from the platters emerging from the kitchen, chunks of beef sitting in a thick steaming puddle of brown gravy, surrounded by potatoes and dotted with barley, Lincoln thought it was probably a wise choice. Very few people had time to cook like *that* anymore. The aroma alone made his mouth water, and he had just had lunch!

Mellie was surprised when Lincoln slid into their booth, but Valetta covered her daughter's hand and quickly introduced them. "Mellie, sweetie, this is Mr. Lincoln Cameron. He's an old family friend."

Mellie's assessment of the stranger was swift and concise. "We already met. And you don't look that old—you look like a pirate."

"Mellie!"

"No, don't," Lincoln stopped Valetta, stroking his five o'clock shadow. "You know what, Miss Mellie? So many people have told me that, I am beginning to wonder if maybe I was, in a past life."

"Hey, we learned all about that in school. *Re-in-car-na-tion,* my teacher called it. Do you really believe in that kind of stuff?" Mellie asked, squinting up at Lincoln.

"Reincarnation? Not really, but like I said, sometimes I wonder. How about you?"

Mellie thought about it. "No, I don't think so, either. But maybe."

Lincoln nodded. "Smart girl. Always cover your bases."

Mellie shrugged as she began to dig through her backpack, apparently unconcerned that she didn't get his meaning. Lincoln watched as all manner of things began to appear on the table: a battered pink Barbie pencil box; two nubby erasers; a pink pencil sharpener; dirty tissues; clean tissues; and a battered box of cherry cough drops. The tools of the trade, he mused. Amused to notice, too, that although Mellie was busy setting herself up for some serious coloring, she had not lost sight of their guest.

"How come you know my mom?"

"I live in California."

Mellie was impressed. "Mom, you knew Mr. Cameron when you lived in California?"

Valetta sighed for the questions that were about to come fast and furious. "Yes, California," she said vaguely.

"Oh, Mr. Cameron, do you know my Aunt 'Lexis? She lives in California, too. Right, Mom?"

Lincoln was relieved to hear that Valetta had not entirely hidden her past from her child. It made his job easier. "As a matter of fact, yes, I do know your aunt. Quite well, actually."

Valetta paled. So, she thought, things had not changed all that much. But Mellie gave her no time to think. "My mom told me that my aunt lives in a castle, so she must be rich. I've never met her, but if she lives in a castle, she must be rich as Crustus."

"As rich as *Croesus,* Mellie, not Crustus. And it's not good manners to talk about someone else's money." Valetta's swift warning glance told Lincoln that Mellie was ignorant of her mother's share in that wealth. His faint nod told her that he understood.

"Well, okay. But since Croesus was a king, does that make my aunt a queen? Because I would like to be a princess," Mellie declared, as she opened a huge box of crayons. "Would *that* make me a princess?"

Lincoln liked how Mellie ignored the correction for the importance of the idea. "She's definitely not a queen!" His lips twitched, but outright laughter would not do, he knew. He was saved by a young man with purple hair and an earring arriving at their booth with a basket of rolls and silverware.

"'Evening, Mrs. Faraday, Mellie. Sir." Carefully, the boy set the bread on the table. "Look out, Mellie, here comes your knife and fork."

Valetta shifted her daughter's coloring book although Mellie held fast to her precious box of crayons. "Good evening, Cory. This is Mr. Cameron, an old family friend. He'll be joining us for dinner."

"I figured," Cory said, as he laid the table for three. "Glad to meet you, sir." Solemnly, he took their order, although since there was only one dinner special on any given night, the choice was only out of politeness. Everyone in Longacre knew this. The real choice lay in what to drink. Mellie asked for a cherry Coke and

Valetta ordered an iced tea, no sugar. The young man waited patiently for Lincoln to decide, not surprised when he, too, opted for the iced tea.

"Sorry for the invasion of your privacy," Valetta said to Lincoln as Cory walked back toward the kitchen. "I thought I had better explain who you were before the rumors started. Everyone Cory serves tonight is going to ask."

Lincoln was amused. "Do you think that calling me an old family friend is sufficient to stop rumors from spreading?"

"Not really." Valetta smiled faintly. "It will be interesting to see who everyone decides you are, by the end of the night. It's like that child's game, Telephone."

"Oh, I love that game!" Mellie said, absorbing every word the adults spoke even as she colored a page of monkeys pink.

"I know you do, sweetie. Do you remember how to play, Lincoln? You whisper a sentence in the first person's ear and send it down the line until the last person repeats the sentence aloud—usually a totally garbled mess and complete corruption of the original."

"Something like my job," he said with a faint smile.

"Well, yes, that's true, isn't it?" Valetta agreed, unable to resist a small chuckle.

"Why? What do you do, Mr. Cameron?" Mellie wanted to know, all ears, although she continued her coloring.

"I'm a newspaper reporter."

"Like my mom?"

"Something like, or so I've heard. Alexis did tell me a little of what you've been up to," he said, answering Valetta's curious look.

Valetta shook her head, her white hair waving. "Don't let him fool you, Mellie. Mr. Cameron is a whole lot more than a reporter. Mr. Cameron runs the *L.A. Connection,* a really big newspaper out in California. He's the editor in chief."

"What does that mean?"

"It means I don't do the actual reporting, anymore, but I used to."

Mellie was confused. "Then what do you do?"

"The easy part. I boss the reporters around and go to luncheons and parties and accept awards," Lincoln explained. "Hey, that can be work, too." He laughed.

"Parties aren't work," Mellie said, disbelieving.

"I suppose that the parties you go to aren't, but the kind of parties I attend can sometimes be a good deal of labor."

Amazed, Mellie shook her head. "Maybe you should come to some of ours. My mom and I have great parties, especially pajama parties. They're the best. My mom bakes brownies and lets me and my friends build tents in the living room and stay up as late as we want, while she goes to sleep."

"I would be honored."

"Oh, but I forgot. You can't. They're for *girls only.*"

"Ah, well, another time, perhaps. When your parents have a grown-up party."

"We don't have that kind. I don't have a father," Mellie solemnly confided.

Now it was Lincoln's turn to be shocked, a fact which did not pass the young girl by. "If you're my mom's friend, how come you don't know that?"

"A very good question," Lincoln answered cautiously. "I guess your aunt Alexis neglected to tell me."

"Oh. Well, my dad's name was Jack Faraday and he

was a doctor and he died before I was born," the little girl offered, proud to impart such grown-up information.

Although his gentle words were directed at Mellie, Lincoln's eyes fastened on Valetta. "I didn't know. I'm sorry to hear that."

"I didn't know him," Mellie confessed. "He died in a car accident. That's why my mom has white hair. The minute he died, her hair turned white, and nobody knows why," she said with a dramatic shake of her head, "not even the doctors."

Lincoln looked at Valetta's silky white hair with something akin to sorrow. "It used to be a reddish-brown, a sort of coppery color, right?"

Uncomfortable under such scrutiny, Valetta would have liked to change the conversation, but Mellie was oblivious. "Yup! Just like mine," she said proudly. "But she's still pretty, don't you think?"

Lincoln looked directly into Valetta's gray eyes. "I have always thought so," he said quietly.

Blushing profusely, Valetta fumbled with the bread basket. "Lincoln, would you like a roll? They're fresh. Jerome bakes them every afternoon."

Valetta's voice was a low plea to change the topic and Lincoln nodded as he reached for the bread basket. He had so many questions, now that he realized how much Alexis had not told him, *and he would have answers.* But it didn't have to be right then.

Mulligan Stew was not his usual fare, but as Cory arrived with their plates, Lincoln decided that if it was hot, he wouldn't complain. Cautiously, he lifted his fork. "This looks pretty good," he said politely.

"Everyone says that Jerome is the best cook in Longacre," Mellie confided, setting aside her coloring book.

"That's because he's the only cook in Longacre." Valetta smiled as she speared a green pea.

"No, Mom, there's Randy's Café. Did you forget?"

"No, I didn't forget, Mellie, but with Randy's leg broken in two places, who knows when she'll reopen. Ordinarily, she takes the burden off Jerome serving all these people," Valetta explained to Lincoln. "Unfortunately, she fell last month, sledding with her youngest."

"And me! I was there, too!" Mellie said importantly. "I saw the whole thing and ran for help. She didn't even cry! *I* would have cried," she confided.

"Well, Jerome Crater's Mulligan Stew suits me just fine," Lincoln said over another forkful of beef. "This really is good, in fact, it's terrific! And I haven't had a Parker House roll in years. And here he was, talking as if he were some local yokel short-order cook. This meal makes him *a chef,* as far as I'm concerned. Now that I think about it, I wonder if he was making fun of me!"

"When was this?"

"When I arrived, this afternoon."

Valetta was amused. "Did you treat him like a local yokel? Because if you did—"

"I did nothing of the kind!" Lincoln said indignantly.

But privately, Valetta thought that could happen without Lincoln intending it. The way he talked, the way he held himself, the expensive clothes probably purchased on Rodeo Drive, perhaps even in Italy.

Valetta glanced across the table at the fine silk of his shirt. Yes, definitely handmade in Italy. It all bespoke a lifestyle that was alien to this small town.

And speaking of small towns, what was Lincoln doing in hers?

Chapter Four

"That was a terrific birthday cake Jerome baked for you, last night. Mr. Crater *is* something of a chef."

Having spent a truly uncomfortable night on Valetta's couch, Lincoln thought his effort at civility the next morning, as he sat at Valetta's kitchen table, was commendable. He just wished she thought so. Busy at the stove scrambling eggs, her muffled agreement was almost inaudible. He was undeterred. Awaiting his breakfast, he thought hard and fast, determined to break through her wall.

"And so many candles! What an old lady you are," he teased. "Thirty, was it? Good grief, where does the time go?"

The sour look Valetta sent Linc only made him smile. "And Castor and Pollux—I mean, your friends,

Ben and Andy—they seem like nice young men. And that Patty, I'll bet she's a real ball of fire."

"Hmm." Valetta ignored him for the flurried entrance of her daughter accompanied by her yellow dog and two black cats Linc hadn't noticed until that moment. Someone here likes animals, Lincoln thought, smiling at the birdcage tucked safely in the corner of the kitchen.

"Here's your lunch box, Mellie," he heard Valetta say as Mellie mumbled a sleepy good morning. "And here are your eggs. Toast is coming up in one minute."

Reaching for the salt shaker, Mellie glowered.

"Good morning," Lincoln greeted the little girl's chary stare. He guessed he would have felt the same way. It was one thing to meet and greet a stranger in a restaurant, but when *said stranger* turned up at your kitchen table the next morning…

Her first words proved him right. "How long are you staying?"

A good question. "A day or two, at most. I have business to discuss with your mother."

"Don't you like it here?" Mellie asked, switching gears abruptly.

"I do like it here, very much. It's very pretty, what little I've seen of Longacre. But I miss my own home, and my job, and they're both back in California. Have you ever been—"

"And guess what? I have one, too," Valetta said as she set a plate of toast on the table with a sharp clatter. She would *not* have Linc prying into their lives. Just because she was polite enough to offer him a place to stay did not give him special rights. "So enough talk. Pay attention to your breakfast, Mellie. You still have your chores to attend to, don't forget. I'll go get my things, and while I'm at it," she added, sending Lincoln a heated look, "I'll try to figure out a good time for us to talk."

"Chores?" Lincoln repeated as he watched Valetta leave the kitchen.

Mellie's face was a picture of long-suffering. "Change the cat water, fill their bowls with dry food, and refill the birdseed cup."

Lincoln glanced at the menagerie waiting patiently for their mistress. "May I help?"

"Better not," Mellie said, as she munched her toast. "Mom might get mad. She has this thing about being responsible." Finishing her toast, Mellie pushed back her chair and dashed to the cupboard where a big bag of cat kibble was stored, next to an even bigger bag of dog food. Carefully, she filled the animal bowls and put away the bags. Just as carefully, she scraped her plate and stored it in the dishwasher. That done, she solemnly informed Lincoln that she had to brush her teeth. Lincoln nodded into the air because she was already gone, passing her mother in the hall.

"Well, Linc," Valetta said, returning with her coat, "how are you going to spend the day? You're welcome to stay here, of course," she added, halfheartedly.

Your enthusiasm is overwhelming, Lincoln thought, amused at the uncertainty in her voice. "Alexis told me a little about your newspaper—she's very proud of your accomplishment. I would like to be able to tell her about it, firsthand…." If Valetta didn't believe him—and she didn't look as though she did—a little honey might go further than the vinegar of truth. "I'd love to get a close-up look for my own sake, too. If you didn't mind, of course."

Valetta most certainly did mind! No way was she going to spend the day with Lincoln Cameron peering over her shoulder. "Um…not a good idea," she said quickly. "Your big name…you would probably make everyone nervous," she added lamely.

Mostly you, Lincoln guessed. "You know, of course, that I am supremely qualified to help out."

"Too qualified," Valetta said, sending him a curious smile.

Linc shrugged. "It is what I do. You can't fault me for that."

"Your first love, *your only love,* I remember you used to say. Are you married, Linc? I didn't even think to ask. A wife and kids in your life?"

"Unmarried, no kids," Lincoln said briskly.

For the first time since Lincoln had arrived in Longacre, Valetta sensed a trace of discomfort in his voice. Even his smile seemed a bit forced, sort of lopsided. The look on his face suggested that *she* was now prying, so she did not press the issue.

"Linc, obviously I can't speak to you now. I have to get Mellie off to school, and then I must get to work. I have a deadline to meet. Let's plan to sit down this evening, after Mellie has gone to bed. Well, after dinner, her homework, a quick game of Scrabble and her bubble bath." She smiled helplessly. "Last night…my birthday party… Sorry, but we're a bit off schedule. If I had known you were coming…"

"Don't worry, if I have to stay the extra day or two, it's no big deal."

"I wouldn't dream of holding you up."

Lincoln smiled. After years surrounded by syco-phants, Valetta's honesty was refreshing. Why then, did he feel sad? "I get the picture, Vallie." He grew sadder still, when she winced at his use of her old nickname. "Don't worry about me. I can take care of myself."

"I never doubted it." Her reply came hard on the heels of Mellie's return, her coat buttoned unevenly, her hat crooked, her red scarf trailing on the floor. A little girl in definite need of help. "Oh, Mellie!"

"Allow me," Lincoln offered, surprising them both. Kneeling before Mellie, he made short shrift of the coat buttons, straightened her hat and knotted her scarf. Rocking back on his heels, he noticed Valetta staring. "For goodness sake, Vallie, I *do* know how to button a coat!"

Her throat dry, Valetta nodded. Feeling mischievous, Lincoln strolled to her side, took hold of *her* parka and politely held it up. But when he tried to do up her buttons, Valetta quickly stepped back. "Thanks," she smiled drily, "but I'm pretty sure I can manage."

Lincoln opened the front door with a smile of his own. "Have a good day, then, ladies. I'll be waiting here when you get home."

Valetta followed Mellie out into the snow and climbed into her battered truck, wondering what had just happened. But her wayward thoughts were forgotten listening to her truck screech as she tried to start it up. She had to turn it over three times before the engine caught, and then she had to warm it up a full five minutes before she dared to drive. Disgusted, she made a mental note to check out the automotive ads in next Sunday's paper. Enough was enough! The last time she had needed a car, Jack had materialized with this monster, but she always thought she would like to own something a little more *mommy friendly* and less of a gas guzzler, perhaps a Honda CRV. And while she was at it, she might even treat herself to a paved driveway, next summer. One you could really shovel clean in winter and that didn't boast rivulets of mud when the April sun finally melted the snow.

Listening to Mellie chatter as they drove into town, Valetta's list grew. Okay, so maybe it was time to get in a plumber to fix that leaky shower. And while she was at it, perhaps she should get Rico Suarez to finish painting the living room. As for that layer of dust…

Hey, Lincoln Cameron appears on the scene and suddenly she sees dust balls in every corner and wants to repave the driveway? Why was she worried about what *he* would think? He was only staying a day or two, until they had a chance to talk about whatever it was that brought him here.

Alexis sent him, no question! Her sister was trying to interfere with her life again. The last time, two years before, she had invited Mellie to come visit. It was summer vacation; Alexis would take her to Disneyland. Not trusting her sister, Valetta had politely declined. All she had to do was recall the time Alexis had offered to send Mellie to boarding school *if they would only move back West…* Alexis arguing that a girl with Mellie's background—*and future*—should have only the best. Valetta had laughed, but it hadn't taken long before they were enmeshed in another full-blown squabble. They didn't talk for at least a year after that little skirmish! Their relationship was colored with many such eruptions, but Valetta wanted Mellie's childhood to remain untainted by her birthright, which, as far as *she* was concerned, Mellie was going to be kept ignorant of for as long as possible.

But Alexis wanted Mellie. That was the crux of the matter, as Valetta saw it. With no children of her own, her sister was scheming to get her hands on Valetta's daughter. No doubt Alexis wanted to groom the heir to the Keane Empire, but Valetta was determined to keep Mellie's childhood simple. Foolish Alexis, sending Lincoln Cameron to do her dirty work! Well, he was welcome to try, but Valetta was wise to their tricks. Tonight, after Mellie was sleeping, she would hear Lincoln out, smile politely and send him on his way.

Lincoln stood at the window and watched as Valetta and Mellie drove off. He stood even longer, in a brown study as he watched the gathering clouds. Scanning the leaden, gray sky, he guessed it was going to snow. Although the ground was an icy patch of white, he didn't think he had actually seen a snowfall in some years. True, he was a sportsman, but his idea of fun was lying on a lounge chair by a pool, after a rough game of tennis. Skiing wasn't high on his list—hell, it wasn't even *on* his list!—unless it was over blue water. Alexis liked to say it addressed his holier-than-thou desire to *walk* on water. Nevertheless, he shied away from the Alps and had never even been to Switzerland, except to dine—once—in Zurich, on business.

Still, as he scanned the woods just beyond the narrow driveway, Lincoln allowed that it might not be such a bad thing to spend some time in New England. It might even be rather quaint to sip some cocoa and watch—from the safety of Valetta's snug little house, of course—the lacy, fat snowflakes catch in the tall pines or drift down to turn the lumpy, brown ground into a smooth, white blanket. Mellie probably adored the snow. Cute kid. No doubt she owned at least a half a dozen sleds, and he'd bet his last dollar Vallie was a pretty mean sledder, herself.

Vallie. She'd winced when he called her that. She probably hated to be reminded that she had any past beyond Longacre, much less one that included him. But she did, and he would claim it, even in the simple calling of her name.

And damned if she didn't have a past he was ignorant of!

A child!

A husband. Dead for years, if he understood Mellie correctly, in a terrible accident. But even so.

And Alexis had *never* said a word! Not a single blessed word in all the years Valetta had been gone—not a word about Valetta's marriage or the birth of her child, much less the death of her husband. How could Alexis have allowed her own sister to have borne such grief alone? As coldhearted as Lincoln could be, he would never have been so callous. He would have flown to her side, had he known.

And to allow Valetta to live in such squalor, he mused, as he studied the shabby kitchen while Mellie's cats jumped up on the counter and studied *him.* Well, not precisely squalor, Lincoln chided himself with a short laugh. But there was no hiding the fact that the once-rustic oak kitchen cabinets were battered, that the Formica table where they had shared their morning coffee was badly chipped, and the shiny vinyl-covered chairs were dull from overuse. And a certain little girl seemed very capable of adding to the disorder, if the crayons, coloring books, sticky tape and glitter bottles strewn across the kitchen counter were any indication.

Beyond that, though, he had to admit that the place did seem clean. The appliances might be dented but they did shine. And if the floor tiles were faded, nonetheless they seemed to have been recently waxed. No doubt kids *were* messy, he thought, as he left the kitchen, amused when Mellie's dog, Yellow, followed on his heels. Okay, you mangy dog, he thought with a smile. We can be friends for today. But you really do need a bath.

Lincoln knew it was a violation of every canon of good manners, but his curiosity was so strong that nothing was going to stop him. He couldn't resist—he wouldn't be human if he had—the opportunity to explore, if not the nooks and crannies of Valetta's home, the corners of her life. He'd been relieved by her invitation to stay in her home. He was on a hunt, not to ferret out the secrets hidden away in her bureau drawers—he wasn't dishonorable—but the display readily available to the observant eye, the treasures she had accrued that gave her life meaning, the mementos that defined her. He wanted a glimpse of her keepsakes and trophies and the pictures she had framed so that he could grasp the construct of her life.

The living room was in a similar state of shabbiness. Recently painted, but not quite finished, it was furnished with the green couch with which he was already familiar, a love seat he'd missed the first time, and a worn but colorful ottoman that had never matched the sofa in the first place. Dried flowers of no distinct bouquet filled a huge, dusty vase, an indifferent attempt at a potpourri. He suspected they were flora plucked during a long-forgotten country walk. Bookshelves filled to overflowing with dust-laden murder mysteries made the room seem more untidy than it was. Scatter rugs were just that—scattered, with no rhyme or reason—over an old pine floor that had unfortunately been painted. One rug seemed a dull gray, with a bit of brown thrown in for highlight, and the other a dull brown with a bit of red for color. Valetta's talents evidently did not run to decorating, he decided. It never occurred to him that Valetta's lack of free time could factor in.

On a battered upright piano tucked away in a far corner of the living room, the only part of the room that seemed dusted, Lincoln found what he was looking for: a vignette of framed pictures. Valetta, the beautiful bride, embracing her handsome groom; Jack mugging it up for the camera; Valetta caught unawares reading a book. Then, a later set of pictures: a vitally pregnant Val, Jack's brawny hand splayed tenderly across her swollen belly. It must have been taken just before he died. And her hair, her beautiful copper curls caught up in a topknot.

Crossing to the other side of the piano, he found a different set of pictures on display: the newborn Mellie swaddled in her unsmiling mother's arms; baby Mellie learning to walk, Valetta learning to smile again; the toddler at nursery school; mother and daughter at the beach. The absence of Jack stood out, her father long gone, as Mellie had said the night before, this spare collection of cellulose acetate all she knew of him.

And Valetta's hair was white.

Unable to resist the impulse, Lincoln turned back to the bridal pictures. How beautiful Vallie had been that day, her ivory veil a gauzy halo framing her delicate features. She positively glowed, Jack at her side, his hand possessively covering hers. A handsome young couple looking forward to their future, their happiness the yardstick of Valetta's loss. Linc turned away in a miserable pique of sorrow and jealousy—sorrow for Jack's death and Valetta's loss, jealousy for their past.

Overwhelmed by emotions he didn't understand, Linc was suddenly desperate for air. Moments later, every warm article of clothing he owned was on his body. Scrounging around in the hall closet, he came up with some oily black boots. Scarves and hats and gloves of every color lay in a basket by the door. Choosing red, a shade he never wore, he layered himself as best he could, knowing it was cold outside. Admiring his red mittens, he held open the door for Mangy Yellow—as he decided to secretly call Mellie's dog—and together they marched down the road.

At first, Lincoln set a slow pace. Shocked by the cold air, his frosty, white breath came in cold spurts and the tip of his nose felt raw straightaway. The bitter chill threatened to turn him back, but the sound of the snow crunching beneath his borrowed boots was strangely appealing. A long, thick branch made for an excellent walking stick, and he set a brisker pace for himself, knowing he would warm up if he did. In good shape, he began to enjoy the hike. Thrilled to be out and about at this unusual hour, Mangy Yellow yipped by his side, so excited that he was up and down the road long before Lincoln was halfway. As the tempo warmed him, Lincoln began to enjoy the deep silence of the countryside, the awesome pull of the woods, the faint chirp of the few birds that hadn't gone South. The tall pines that surrounded him were gray-green sentinels that rustled a discreet salutation to the stranger in their midst. The lightly falling flakes that stuck to his lashes were a gentle greeting and he discovered that—of all things!—he actually liked the feel of the cold ice as it brushed his cheeks.

At some point, his feet turned up the mountain and he began to explore the woods. It was a zigzag sort of effort because, although Mangy Yellow was a spirited companion who would have led him astray, Lincoln wanted to keep the road in view. The towering forest was a dramatic contrast to the gray stone cities and white-hot beaches he was used to, and he felt vaguely uncomfortable as he marched through the woods. They seemed ominous, their solitude unfamiliar and unsettling.

As he walked, his head began to fill with questions, a surprise because, in general, he was not given to introspection. Only now, as he gazed up at the pines and scanned the forest canopy, he wondered why he hadn't made more of the curveballs he'd been thrown in his life. He had rather enjoyed facing challenges, so why, then, had his life become so steady and safe and predictable? Were there no surprises left in store for him, no real excitement to be had beyond the making of a deadline? Here on the cold side of the planet, why did his brain begin to race with these thoughts? Disturbing his orderly life was something he would prefer not to do. But reaching out to scrape his mittened hand along the rough bark of a pine tree, he couldn't help wonder if this was the reason Valetta had refused to leave Longacre. Was the heady scent of pine that assailed his senses the reason Valetta declined to return to California, the real reason she'd remained in Longacre after her husband died? Did she feel—*know?*—that everything

Mellie needed was planted here along this country back road?

Another pause in his steps. Why had he *really* been sent to Longacre? Had Alexis come to realize that she was losing the battle to pry her sister from these shadowy woods? After so many fruitless battles, had Alexis come to recognize that the roots Valetta had set down in Longacre were not easily transplanted? As suddenly as the thought came, Lincoln knew he was right. He was just Alexis's pawn in a game she played with her sister. The question was, did Valetta know?

Depressed, he lost enthusiasm for his walk and headed back down to the road, Mangy Yellow trailing closely behind. When a truck pulled up, a moment later, Lincoln skirted the shoulder.

"Hey, buddy, need a lift?" the driver shouted from the cab of the battered pickup. About thirty, dressed in well-worn coveralls and a red check work shirt, his black beard shaggy, the driver presented a menacing appearance.

"No, thanks," Lincoln declined politely, "I have a companion." Mangy Yellow lifted his head alertly, almost as if he knew they were talking about him.

"No problem. That's Mellie Faraday's pup, if I'm not mistaken."

Taking a second look at the driver, Lincoln reconsidered the offer. "That he is."

"Come on up, boy!" he called to Yellow with a click of his tongue.

"Thanks," Lincoln said as he followed the dog, grateful for the blast of warm air that greeted him. "I forgot to save anything for the hike back. Lincoln Cameron, here."

"Oh, I know that!" The young man grinned as he stuck out his hand. "I'm Rico Suarez. I live down the road from Valetta and Mellie, about four miles past. But that's not why I know who you are," he said with a knowing smile.

Lincoln sighed as he fastened his seat belt. "I'm sure the word was out the minute I sat down to lunch at the diner. I'll bet everyone in Longacre knows how I take my coffee."

"Black, no sugar?" Rico laughed as he put his truck in Drive.

"Just drop me off at the Faradays', when you drive past," Lincoln requested, his mouth a wry grin. "I left my rental car parked there."

But Rico was of a mind to get friendly. A stranger in Longacre was exciting news. "Hey, Cameron, why don't you join me for breakfast? Lunch, actually, if we can persuade Jerome to make us something, seeing how it's coming on to noon."

Lincoln was about to speak when he heard the low, distant keen of a whistle.

"There you are," Rico said with satisfaction. "My inner clock speaks. That's the firehouse whistle. It goes off every day at noon to let the farmers know it's lunchtime. Although now that I think about it, most of them carry cell phones nowadays, so I guess it's more tradition than necessity. But look, if you come with me to Jerome's, you'll get to meet some of the locals."

"You mean some more of the locals. I was there last night, so they'll get to give me another looking over."

Rico laughed. "That, too. But hey, you look like a good sport, and we don't get too many visitors this time of year, so it's kind of exciting to have a stranger turn up. Breaks up the winter, if you know what I mean. I'll drive you back to the Faraday house later, I promise. I'm coming back this way."

Lincoln gave in with good grace. The rumble in his belly said it was a wise choice.

Chapter Five

Two hours, one tuna sandwich, a slab of apple crumb pie and three cups of coffee later, Rico dropped Lincoln back at Valetta's house, well fed and exhausted. For a small town, there had sure been a crowd at the diner, he thought as he lay down on Valetta's worn couch for a quick nap. But Rico had been right. He had introduced Lincoln to quite a few of the townspeople and discovered in the process just how much they all cared for Valetta and Mellie Faraday. Curiously, the idea reassured him.

That was his last thought before he nodded off. Next thing he knew, Mellie was standing beside him, blinking owlishly into his face, her candy breath tickling his cheek while Valetta stood beside her daughter, trying not to laugh.

"Had a hard day?" She grinned.

Lincoln blinked back, unable to speak for the oddest dream he had been having. He was reaching for Vallie, pulling her into his arms…

Quickly, he sat up and shook the sleep from his head. "What time is it? I haven't felt this tired in years."

"Then I guess dinner isn't ready," she said with a wry twist to her lips.

"Dinner?"

"Mellie was betting that you might have something waiting on the stove. Kids are always hungry, at least this one is. It's got something to do with growth hormones. Never mind." She sighed when she saw his look of confusion. "It's nothing you would know about. Anyway, I told her not to count on it. Tell the truth, Lincoln, when was the last time you actually turned on a stove?" When she saw his embarrassed grin, she laughed. "That's what I thought."

"Sorry, my dear, but your momma's right. Cooking is not one of my talents."

Mellie was flabbergasted. "You mean, you don't know how to cook?"

Lincoln was indignant. "I suppose I could, if I wanted."

"You could not!" Valetta grinned.

"I'm a very busy man, is all," he said, defensively. "Back home," he said to Mellie patiently, "I have all the right appliances, and an excellent housekeeper who gets paid a great deal of money to put them to good use. You have to understand, I often get home at ungodly hours, so Rita cooks for me."

"What's an *ungodly hour?*" Mellie wanted to know. "Does it mean that God is asleep?"

"No, honey, it means that everyone but me is

asleep! For instance, three o'clock in the morning is an ungodly hour."

Mellie was astonished. "You mean that you stay up until three o'clock in the morning? I'm not allowed to do that even during a sleepover!"

"Of course not, but sometimes there's an emergency."

"Are you a doctor?"

"I'm a newspaper man, remember?"

"But how could there be an emergency at a newspaper at three o'clock in the morning if everyone is sleeping?"

"You'd be surprised," Lincoln said sardonically.

"Mellie, honey, you're forgetting that there are different time zones all over the world."

"Precisely," Linc nodded. "That's why Rita is always there for me, ready to cook at a moment's notice, although sometimes, if I'm very late, she leaves something on the stove for me to heat up before she goes to bed."

"You mean she *lives* with you?"

"Yes, of course. She's a live-in housekeeper, so she has to live with me," Lincoln explained as he searched under the couch for his shoes.

"Are you and Rita married?"

"Goodness, no," Lincoln laughed as he retrieved a shoe. "Rita is old enough to be my mother. She has her own room and bath, four weeks' vacation, and all the food she can eat. Not to mention that she spends half her time in front of the television watching the soaps with her girlfriends while I'm at work. For goodness' sake, Valetta, haven't you brought this child up to the ways of the world?"

"Apparently not *your* world," Valetta chuckled as

she headed for the kitchen. "But you'll be glad to know she does just fine here in Longacre."

Thirty minutes later, the threesome was sitting at the kitchen table eating the juicy hamburgers Valetta had broiled, and French fries dusted with Cajun spice, just the way Mellie liked them.

"Oh, yes, I met him, too," Valetta heard him say as she got up to get more apple juice.

"Mom, Mr. Cameron says he met Ranger Davey at Jerome's this afternoon."

"You met Davey Hartwell?" Valetta asked, tensing as she returned to the table with the container.

"Rico introduced us. Is there something wrong with that?" he asked, sensing her apprehension.

"No, of course not," Valetta said quickly. "It's just…Davey and Rico, both in one day? You *have* been busy." Why she found this disconcerting she couldn't say, but she did.

"Mr. Hartwell is my favorite forest ranger," Mellie confessed, waving a dill pickle. "He comes to our school every spring and tells us about forest fires and how they get started and how not to—"

Over Mellie's meandering monologue, Valetta and Lincoln shared pointed looks, their tempers flared for reasons neither could articulate. If *she* had to say, Valetta *might* admit to a slight pique of jealousy at the way Lincoln was insinuating himself into her life. The way he had shown up in Longacre unannounced was bad enough, but now he was sleeping on her couch, joking with her daughter, making friends with her friends… And doing *nothing* to endear himself to *her*! One would have thought…

What would one have thought? Valetta asked herself

as she watched him tease Mellie, who seemed to hang on his every word. How handsome he still was? How her heart had beat a little faster when she discovered him in the diner the night before? How her hand burned at his slightest touch, even passing him his coffee this morning? How she longed to run her hand along his jaw and discover the bristly softness of his beard?

Oh, how she wished he would leave Longacre! She really did. Memories were surfacing far too quickly, one after another, recalling to mind the girlish longing that made up much of her history with this man. All one-sided, of course, and painful. Painful...but still compelling. *Compelling?* Was she *still* caught in the grip of her girlish fantasies? Did she still wonder how it might have been if she hadn't run away that rainy night? If she hadn't allowed Alexis to tarnish her friendship with Lincoln. If she hadn't met Jack...if she hadn't had Mellie...if she hadn't remained in Longacre. Would he have come to love her, as she had loved him, all those years ago?

Tell the truth, silly girl, didn't you remain in Longacre after Jack died, as much to avoid Lincoln as to create a home for Mellie?

Tell the truth, silly girl, aren't you still just a little bit in love with this man?

Neither said a word as they cleared the dishes while Mellie ran to get her homework. While Lincoln loaded the dishwasher—doing it wrong, Valetta was annoyed to see—and swiped down the counter—leaving crumbs, another irritation—Mellie returned with a pile of books and spread them across the kitchen table.

Watching their heads bent over Mellie's math book, Valetta's gleaming white hair brushing Mellie's red curls, listening to their gentle murmurs and soft laughter, Lincoln was overcome with a sentiment he dared not define. Escaping to the guest room Valetta had finally—reluctantly—offered him, he lay across the bed, his long legs extended beyond the bottom edge. He clasped his hands behind his head and mulled things over. If Lincoln was forced to admit to anything, he would have to say that he was insulted at the way Valetta rejected him at every turn. Unfortunately, her disregard didn't seem much of a check on his feelings for *her*. If there was one thing he knew, it was when he was attracted to a woman, but his disquiet at the notion knew no bounds. Feelings for a woman he hadn't seen in over a decade? He was incredulous at the idea. Confused and tired, he went to bed early, ignoring Mellie's shout an hour later, inviting him to join them for cookies and milk.

Feeling better rested for the good night's sleep on a real bed, Lincoln was the first one downstairs the next morning. Having mastered the workings of the coffeepot in a vast ten minutes, he had the coffee perking in no time, and had just begun a search for the cereal when Valetta joined him in the kitchen. Apprehensive, even so, she accepted the cup of coffee he handed her, grateful for anything hot.

"We were supposed to talk last night," she reminded him.

"Sorry, but I was overcome with jet lag." He could see the worry writ across her face—he would have to stay another night.

"But you napped on the couch earlier. You shouldn't have been so tired."

Lincoln shrugged. "I must be getting old."

"Sure, sure."

"No, really. The last time I flew, I think it was to Paris. Yes, Paris. It took me three days to get back on my feet. I almost had to cancel a meeting."

"Lincoln Cameron *cancel* a meeting?" Valetta snorted. "Now I know you're joking."

"I did say *almost*." Lincoln smiled. "But honestly, I was pretty tired. Today, though, I feel great."

"I can see that," Valetta said wryly. "Showered and shaved, and it's only seven-thirty."

"This is late for me. I'm usually at my office by five, and I'm reading news dispatches on the way in. But that's in Los Angeles. I figured you had a more modest schedule here. Not that I haven't already watched the news." He laughed. "Glad to see you have satellite TV."

"I must remember to send you the bill."

Lincoln smiled. "It *is* my job to be on top of the news," he explained. "Perhaps you'd like to trade stories sometime, seeing as how we're apparently in the same business?"

"Not quite," Valetta retorted as she began to make Mellie's lunch. There was no way she was going to let him cozy up to her.

But almost as if he could read her mind, Lincoln ignored her little dig. "I've decided to leave my car behind and hitch a ride into town with you and Mellie. To see the sights," he said lightly as he filled his own mug.

Valetta had skepticism written all over her face. "At seven-thirty in the morning? And besides, we have no sights!"

"That's what you think." Tasting the weak tepid brew, he almost choked. "Shoot, this coffee is *awful!*"

Spilling her coffee down the drain, Valetta smiled. "I

was trying to be polite, but I was right, you know absolutely nothing about cooking and it looks like you can't even boil water. If you clean the pot, I'll show you how to do it. You *do* know how to clean a coffeepot, don't you?"

Lincoln sent Valetta a look that was cutting. "I think I can manage."

"You can't blame me for asking."

"Listen, Valetta," he began softly. But whatever Lincoln was going to say was lost in the flurried entrance of Mellie, Mangy Yellow trailing closely behind. The routine was the same as the day before: breakfast, chores, book bags and lunch. They had no further chance to talk until Valetta had dropped Mellie at school.

"'Bye, sweetie."

"'Bye, Mom." With a quick kiss to her mother's cheek, Mellie ran across the basketball court, through its broken fence and up the school steps, joining some of her friends midway.

"And where do *you* want to be dropped?" she asked Lincoln as she waved to Mellie. "It's close to nine and I have to get to work."

"I'm meeting Rico, so Jerome's diner will be fine, thanks, although a car dealership might be more appropriate," he said flatly, unnerved by the strange sounds that had been coming from Valetta's truck as they drove to town.

Meeting Rico? Her lips pursed, Valetta said nothing as she pulled up to the diner. *That's* why he didn't need to use his own car; he already knew how he was getting back to the house. There he was again, trying to befriend her friends, worming his way into her life, and she had no idea why. "Lincoln, we must talk this evening."

Lincoln appeared not to have heard her. "Vallie, why are you driving this tin lizzie?" he asked as he unfastened his seat belt.

"Because I'm a little short on funds? Linc, are you trying to change the subject, because if you are, it won't work."

"Valetta Keane, you are the most suspicious woman alive! It was just a simple question."

"The name is Faraday," she snapped, her face a dark scowl. "And what I drive is of no concern to you. But if you must know, our printing press died in January and obviously had to be replaced at once. On top of that, we lost out on a big commission we were counting on. Then the price of ink went up, which *you* know better than I. The list is endless."

"Come on, Valetta! Those are just excuses. If you won't think of yourself, at least think of Mellie. This tin can sounds like it's going to die any minute, maybe at a bad time, maybe in the middle of a blizzard! Then what?"

"I have a cell phone."

"You know damn well they don't always work in the mountains, and besides, that's not what I meant."

Valetta leaned back with a heavy sigh. "If you must know, I can't afford a new car. I'd have to take out a loan, and I'm already carrying a mortgage. I'm a single parent, don't forget."

"A single parent?" Lincoln was dumbfounded. "You're a damned heiress, don't *you* forget! You can afford to pay cash for a Jaguar—make that a garage full of them! Make that *the whole damned factory!*"

"You know, Mr. Cameron," Valetta said with a short

laugh that sounded brittle even to her ears, "I thought I was doing a good job of running my life until you showed up. Let me clarify a few things. Whatever money is waiting for me in the Bank of California is going to remain in the Bank of California. Keane money comes with far too many strings attached. If I used that money, I would have to make explanations to Mellie that I'm not ready to make. Mellie doesn't know anything about her connection to the Keane family. I decided a long time ago that I don't want her to know about her connection, or her inheritance, until she is ready to handle it. And that's a long way off."

"Meanwhile, you let her go *without* because of your damned pride! I don't get it."

Valetta couldn't believe what she heard coming from Lincoln's mouth. He was just like her sister. But she would not let him anger her the way Alexis did. "First of all, would you please stop cursing? Secondly, Mellie is not going without," she said quietly. "You make us sound like we're on a bread line, for heaven's sake, and that's exactly what scares me about touching Keane money! You and Alexis think exactly alike, you both equate success with wealth. Well, let me tell you something, Lincoln Cameron. Mellie Faraday has everything she needs right here in Longacre, so stop criticizing me. When I think we need a new car, I'll buy one, and I'll go to the bank and take out a car loan just like everybody else!"

"But you're not like everybody else!"

"I am, here in Longacre!"

"Tell me, did Jack go along with this…this nuttiness?"

"You leave Jack out of this! He's not the one who

has to decide. And unfortunately, his insurance policy was very small. We were just about to change it when…" Valetta shrugged. "We never got around to it."

"I'm sorry, Valetta, about Jack and all, but I still don't understand. It hurts me to see you go without and not be allowed to help you. Okay, okay," he said, holding up his hands, "you're not going *completely* without, but then, what do you call it driving a ten-year-old car?"

"It doesn't matter what I call it, I just wish you wouldn't make out like we're poverty-stricken. And since it's not your problem, Linc, I would appreciate if you backed off. Now, please," she said, pointing at the door, "…out! I have to get to work."

Stepping carefully onto the sidewalk, Lincoln tried to avoid sinking his feet in the snow. What damage water could do to Italian leather didn't bear thinking about. But it was too late.

"Longacre be damned," he fumed as he felt the bitter, wet chill seep to his toes. "This subject is not closed!"

"Oh, it's closed all right," Valetta snapped, wishing the door didn't squeak quite so much when Lincoln slammed it shut. Gnashing her teeth as she drove away, Valetta determined that she would speak to him that very evening. The sooner she knew what he wanted, the sooner she could send him on his way.

But the next opportunity to speak to her visitor was closer at hand than she thought. She wasn't sitting at her desk more than ten minutes, sorting her mail, when she found him standing in the threshold of her office, his arms folded across his chest, his tall figure threatening to dwarf the room.

"Nice place you have here."

Startled, Valetta jumped to her feet. "What are you doing here? I thought you were meeting Rico."

"Oh, that male bonding thing can wait," Linc said, his voice a lazy drawl as he strolled around her tiny office, examining the pictures and plaques on the wall. "This is much more interesting. A little small, but Alexis would get a real kick out of this place."

"Hush, now!" she whispered, rushing to close her office door. But Lincoln caught her arm as she passed, anger flaring in his eyes. "Nobody in this one-horse town knows who you are, do they, Valetta Keane Faraday?"

Blushing furiously, Valetta tried to pull away, but Lincoln held firm, his grip like a vise. "That's what I thought. Which makes me very curious, Vallie. Like, for one thing, how are you going to explain me? Who are you going to say I am?"

"My explanation of old friend is fine," Valetta said, her chin high. "I wasn't expecting you, remember?"

"I remember. But forgetting about me for the moment, why all the secrecy about *you,* Vallie? You couldn't possibly be ashamed of your past, could you? You hardly had one, you were so young when you left. So it's got to be Alexis. I'm right, aren't I?" he said when he saw two pink spots dot her cheeks. "It *is* Alexis. Tell me, Valetta, was she really so difficult?"

"The very worst sister imaginable!"

"But Valetta, that was *years* ago."

"So what? If she's changed, I haven't heard! She's a tarantula. Poisonous. Don't you see? She wants Mellie! She sent you to get Mellie."

"That's not true! Mellie's name was never mentioned. I didn't even know you had a daughter until days ago!"

"Can't you see? She's running circles round you. *She is,* Lincoln, don't look at me like that. I know how she operates, and you should, too, after all these years. She pats you on the head, makes you feel good—lots of perks in your line of work, aren't there, Lincoln?— pretends that *you're the only one* who can understand her. Happy to make her happy, you jump as high as you can, forgetting that, every so often, she likes to remove the safety net!"

"I won't even honor that with a response."

"Oh, really?" Valetta snorted. "Then why are you here?"

"Alexis asked me to deliver you a message."

"Oh, please. As if she couldn't pick up the phone herself!" Valetta was so disgusted she could barely contain her anger. "I can't believe that with all your business savvy, you can't see my sister for what she is, but okay, fine, if you want to live in a state of denial, go right ahead. Just don't ask me to join you."

Caught off guard by her anger, Linc strove to be convincing. "Valetta, I give you my word, that's not why I'm here."

"I don't believe you!"

But Valetta heard the ring of truth in his voice. Reining in her temper, her eyes narrowed. Perhaps her take on Mr. Big Shot Lincoln Cameron was wrong. She was, after all, holding on to an image formed by an eighteen-year-old. Now she was older and more knowledgeable, perhaps she owed him a second look. He might be terrific at his job, but quite possibly not good at understanding people.

His warm breath on her cheek, as he leaned forward, made her lose her train of thought. Lincoln, too, must have felt the sudden and unexpected spark that jumped unbidden between them, if the frown on his face was any indication. But her own response concerned her more. "Let me go, Linc."

She didn't know why, but his touch was upsetting. Ten years ago she would have fallen to her knees in gratitude and adulation. Now, she was plain humiliated. Was she such an easy mark? Had she sent signals, unaware? Was she that desperate for attention? Who did he think he was, anyway, to march in like this, unannounced, and try to seduce her? No way was she going to fall victim to the Cameron charm. Thankfully, a light rap on the door prevented that danger.

"Mrs. Faraday, Joe Ronin is on line three."

Sending him an irate look, Valetta picked up the phone. Quietly, Lincoln left the office.

"Hey, hello there," he called out to the young man who'd delivered the message. "Benjamin, isn't it? We met the other night, at the little birthday party for Mrs. Faraday."

Ben was pleased to be remembered. "Yes, sir, we did. I didn't think you'd recall."

"No, no, of course I did," Lincoln assured him.

But he was more interested in the printing press that occupied the center of the room, humming importantly. Interested, too, in the people who occupied the battered desks piled high with manila folders, strewn with paper clips and rubber bands and littered with the requisite foam coffee cups without which no office was complete. In the far corner a coffeepot promised something hot, although if it was like anything Linc was familiar with, it was a bloody awful brew. Beside it sat a box of doughnuts, half empty. Sugar for breakfast, the American way.

The room seemed disorderly, but Lincoln's trained eyes could tell there was method to the madness. Around the office, people were in various states of conversation, or hunched over their desks engrossed in writing. Above all else, there was a bustling feel in the air, a crackling of energy.

"Ben, since Mrs. Faraday is occupied, I was wondering, would you mind introducing me around? That is, if you're not too busy?" Lincoln had a feeling that if he wanted to know what was going on, he'd better seize this opportunity. He was pretty sure he'd get a clearer picture of things if Valetta were out of the way.

The man looked past Lincoln's shoulder to see what his boss might have to say about this, but Lincoln discreetly blocked his view. Charmingly, Lincoln extended his hand. "I'm Lincoln Cameron."

Ben returned his handshake. "You're the Pulitzer prize-winning editor who runs the *Los Angeles Connection*, right?"

"I'm afraid so," Lincoln said, embarrassed by Ben's weighty veneration.

"I knew you looked familiar when I saw you at Jerome's, but I didn't want to ask. Hey, Andy, c'mere. Listen up, everybody!"

Barely able to contain his excitement, Ben called the entire office to attention. "I was right. This here *is* Lincoln Cameron, the editor in chief of the *Los Angeles Connection!*"

"No kidding?" someone said doubtfully as she munched on a doughnut.

"Ben, is this another one of your lame jokes?"

"No! Take a look. Go ahead, go online and find out for yourselves." Nodding excitedly, he waved his hand.

"Do you remember my partner, Andrew Buchanan? They call us Castor and Pollux because we're always together, like the stars."

"Are you *really* the famous Mr. Cameron, the editor in chief of the *L.A. Connection*?" Andy asked, his eyes a disbelieving squint as he extended his hand.

Lincoln saw he was going to have to combat his fame. "Don't pay him any attention," Ben said. "He's just jealous that I recognized you first. If you still want to look around, I'd be glad to give you the royal tour. Not that there's all that much to see."

"There's always something to be learned at a newspaper, no matter the size."

"We *have* been getting some good reviews lately," Andy said proudly.

Politely, the two young men escorted Lincoln around the office and introduced him to the staff. A lovely blind woman was working on a specially adapted computer that must have cost Valetta the earth to provide.

"This is Ellen Hartwell."

"Any connection to Davey Hartwell, the forest ranger? His sister, maybe?"

"His wife!" Ellen laughed. "But I do have my own identity." It was her job, she revealed, to solicit ads.

"Well, somebody has to pay for ink," Lincoln laughed.

"Oh, and I write, too, freelance. And I've been known to teach a class or two at the local college."

Another woman, Julie Berry, quite a bit older and very intent, waved absently as she scribbled away at some copy. Apparently she hadn't computed the great editor's arrival, and Lincoln was relieved not to have to do his modesty number. While they walked about, Ben told Lincoln that the staff was larger, but that some of them were absent. Jay Logan and Kirin Red were out making deliveries and would not be back till later that day. Oh, and Flossie McGowan had called in sick. She handled the upstate news desk. That comprised the staff. Except for Gertrude, of course.

Ben and Andy turned as one to the printing press standing in the center of the room. "Meet Gertrude, our state-of-the-art resident foxy lady, and no, there is nowhere else to put her. Mrs. Faraday is thinking of moving us to bigger offices," Andy explained apologetically, "but it's always about money, isn't it?"

Not for Valetta Keane, Lincoln thought to himself. Another reason to wonder why Valetta refused to use her wealth, since her fledgling paper seemed so desperately to need it. He would ask her when they were alone. There were many things he would ask her, when they were alone.

"Mr. Cameron!"

Uh-oh, time's up, Lincoln thought ruefully, when he heard Valetta sharply call his name. "Ah, Mrs. Faraday, these gentlemen were good enough to introduce me around while you were on the phone," he said amiably. "You have an impressive staff."

The glare Valetta sent Ben and Andy was enough to send them running.

"Now, now, Vallie, they were only being polite."

"I don't pay them to have good manners!" Valetta said crossly. "I pay them to report the news."

Angry as she might be at his sneaky invasion, Lincoln knew she would not make a scene. "Well, now you don't have to trouble yourself showing me around," he said wryly, as he shrugged into his jacket. Ignoring the frosty look that said she hadn't planned to, he brushed past her and opened the door.

"Perhaps you would like to join me for lunch? Is Jerome's diner the only place in town to eat?"

"Randy's Café is closed. She broke her leg, remember?"

"Ah, yes, so you said. Well, then, I guess Jerome's is where I'll be, if you get hungry."

"I bring my lunch, remember?" she said with a toss of her head.

"Ah, yes. Your little economy," he said blandly.

Buttoning his thin jacket against the cold air, Lincoln ignored her glare. "Brr, it's cold here. I think I might have to order some warm clothes, if I'm staying awhile. A parka, gloves, boots… I hadn't planned on a long visit, but it's been so interesting visiting here today, I'm tempted. Perhaps it would be a good idea if I rented a room," he said, a small smile on his lips.

"Lincoln, no!" She didn't want him to stay in town long enough to need a room.

"Now, now, Valetta, don't insist. You know I can't stay with you indefinitely, it wouldn't be proper. Really, Vallie, you aren't thinking or you wouldn't even suggest it. We wouldn't want to get the gossipmongers going, now, would we?"

"Lincoln!"

"No worse than they already are, anyway. Any suggestions?"

"Lincoln!"

"I didn't think so. I could use some gloves, too," he murmured as he stepped out into the watery sunlight. "Didn't I see a dry goods store on Main Street?"

Chapter Six

Leaving *The Spectator,* Lincoln strolled down Main Street, finding the dry goods store with no trouble. In a town the size of Longacre, it was no trouble to find anything, he thought, feeling oddly cheerful as he entered the store, its overhead bell announcing his arrival.

"Hi there. Can I help you?"

Lincoln turned to find a tall, angular woman staring at him from across the store counter. Her hair a mélange of bright orange curls, her lipstick a slash of red, her clothes were a rainbow of color and texture. Linc guessed she was the town eccentric.

"Patricia Carmichael. We met the other night," she said, stretching her hand across the counter. "But everyone calls me Patty. You're Lincoln Cameron, Valetta's friend from California."

Lincoln smiled. "There goes my air of mystery."

She appreciated a man with a sense of humor, and it was even better when he had the wit to use it.

"I guess it's pretty quiet here in the middle of February. Not that you wouldn't have scoped me out in August!"

Patty laughed. "How true. The problem is that we don't have a ski lift. No ski lift, no tourists. No tourists, no winter income. We close down for the winter, so you do sort of stick out. They come in the summer—the tourists, I mean—for the mountains. Our population quadruples on July 4, but that's true of all the towns, hereabouts. We might not have a ski lift, but we do have the most beautiful mountains and lakes. I own a bed-and-breakfast, and it's already booked from Memorial Day Weekend right through to Labor Day, and has been since Christmas. I don't know why, but people start to think about summer around that time. Must be cabin fever."

"In Los Angeles, we have the opposite problem. The hotels in Palm Beach are filled to the rafters this time of year, people soaking up all that sunshine."

"I wish!" Patty chuckled. "So now, Mr. Cameron, what can I do for you?"

"Well, Mrs. Carmichael, I brought a suitcase of clothes, but unfortunately, I wasn't thinking *snow*. I got on the plane wearing nothing but this thin jacket, so I could use a jacket, for starters."

"Call me Patty and I'll see what I can do. Call me Mrs. Carmichael and I'll have to show you the door."

"Okay, Patty, and you call me Lincoln."

"A deal." Pleased, Patty led Lincoln down the aisle. "Looks like you could use a sweater, too, Linc."

"Do you carry any?"

"I do, but…" Glancing at his huge shoulders, she shrugged. "Let's start with a jacket. Here, try this on for size. And while you're at it, tell me what brings you to Longacre. That is, if you want the town to get the story straight." She winked.

Lincoln slipped his arms into the heavy, lined jacket and marveled at the perfect fit. "Thanks, Patty, you just saved me a great deal of trouble."

"You mean I saved you a phone call to L.L. Bean. No matter," she said with an easy smile. "Let's try these gloves on for size. They don't quite match, but they're guaranteed to keep you warm. So, how long are you staying?" she asked as she watched him wriggle on the gloves.

"I wasn't skirting your question." Lincoln smiled as he flexed his huge hand, but the sheepskin glove fit perfectly, too. "These are fine, thanks. You have a good eye."

Patty wasn't fooled. "Hey, look, I'm no busybody, but if you're planning to stay beyond tomorrow, people are going to talk. Okay, okay, they already are. But it does seem like you're in for the short haul, given that it's going to snow another four inches tonight. So if you're planning to stay, you'll want to have some boots, too—as opposed to those fancy moccasins you're wearing. Now, boots I've got in all sizes. It's the one thing I stock all year round. The mountains, my friend." She grinned at Lincoln's blank look. "The spring rain, summer hikes, fall harvest, winter snow—the weather keeps me in the boot business all year round. I don't need a ski lift to earn a living."

Half an hour later, loaded down with two thick cable-knit sweaters, a pair of long johns and an assortment of other rugged winter attire, Lincoln was ready to pay.

"Any idea where I can rent a room?" he asked as he handed Patty his credit card.

"What's wrong with Valetta's? She's got a real nice house."

"Her house is lovely," Lincoln agreed, "but I don't want to be a burden. They have their routine and I don't want to interfere."

"So you and Val aren't such good friends, then? Her sister must have sent you."

Lincoln hesitated to confide in a stranger but something told him that Patty would make a good confidante. He even had his suspicions about her ignorance of Valetta's real identity, but since he couldn't be sure, he dared not reveal Valetta's past. Thus he told Patty a little—a very little—of their history and how Valetta's sister was...requesting...her return home.

"If she doesn't want to return home, why don't you accept that?"

"She doesn't know the whole story. Look, I'm just the emissary but I'm hoping that when she does know everything, she will reconsider. And I'm thinking about Mellie, too. I'm not sure how much the child appreciates my presence. Why should she? I'm just a stranger passing through, as far as she's concerned."

Patty nodded, impressed by his sensitivity to Mellie. "All right, I don't usually do this midwinter, but I suppose I can rent you a room."

"I wouldn't want to impose."

"My door is open any season to a cash customer. It's just not that common this time of the year."

Lincoln was relieved. "Good, because you have one knocking at your door."

Patty was surprised. "You would rent the room, sight unseen?"

"I may be going on instinct here," Lincoln laughed, "but I think I can trust you."

They spent the next few minutes discussing the details, and when they had settled on the terms, Lincoln told Patty that he would move his stuff in that very night, right after dinner, if she didn't mind. He wasn't staying long, but he did have a small valise and a laptop, and some clothes, now, he reminded her, nodding at the three shopping bags on the counter. The particulars settled, Lincoln then headed over to Jerome Crater's to warm himself with a bowl of soup. Minutes after he'd ordered, Rico joined him.

"Hey, buddy," Rico said, sliding into Lincoln's booth. "Smells good. What's on for today?"

"Rico! Good to see you. Have a seat," Linc grinned as Rico shrugged off his jacket. "Jerome's really on top of it, today. The luncheon special is onion soup."

There was no need to explain further, because Jerome was already headed their way, the aroma of the steaming bowl of soup he carried filling the air.

"Thank you, Jerome," Lincoln said, as Jerome set the bowl on the table. "This smells wonderful."

"It's pretty good if I do say so myself. I suppose you want some, too?" he grumbled to Rico.

Rico laughed good-naturedly. "Well, if it wouldn't be too much trouble, old man."

"It ain't no trouble," Jerome groused, "but I'm serving it for dinner, too, so don't go ordering any later tonight or I won't have enough."

"Don't worry, I won't be here," Rico told him. "Nancy wants to stay home tonight and watch some cable."

"Exactly what I was planning." Lincoln nodded. "I can't lose too much sight of the rest of the world. And I'm moving into Patty Carmichael's this evening, so I won't be here, either," Lincoln told Jerome, figuring it was best to let them know before the grapevine embellished it.

Rico was surprised. "No kidding? Patty is opening up in the middle of winter? That's pretty amazing. On the other hand, you'll be eating here a lot because Patty doesn't cook for beans, and Chuck hates the sight of a store. They're here three, four times a week, at least. Except in the summers when they serve a continental breakfast to their guests."

"Now, that's not fair," Jerome frowned, as he returned with Rico's bowl of onion soup. "I taught Patty how to roast a chicken last winter, and she did just fine."

Rico's brow quirked as he buttered a piece of crusty, warm bread. "Well, if that's so, maybe you can teach my Nancy how to use a stove."

Lincoln was intrigued. "You know, that might not be a bad idea, Jerome. Something to think about, starting up a cooking school. With a few technical adjustments, you could even do it right here at the diner. I mean, this soup is amazing."

"Linc here may have an idea," Rico mused. "It could just happen, Jerome. You might have to change the layout a bit, but I'd be glad to help with the carpentry and stuff."

"And, if you wanted to update some of your equipment, I'd be happy to back you," Lincoln offered.

"Back me?" Jerome frowned. "Like in a loan, you mean?"

"You could set the terms yourself, whatever was convenient. I trust you."

"Some businessman you are, trusting your money to a total stranger."

"You're Valetta's friend." Lincoln shrugged. "That's good enough for me. Besides, you are one terrific cook. Like I said, this soup is amazing. Anytime you want to open a restaurant in L.A., just let me know."

An hour later, Rico dropped Lincoln at the Faraday house. Mangy Yellow attacked Lincoln the moment he stepped through the door. "Whoa, down boy." Lincoln laughed as he bent to scratch the puppy's ears. "Okay, okay, but it's only going to be a short walk."

Freedom! Mangy Yellow dashed past Lincoln's legs, leaving his new master to follow behind.

It was getting on to five o'clock and Lincoln was pretty much packed, his belongings loaded in the back of his Jeep, when he had the inspiration to make dinner for Valetta and Mellie. Remembering Valetta's disparaging comments on his culinary skills, or the lack thereof, he decided not to worry over this spurt of possibly misplaced enthusiasm and went to investigate the kitchen.

The kitchen was a real mystery, but determined to prove himself, Lincoln bravely poked about, examining every box in the pantry until he settled on spaghetti. Putting water up to boil exactly as directed, the pasta was soon bubbling away. He even found a can of sauce to go with it. Hey, this cooking stuff was easy. Feeling smug, he poured the sauce into a second pot. Piece of cake. Why in the heck did women complain about having to cook? Not that he'd ever lay claim to Beef Wellington, but still, what was all the fuss about?

Knowing that Valetta and Mellie wouldn't be home for another thirty minutes, he decided he had time for a quick phone call, a long overdue call to California.

Three thousand miles away, he could hear Alexis Keane catch her breath. "Lincoln! It's about time. I've left you four messages. Why haven't you called?"

"Alexis, I've only been here one day!"

"Two days, actually," she corrected him brusquely. "That's how long I've been waiting by the phone."

"Well, I know you want to know what's going on," Lincoln said slowly, "but there's nothing to report, yet. Valetta and I haven't had a chance to talk. Things keep cropping up. But we're on for tonight."

"I'm very impatient, Lincoln. I have a time frame. I hope you haven't forgotten that, in the excitement of your travels."

Lincoln winced at her ill-concealed sarcasm. "I'm aware of that, Alexis, but surely you didn't expect me to get off the plane and throw everything at Valetta all at once? Valetta is a strong-minded woman. It will take some persuading to get her to return home." If California *was* her home.

"How *is* Valetta? And Mellie, what is Mellie like? Does she look like her mother?"

"Hold on there, Alexis! Valetta and Mellie are fine. Mellie is a spunky little girl, just like her mother." Lovely, just as lovely… He was glad Alexis wasn't there to see his face turn red. He would have had to explain things he himself didn't understand.

"Lincoln, are you still there?"

"Yes, I'm here, just thinking."

Listening to Alexis drone on and on, Lincoln began to wonder if Valetta had been exaggerating about her sister. Maybe there was some basis for her distrust of Alexis.

"If the price is right…we just have to find her price…."

Her price? Was the woman lost to all sense of propriety? "I don't know about that. This is her child you're talking about!"

Alexis must have sensed Lincoln's distaste because she immediately backed off. "I was referring to private schools," she said cautiously. "Horseback riding lessons, the culture, the arts. Whatever the child wanted would be at her fingertips if Valetta came back to California. Would Valetta seriously deny her child the advantages that she herself had?"

"I haven't asked her, but she might. She doesn't talk about her own childhood in precisely those terms."

"Well, *do ask her,* and in just those terms!" Alexis's exasperation could be felt across the continent.

His hand clenched on the phone, Lincoln forced himself to speak calmly. "Alexis, you sent me here on a mission of some delicacy. You have to trust me to relay your message at the right time, *and in a manner appropriate,*" he emphasized. I just wish I knew how I was going to accomplish that, he thought as he heard a car door slam. "Look, Alexis, I have to go, Valetta and Mellie just drove up. I'll call you tomorrow." Clicking shut his cell phone, Lincoln grinned as the front door flew open. "Welcome home, ladies."

Mellie returned his cheerful smile with one of her own. "Hi, Mr. Cameron. What's burning?"

An hour later, sitting snug in Jerome's *smoke free* diner, the Faraday women waited patiently for their second dinner. Still reeling from his culinary humiliation, Lincoln recalled how he'd raced to the kitchen, Valetta and Mellie hot on his heels. Waving the billowing black smoke from his face, he grabbed a dish towel and threw the burning pot into the sink. Blasting it with cold water, he shouted for Valetta to shut the gas jets while Mellie rushed to fling open the back door.

Collapsed against the sink, he stopped to catch his breath while the Faraday women eyed him doubtfully from the back porch.

"Hey, Mom," Mellie said quietly when the excitement had subsided and they had all gathered at the stove. "Didn't you just get these pots a few weeks ago?"

"On sale, too," Valetta sighed, as they stared into the black hole of mush that had once been a boiling pot of pasta. "What exactly were you trying to do, Lincoln?"

"Make dinner?" he offered bleakly. "Meatballs and spaghetti?"

"Where are the meatballs?" Mellie asked curiously.

"In the sauce pot?"

Uncertainly, they peeked into the second pot. Any evidence of red sauce was lost in the hard, brown sludge that covered the bottom of the pan.

"I'll replace the pots, of course," Lincoln assured Valetta as they settled down in Jerome's Diner. Chicken potpie and a side of broccoli slaw. Buttering a whole wheat roll, Lincoln wondered if he could coax Jerome into relocating to Los Angeles.

"Two pots in one day?" Valetta said weakly as she fiddled with her fork. "I wonder if they came with a warranty."

"Don't worry. I said I would replace them." Maybe Jerome would even agree to be his private chef. He could name his price—

"Lincoln!"

Lost in a culinary fantasy, Lincoln didn't hear Valetta call his name until she rapped on his knuckles.

"Sorry. You were saying something?"

"Where were you? I called your name twice."

"Sorry. You wouldn't believe," Lincoln apologized with a rueful smile.

Valetta frowned but she didn't press the matter. "We were trying to tell you that Mellie begins soccer practice tomorrow, right after school."

"So soon?

"They start early here."

"Well, since we're talking plans, I have something to tell *you* ladies. I didn't want to say, what with the mess I made of your kitchen and the chaos, but... I've taken a room."

"A room?" Mellie perked up. "What room? Taken it where? How did you move it? Where did you put it?"

"Hey, silly." Lincoln grinned, ruffling her red curls. "I didn't take it anywhere. It's a saying. It means that I've *rented* a room."

"Oh, yeah, I knew that," Mellie said with a blush.

Unsure if she really understood, Lincoln let it slide. "Patty Carmichael has agreed to rent me a room," he explained. "I'm already packed. When we get back to the house, I'm driving over to Patty's with my things." Lincoln almost laughed at the relief that crossed Valetta's face, alongside her consternation.

"I don't understand why you're staying at all," she said bluntly.

Even Mellie heard the disapproval in Valetta's voice. "Hey, Mom, don't you want Mr. Cameron to stay?"

From the mouths of babes, Lincoln thought wryly, as he watched Valetta flush.

"Naturally...what a question...of course, I do," she floundered.

"Mellie, your mom was just caught by surprise,"

Lincoln explained. "It occurred to me that it would be nice to spend some time here. If I stayed a few days, I would have the opportunity to get to know you both better. And you, little miss, could get to know me."

"But you do know me. I'm Mellie, I'm almost ten years old, I like school, and I have no dad. And I love chocolate cake," she added thoughtfully.

"It's that simple?" Lincoln laughed, following her greedy eyes to the chocolate layer cake resting on the counter. Jerome had been positively inspired today.

But Mellie was gone, having slid from the booth to find Jerome and beg a slice of cake.

Lincoln reached across the table and chucked Valetta's chin, a glancing touch that she spurned. "Come on, Vallie. I'm only going to stay a few more days. You don't have to act like I just delivered you a writ of execution!"

"Lincoln, I don't know what scheme you and Alexis have concocted, but be advised, it won't work! I want you to leave as soon as possible. I'd tell you to leave right now if they hadn't predicted more snow."

"Nice of you to think of me," Lincoln observed, a shade sardonic as he leaned back. "Sorry, Vallie, but I can't leave Longacre until we sit down and talk."

"We're sitting, now." She glared at him.

"I mean alone, somewhere private, where we won't be interrupted and I can tell you what's going on in California."

"A message, then, from Alexis?"

"Of course. I told you when I arrived that I didn't know your whereabouts until she told me last week."

"Alexis knows darn well that I want nothing to do with her. An occasional phone call is more than enough."

"Vallie—" Lincoln left off as Mellie returned to their table, balancing a loaded cake plate.

"Mom, look! Jerome gave me the biggest piece!"

"Hey, are you going to eat that all by yourself?" Lincoln marveled.

"I guess I could share, if you wanted some..." Mellie's voice trailed off. "Mom, you want some, too?"

"None for me, thanks, honey. I'm counting calories."

"Well, I'm not, so I guess I'll go get the other half of that cake!" Lincoln laughed as he rose to his feet and headed for the counter.

"I like Mr. Cameron, he's nice," Mellie decided, as she picked up her fork.

"Mellie, you have the oddest way of resuming a conversation as if it hadn't ended ten minutes ago. Besides, you only think he's nice because he didn't ask for a piece of your cake!"

"That, too, but he is nice," Mellie insisted. "He promised to take me hiking tomorrow, if it doesn't snow too much. And if you said it was okay. He bought work boots at Patty's—did you see them?—and gloves, too. And did you see his new jacket? I'm glad he's staying. Hey, maybe Aunt 'Lexis could come visit, too."

Valetta almost choked on her tea. "I doubt it. Your Aunt Alexis doesn't like to travel."

"How do you know? Maybe she's changed her mind. You haven't seen her in a hundred years."

"We do talk."

"Well, I think we should ask her."

Valetta was amused and horrified at the same time. "Honestly, Mellie, I can't see your Aunt Alexis wearing work boots and riding in a pickup truck with Yellow. I'm pretty sure she's not too crazy about dogs. And the last time I heard, she drove a Mercedes-Benz, and she doesn't even drive it, she has a chauffeur."

"Maybe her chauffeur could drive her here. Then she wouldn't need work boots. And Yellow could sit on my lap."

"Who wouldn't need work boots?" Lincoln asked as he returned to the booth brandishing a huge slice of chocolate cake. "Here, Vallie, I brought enough for you, too."

"Liar!" Valetta snorted, as she eyed the mouthwatering mountain of fudge.

"No, really, I did!" Lincoln protested, setting the plate between them. "So, who won't need work boots?" he asked as he forked a piece of cake and tried to feed Valetta a bite.

Just this once, she promised herself. Chocolate! Almost better than—

Lincoln laughed, almost as if he knew what she was thinking. Damn that man!

"We're talking about my aunt 'Lexis. I want her to visit, but Mom says she won't because she's too old."

"I did not say that!"

"Then why doesn't she ever visit us? Doesn't she like us?"

"How can she not like you, Mellie? She's never even met you!"

"Then why does she send me Christmas gifts and birthday presents?"

Carefully, Valetta hid her dismay. Whatever lay between her and Alexis had nothing to do with Mellie. "Hey, kiddo, what if I think about it?"

Mellie rolled her eyes as she pushed away her plate. "Oh, Mom, whenever you say you're going to think about something it always means *no*." Visited by inspiration, Mellie brightened. "Hey, if Aunt Alexis won't come here, why don't we go there?"

"To California?"

"Yeah! Maybe she would take us to Disneyland. Do you think she would take us to Disneyland, Mr. Cameron?"

"Hmm. Alexis Keane on the Matterhorn Bobsled? Now, there's a sight that might be worth the trip."

Biting her lips, Valetta managed to smother a laugh. "Well, whatever we decide, my darling daughter, you still have homework to do, so let's call it a day, shall we?"

Knowing that Valetta wanted to end the conversation, Lincoln didn't protest. It must be hard to explain these things to a nine-year-old going on twenty. He didn't envy her the job. "Okay, ladies, if you give me a minute, I'll go ask Jerome to put the meal on my tab."

"Your tab?" Valetta frowned.

Lincoln was nonchalant as he shrugged on his parka. "When he heard I was going to stay an extra few days, Jerome offered to set me up an account. He said everyone did it, it made life easier. He says he keeps a book, but I think it's all in his head."

Disconcerted, Valetta watched as Lincoln marched down the aisle, bidding everyone a cheerful good-night. She was doubly horrified when Mellie ran after him and slipped her small hand in his. A tab, indeed! She would set up this meeting with Mr. Lincoln Cameron as soon as possible!

Unfortunately for Valetta, Lincoln was suddenly of no mind to hurry back to California. Sure, he missed the palm trees and the sun, but he was beginning to like Longacre, beginning to enjoy meeting the odd friendly face as he strolled down Main Street. There was unexpected pleasure to be found lingering over a cup of coffee, shooting the breeze in Jerome Crater's overheated diner, no one asking anything of him but some good, old-fashioned conversation. It was a relief not to be cornered by a rookie reporter begging for a deadline extension, or pleading for help with a tricky interview. No requests littered his desk to deliver a speech halfway around the world, when more and more of late, he'd discovered he would rather be at home with a good book. Hidden away in Longacre, he suffered no embarrassing calls from women—younger and younger, he'd noticed lately—women he hardly knew whose greatest hope was to warm his famous bed. And when had *that* started? Where, he wondered, were the women he used to know with whom he had a history longer than an hour? Had they left the city? Left the country? Married?

Married?

He looked sharply at Valetta as she caught up with them, her pretty nose in the air as she shrugged on her coat. Watching her adjust her hat made him shiver.

"I'll go warm up the car."

Chapter Seven

Sports talk. Patty listened with some asperity as she served her husband and their houseguest a late-night snack. "Mr. Cameron here—Lincoln—isn't sure how long he's staying," she interrupted them as she set a plate of cookies on the table.

"None for me, thanks," Lincoln declined, his hand on his belly. "I just wanted to thank you for putting me up. I had a full meal tonight at Jerome's."

"Let me guess." Chuck smiled. "Ah, yes, it was *killer chocolate cake* night."

"How did you know?" Linc asked, then shook his head. "Is he as regular as rain?"

"You could set your clock. And you just couldn't resist one little slice, could you? Don't feel bad. No one can."

"I wouldn't, if it was *one* slice," Lincoln said ruefully. "I think it was more like two."

"Be warned." Patty laughed. "Tomorrow is Friday, so it's fish fry and lemon meringue pie. I'll be there, that's for sure, but you might want to stay away if you're watching your waistline."

Reaching for a cookie, Chuck had to agree. "Jerome is a great cook, but you can't eat there every night. I always tell him he should go into business and he always tells me he is. But what I mean is a fancy restaurant in Albany."

Lincoln nodded. "I think we're on the same wavelength. But I offered to set him up in California."

Patty shook her head. "If Jerome left Longacre, he'd be a fish out of water. This is his home and we're his family. He's cooking for *us,* don't you see? And another thing, he's getting old. He might not be using that walker, but I've noticed that he does use his cane more and more."

"Come to think of it, I've noticed that, too," Chuck mused.

"There might come a day when he won't be able to run that diner, and the truth is, I don't think it's all that far away."

"And here I was foolish enough to suggest he start a cooking school," Lincoln told them, mortified by his tactless suggestion.

"Well, I don't know. That might not be a bad idea," Patty said thoughtfully, "*if* he had an assistant. It would allow him to keep his hand in the business and ease up on other things at the same time."

"Food for thought, no pun intended." Chuck yawned as he rose to his feet. "Well, I don't know about you two, but I'm for bed. I've got to get an early start tomorrow. Heading up to Plattsburg to see a man about a cow."

"A cow?" Lincoln repeated as he helped Patty clear the table.

"Patty and I live here in town so she can run the store and this here B and B, but we also own a dairy farm about eight miles outside of town. Small, but mine own, as the saying goes. You don't get rich milking cows, but it's honest work. This place gives us extra income."

"Truthfully, we'd rather live on the farm, but the oil burner went two years ago," Patty said with a frown. "But we get by."

"We get by because we have no kids to worry about. Not yet," Chuck winked. "We figure if we take our time having kids we can save a few dollars, although I hear that's a pipe dream."

Lincoln had much to think about later that night, as he settled down in the pretty room Patty had assigned him. Patty had been pleased to inform him that since it was off-season, she was able to give him the only room with a private bath. Immaculate, if a bit fussy for his taste—the yellow, flowery wallpaper, the carpet an odd design of red cabbage roses, the curtains of white linen—it was something straight out of a country life magazine. He didn't dare touch the lace doilies for fear of offending her, but he did move the vase of dried flowers from the narrow nightstand to the windowsill and replace it with his traveling clock and three cell phones. Two for work—domestic and international— and one for private calls. He had a feeling that Patty would have been amused.

The next morning, she served him a lumberjack's breakfast that was more pleasing news. Then off to open her store, she wished him to have a good day. He would, thank you, Lincoln said, as he lingered over his coffee and the local shopping flyer, wondering if he could have *The Spectator* delivered while he was there. Intending to spend the whole day at Valetta's office, scoping out her newspaper, he made a mental note to inquire. But he didn't say this to Patty. He was pretty sure that Patty would call Valetta the minute she could, if he revealed his intention. The moment she was gone, though, he planned to head over to *The Spectator.* Not, though, before he took a moment to call Alexis.

"Well? Any news?"

Lord, the woman didn't waste any time, did she? "Good morning to you, too, Ms. Keane," he said crisply.

"Let's skip the niceties, Cameron. You know damned well I've been up for hours. Doing your work, I might add."

And whose work am I doing? he forbore to ask.

"Sorry, Alexis, but I've nothing to report. I'm inching my way toward a conversation with your sister, but like I told you yesterday, a matter of such delicacy has to find its moment. And it's not a conversation I want to have when Mellie is around, which she is a good deal of the time."

"Ach! Maybe I should call. This is taking far longer than I like."

For some reason, that idea bothered Lincoln. "I thought from the beginning that you should do so," he said slowly, "but since I'm already here... Be patient, Alexis. We'll come about. Tell me, though, have you ever thought about coming East?"

"To New York?" He could almost hear her gasp. "Don't be ridiculous! I don't do snow!"

Trudging down Main Street in his new work boots, fresh snow coating the sidewalk, Lincoln was thrilled to find his feet warm and dry. Wriggling his gloved hand, he waved hello to everyone he met. Lord, what a greenhorn he must seem to these people, he realized, as they sped by in their pickups. He'd never seen so many damned Ford trucks in his life! Not a single Porsche in sight! What *was* he doing here? If he were honest, he could have relayed Alexis's message anytime the last couple of days—not tactfully perhaps—but delivered, nonetheless. Why was he stalling? Why were his feet not pointing west, toward California?

Distracted by his thoughts, Lincoln would have walked right past Valetta's office if the words *The Spectator* hadn't been boldly painted across the glass window. The storefront was so dated, it might have better housed an antique shop than a modern newspaper. Stomping his boots free of snow, he swung the door wide, amused when heads turned at his entrance. "Good morning, all," he said with a wide grin.

"Good morning, Mr. Cameron," Andrew Buchanan greeted him. "Good to see you again. Can I help you? Mrs. Faraday just stepped out."

Good. *Great.* "No problem, Andy," he said, as he hung up his parka. Rocking on his heels, he stood tall, his hands in his pockets as he surveyed the office. "I don't think she'll mind if I wait."

Andrew looked doubtful, as did most of the staff, but Ben Zuckerman came to his rescue. "We don't mind at all, Mr. Cameron. As a matter of fact, perhaps you would like to give us five minutes of your time and tell us what it's like to run a big newsy like the *L.A. Connection.*"

Bless you, Benjamin, Lincoln thought as he strolled

around the office, although he was careful to sound reluctant. "I wouldn't want to overstep my welcome."

"Are you serious, Mr. Cameron?" Ben asked, incredulous at the idea. "Turning you away would be like telling Randolph Hearst he knew nothing about the printing press. Please, have a seat, let me get you some coffee. We keep a pot going. Perhaps you could talk to us about your experiences when you were first starting out. That would be great, wouldn't it, everyone?"

No question, it would be. When Valetta walked in an hour later, she was witness to an impromptu conversation between the Pulitzer prize winner and her small staff.

"Mrs. Faraday," Ben exclaimed when he saw her walk through the door. "You'll never guess. Mr. Cameron here has been telling us the most amazing stories. Did you know that his first interview as a reporter was with a senator?"

"Imagine, too," Lincoln said, rising to his feet, a wide smile spread across his craggy face, "that one of John Kennedy's first jobs after the war was as a reporter for the Hearst chain of newspapers. So you see, Ben, there's plenty of time for you to learn your craft."

Valetta didn't look as if *she* cared to learn anything except how to strangle Lincoln Cameron, but somehow she managed a smile. "All right, everybody, back to work. Mr. Cameron, may I see you in my office?"

"Oh, Mr. Cameron," Julie Berry called, "you won't forget to show me how to revise that article about dolphins, now, will you?"

"Certainly not, Julie!"

"And you promised to show *me* how to surf the Web for revenue resources," Ellen Hartwell piped up.

"I'm sure Mrs. Faraday will allow me these small tasks."

No one seemed to notice the storm gathering in Valetta's gray eyes. No one, that is, except Lincoln Cameron, who calmly followed her into her office. Her spine rigid, she held the door as he passed and closed it with a clip.

"Dolphins?" she hissed. *"Dolphins?* You are most mistaken, Mr. Cameron, I will *not* allow you that *one small task.* I will not allow you *any small task,* or even a big one!"

"Sorry, Valetta, I didn't mean to get carried away."

"You did to mean to! Oh, listen to me, I can't string two words together, you make me so mad! For heaven's sake, why are you here, Linc? You sure didn't come for the Mulligan Stew!"

"Valetta, if I have had any motive coming to Longacre—all right, yes, I admit I'm your sister's emissary—please believe it is nothing less than benevolent. But you have to admit that you have made my errand difficult—at every turn, I might add."

"Oh, you cad! That is *so* not true! I never asked you here in the first place. And lest you forget, my sister and I are estranged. Your visit smacks of interference."

"Valetta, I have only your interests at heart!"

"Poppycock!"

Poppycock? Lincoln would have laughed if he wasn't so angry.

"Lincoln, I haven't seen you in ten years. That maddening teenager you knew is gone. I'm not a child anymore and it would be nice if you realized it. Have you any idea what the last ten years have been like for me? Mellie is the best thing that ever happened to me. Everything else is window dressing."

"Vallie, I am *not* treating you like a child."

"Oh, but you are, Lincoln. Every time you call me that silly childhood nickname I am transported back a decade. You have been completely paternalistic."

"That's not true!"

"What do you call it, then, flying three thousand miles across the country to deliver a message to a woman you haven't seen in over a decade? Barging into my home like you owned the place, befriending my daughter, intruding into my workplace, seducing my employees with your self-importance and trying to charm *me*—which is *not* going to happen, by the way!" she warned, her voice rising on a note of hysteria.

Lincoln thought for a moment. Had he really been so high-handed? "Alexis begged me to come," he protested, but his argument sounded weak even to his own ears.

"Oh, for goodness' sake, Lincoln, she's old enough to deliver her own messages, don't you think?"

"She didn't believe you would listen."

The look Valetta sent him was pitying. "Lincoln, she's my sister, I would have listened. Maybe not for too long," she added, her mouth a wry slant, "but I would have given her a few minutes."

"I'll tell her."

"Don't bother. Let Alexis figure it out for herself. She runs the biggest publishing empire in the world, surely she can add one and one, don't you think?"

Later, Lincoln would come to believe that it was a trick of light, and perhaps it was. Or maybe it was ten years of missing her terribly, her absence in his life, the void she had left behind and he'd not filled, had never even dared put a name to, until this moment, when, in an instant he was looking straight at her and she was a child of eighteen. And then she wasn't; she was a grown woman with a child of her own.

She had survived tragedy, maybe things he didn't know about, but in her clear, gray eyes he suddenly found reflected the profound strength of a real woman. Whatever it was—that trick of light, a trick of circumstance—suddenly Lincoln didn't know what to think.

Without warning, desire overcame him, and she must have intuitively understood because she sought to step back. But his hands had, of their own volition, curled about her shoulders and drawn her close. She shook her head, but the movement was so faint, Lincoln could be forgiven for taking no notice.

He held her close, so close her breast brushed against his brand-new flannel shirt. His thoughts centered on the fine line of her lips, how much he wanted to touch them, to discover if they were as soft as they looked, Lincoln lowered his head. But a quick glance in her eyes and he saw her panic. He dropped his hands as if he'd been burned, not quite sure what had happened, only sure that something *had.* Mortified, he backed away, but Valetta had already escaped to the safety of her desk.

"Lincoln, go. Please," she begged him, her voice low.

Did she mean for him to leave the office, or leave Longacre? Lincoln didn't know, and he couldn't ask, his throat wouldn't work. But he could nod. He was able to do *that* before he hurried from the room, ignoring the farewells of his newfound friends.

Loaded down with folders, Ben hurried into Valetta's office. "Wow, wasn't *he* in a hurry?" He frowned, surprised by Lincoln's mad dash out the door. "Here you go, boss lady. The proofs you asked for."

"Thanks," she said absently.

But the look of distress on Valetta's face spoke volumes to Ben. "Uh-oh, did you two just have a fight?"

Smiling uncomfortably, Valetta began to sort through the mess on her paper-strewn desk. "It doesn't mean anything. We go back a ways."

"Oh, really? How far?" Ben asked with an impudent grin, and when Valetta said nothing, grew even more curious. "Well, he may be the greatest editor of all time, but his manners are pretty lousy! He said he was going to give us all some pointers about the business before he left."

Shifting through the folders, Valetta tried to minimize Lincoln's hasty departure. "Look, Ben, he must have forgotten. We were discussing some complicated family business. In general, Lincoln is not a rude person. On the contrary, he's famous for his diplomatic skills."

Ben was unconvinced. "Perhaps," he allowed, "but since I pass Patty Carmichael's on my way home from work, maybe I'll stop by and ask him if he can reschedule. Everyone was looking forward to it."

True to his word, Ben stopped by the Carmichael house directly after work. Andy stood beside him, as he always did. Patty opened the door on his second knock. "Castor and Pollux! Hey, guys, what brings you around? We were just heading over to Jerome's. Ah, it's about Mr. Cameron, isn't it?"

Ben smiled, Andy nodded. Neither said a word.

Patty raised a brow. "Mr. Cameron is upstairs, getting ready for dinner. I suppose you want me to call him down?"

"Yes, please," they said in unison.

"Well, come on in, guys, and I'll let him know you're here. Be careful, though, to wipe your feet."

Their boots spotless, Ben and Andy shuffled politely into Patty's living room and sat quietly, waiting for Lincoln to appear. He arrived a few minutes later, smiling at the sight of them perched together like brown sparrows on the edge of Patty's sofa. The way they fidgeted, he guessed they were running an errand that made them uneasy.

"Gentlemen?"

Startled by Lincoln's noiseless entrance, Ben and Andy jumped. "Mr. Cameron."

They were reluctant to speak, but Lincoln was patient as he took the chair opposite them. "What can I do for you?"

Whereas they were known all over Longacre to be garrulous to excess, suddenly the two young men were tongue-tied. Surprisingly, Andy took the lead. "Mr. Cameron, this morning when you visited *The Spectator*, you said you would share with us some ideas on how to raise the bar at the paper."

"Yes, so I did. I remember."

Andy's relief was palpable. "Good, because you see, Mrs. Faraday is so busy lately trying to drum up business, she's left the creative end to us. She reviews everything before we go to press, of course, but she never has any real criticism. Just a few days ago, we were talking about how tired *The Spectator* was looking, lately. That's why we came by. We were wondering…to be honest, we would…the office would like…we would like…"

"Oh, Andy, just go ahead and ask!" Ben said, interrupting Andy impatiently. "Mr. Cameron, we would like to know whether you would be generous enough to give us some lessons in journalism. The entire office is hoping you will. You did sort of mention that you might, this afternoon, and, well, we kind of took you at your word."

Lincoln leaned back and looked at them curiously. "When you say *the entire office,* do you include Mrs. Faraday?"

Ben and Andy exchanged looks. They knew there was tension between Lincoln and Mrs. Faraday, but after discussing the matter, they had decided to ignore it. A pity Mr. Cameron had to mention her name. "Um…no, we don't," Ben said slowly. "But the office is egalitarian so Mrs. Faraday would never override a consensus, and we do have a consensus. It isn't every day that a man of your stature passes through Longacre, and since you are probably going to leave any minute—"

"…and probably not return in our lifetime…"

"You *did* offer," Ben finished bravely.

Lincoln tried to decide what to do. When Valetta got wind of this she would have a fit, no matter what they said. Finding him back in her office would be the last straw. Even if she hadn't forbidden him the premises, she would not be pleased with his presence, not after this morning's episode. On the other hand, he *had* made the offer. It was Ben who inadvertently came up with a solution.

"We didn't expect you to do it on company hours,

of course. We thought maybe we'd meet in the evenings, when you weren't busy." Ben wasn't exactly sure what Mr. Cameron was busy with, but he had better manners than to ask. "Andy and I live above the bowling alley."

Lincoln frowned. "A somewhat noisy venue, don't you think?"

"They close at nine, weekdays. And the rent is cheap." Ben grinned.

"I can believe it," Lincoln said, returning Ben's smile. "Look, what if I asked Patty and Chuck if we could meet here? We'd be a small group, so we wouldn't really be disturbing them."

Ben and Andy were thrilled; he could see it in their faces. It made Lincoln wonder if they had really expected his cooperation. Never mind, they had it, now. And it was a great excuse to stay in Longacre.

"I'll ask them over dinner, give them a little time to think about it and get back to you? Fair enough?"

"More than fair!" they said in unison. Relieved that their mission was over, Andy and Ben bolted for the door. They weren't gone but a few minutes when Patty came to offer them coffee.

"Too late, they've left," Lincoln said. "They made me an interesting offer. Actually, now that I think of it, they didn't offer me anything, but they sure got me to commit! Very clever, those two. They've got the makings of a couple of very good reporters."

Lincoln told her of their request and Patty smiled. "If you want to meet here," she said, her eyes twinkling with humor, "I have no problem with it, and I'm sure Chuck won't, either, but what happens when Valetta finds out? Can't keep it secret, you know. Not in this town!"

"I didn't think to do so," Lincoln said stoutly. "But if we had your permission to meet here, what could she do?"

"A slow burn?" Patty offered.

"Look, Patty, if this puts you in an awkward position—"

"Oh, Mr. Cameron, it's not *me* who's going to be in the awkward position."

Chapter Eight

The next morning, true to his word, Lincoln went calling on the Faradays' to take Mellie on the promised hike. He hadn't seen Valetta since the fiasco in her office, but he wasn't surprised to see her standing beside her daughter as he pulled up in his rental car. Her boots laced, she was ready to accompany them. He looked at her keenly, hoping to divine her thoughts, but whatever they were, she wasn't going to share them. He guessed she wasn't going to spoil the day for Mellie, and he took that as a good sign, a peace pipe, of sorts. That was easier to believe than the idea that she had forgotten what had transpired.

The Faraday women, ready and armed, he thought ruefully as he followed them outdoors to the car. Mellie was so excited she could scarcely contain herself. "Is it all right if Yellow comes with us?" she begged as she glanced at her beloved dog sitting patiently on the porch. "He's a very good hiker and he loves to chase birds. And he's very obedient."

"That's up to you and your mother. For myself, I have no problem with it," Lincoln said, amused at the way the dog sat patiently beside the door, his tail wagging violently.

"Good, because Mom said it was up to you. Come on, Yellow," she called with a whistle.

"Thanks," Valetta said, as Yellow jumped onto the backseat. "She was counting on your soft heart."

"Well, to be honest, I figure he might protect us, alert us to bears or something."

He took Valetta's smile for a good sign. "If that happens, it will be too late."

"Seriously?" he asked, as Valetta handed him a heavy backpack.

"Don't worry, we're not going that far," she said with a grin. "Anyway, it's very rare for a black bear to attack anything more than your sandwich. You're thinking of grizzlies, and they hang out in the Rockies. Sort of near where *you* live…"

"Ha! Ha! Very funny. Look, what I don't know about bears—"

"Could fill a book!" Mellie crowed from the backseat.

"Something like, missy, so don't you go all Paul Bunyan on me." Their supplies safely stored in the trunk, Lincoln slid behind the wheel. "Okay ladies, where are we headed? I have to warn you, I haven't hiked in years, so I hope you haven't planned a treacherous five-hour march through the snowdrifts."

"That's what Mom thought." Mellie giggled as she buckled her seat belt. "She said you looked like you were in pretty good shape, though."

"She said that?" Lincoln asked, his lips twitching, while Valetta found that locking her seat belt was suddenly a complicated affair.

"Yeah, but then she said that since you could never tell, we better take you to a state park that had easy trails."

"Easy trails?" Lincoln laughed.

"Be advised," Valetta warned Lincoln, "a beginner trail in the Adirondacks is still a challenge. Contrary to common belief, the Rockies aren't the only mountains in America."

Valetta rode shotgun and she gave directions beforehand, so Lincoln didn't make any mistakes getting to their destination. Half an hour later, they were parking in Windsor Lock State Park and gathering up their scarves and gloves. A park ranger strode up to them just as Lincoln was adjusting the straps of Valetta's backpack to accommodate his broader shoulders.

"Ranger Davey!" Mellie cried, as she spotted the tall lanky figure striding their way.

"Mellie Faraday, have you grown since I last saw you?" The park ranger grinned as Mellie jumped into his arms.

"Oh, Mr. Hartwell, that was only two days ago!" Mellie reminded him with a giggle.

"Hey then, Miss Mellie, it must be all that milk you're chugalugging! Valetta," he added with a tip of his hat.

"Hello, Davey. You remember Lincoln Cameron, don't you? Our houseguest from California, or rather, Patty's houseguest, now, I should say. He rented a room there."

"Lincoln and I have already met over coffee at

Jerome's. And Chuck already told me about his new house guest."

"Why am I not surprised?" Lincoln said with a comical groan.

"Country ways," Davey apologized as he put Mellie down and held out his hand. "There are very few secrets in a small town."

Lincoln nodded as he smiled back at the ranger. There was Irish blood somewhere, Lincoln thought. But whereas half Davey Hartwell's face was a handsome study of blue eyes and black brows, the right side of his face was a road map of scarred tissue that reached from his brow to his jawline. Must have been a helluva accident, Lincoln thought. Curious how no one ever mentioned it. But then why would they if they saw the man, not the scars.

"Thanks for alerting me to your hike, Valetta. Ellen told me to tell you that dinner was around seven."

Lincoln caught the swift look of amusement that flashed through Valetta's eyes. "Is that the same Ellen Hartwell I met at Valetta's newspaper office?"

Davey was pleased that Lincoln made the connection. "My bride," he said proudly.

"So she said. Lucky man."

"We went to the wedding," Mellie exclaimed. "The whole town was there, and I was the flower girl and I wore a long white dress just like Ellen's, and carried a real bouquet and wore a wreath in my hair. I was beautiful, everybody said so!"

Valetta laughed at her daughter's shameless vanity. "Almost as beautiful as Ellen," she admonished Mellie.

"Oh, no, Ellen looked like a queen!" Mellie solemnly informed them. "She wore her hair all the way down her back, just like Juliet in *Romeo and Juliet*. And she carried a pink bouquet and there were pink flowers in her hair and on her dress, and Mom was her maid of honor, and Patty was—"

"Mellie! You're boring Mr. Cameron," Davey said, but Lincoln could tell he was pleased. "The wedding was last spring, but everyone is still excited, I guess. In particular, a little girl I know," he said with a wink.

"It made the front page of *The Spectator*." Valetta grinned. "So you could say it was something special. Of course, Ellen is something special."

"She had to be to get me to the altar," Davey said, flushing faintly.

"Too true. Lincoln, this Neanderthal was dragged kicking and screaming down the aisle," Valetta teased. "And now all he can do is talk about his *bride!*"

"I would love the opportunity to meet Mrs. Hartwell again," Lincoln said, watching Davey flush. "We hardly spoke two words when we met."

"Good, because Ellen was about to truss a chicken when I left for work. She invited all of you to dinner this morning."

"Sorry, I forgot to mention it," Valetta apologized.

"And I get to play with Pansy's puppies," Mellie said sagely. "Speaking of dogs, where is Yellow?"

Watching the dog lope to their side when he heard his name, Davey bade them good day. "All right, then, folks, I won't hold you up. Have a good time, keep to the path—"

"And don't start any forest fires!" Mellie finished for him.

Davey laughed. "Glad my visits to your school weren't a waste of time, Miss Mellie, not that you have to worry too much about fires this time of year. You folks have a good hike, then." Sending them a nod, Davey climbed into his Jeep and drove away.

The Faraday women thought it was great fun to watch a grown man the size of Lincoln Cameron struggle with a pair of snowshoes, but eventually Linc prevailed. They hiked two hours cross-country, about one and a half hours more than Valetta privately thought Lincoln could do. Not that she didn't think he wasn't in great physical condition. He was, and it stood him in good stead as they hiked across the fields. But she insisted they take it easy, resisting his request for more challenging paths. Lincoln had no idea how sore he was going to feel tomorrow, but she did.

It was a slow trot, but Mangy Yellow gleefully led the way. Lincoln was mesmerized by the beauty of the snow-covered mountains, but he was unused to the heavily laden branches of snow. Uncertain of the path, he took in more than one mouthful, and tolerated Val and Mellie's laughter with good humor. And when the opportunity arose, he sought vengeance in the shallow slope of a hill Valetta didn't notice until it was too late. Together they tumbled down, down, down, landing in each other's arms, while Mellie laughed hysterically at the sight of two grown adults thrashing about in the freshly fallen powder.

"Here, allow me," Lincoln said, extending his hand as Valetta tried to catch her breath.

"I can manage, thanks," she insisted as she scrambled to her feet.

"No, actually, you can't." Lincoln's smile was devilish as he pushed her back down in the snow.

Mellie stood at the top of the hill with Mangy Yellow

and laughed herself silly at their antics although she couldn't hear a word they said.

"I'm sorry to say this, Linc," Valetta said, as she struggled to sit up, "but I think you pushed me on purpose."

"*Moi?*" Lincoln protested, all innocence as he tripped her again. "I would *never* do something so dastardly."

"You…you…" Valetta discovered she could splutter and laugh at the same time. "Let me up, you rogue!"

"Rogue, is it?" Holding her down with one pointy finger, Lincoln could hardly stop laughing. Then suddenly, he was sober as he collapsed beside her. "Ah, Valetta, Valetta, you're…you're beautiful," he said softly, as if he had just discovered the fact.

"You are, too, Lincoln Cameron," she smiled, brushing the snow from his hair. "Even if you do look like a pirate," she added with a wicked smile.

"Thank you," Lincoln said, his finger trailing her cheek. "That's the nicest— Oomph! Ohmygosh, what was that?"

No warning given, no prisoners taken, Lincoln was suddenly bombarded with icy snow down his neck as a scrawny little girl and her thoroughly keyed-up mangy dog clambered on top of him.

"Help!" he shouted, "I'm being attacked by a…a kid…and her wet, mangy mutt!"

Lincoln's breathless cries only made them all laugh louder. If someone were standing at the top of the hill, they could not tell where the Faradays ended and Cameron began. But they would hear the raucous hilarity that spread across the snow-covered field and laugh along with the echoes.

Twenty minutes later, Lincoln brought up the rear of

the tiny parade, his legs dragging, while Mellie trotted ahead, looking for a place to picnic. Jeez, how did she do it? he wondered. Here he was, ready to drop from exhaustion and wondering whether he could be medevaced to the nearest hospital, and she and her dog were gadding about as if there was no tomorrow. And Valetta! If she sent him one more sly smirk over her shoulder…

Valetta kept careful sight of Mellie, but personally she didn't really mind the slower pace meant to accommodate Linc's exhausted stride. She was pretty wiped herself, but Valetta took care to watch Lincoln, too, knowing full well it was the cold air that got you, that the whiplash of frost attacked the best of hikers. More accidents, and worse, were a result of the weakness that followed a long, cold hike that hit your lungs like a brick if you didn't take care.

She led them to a plateau that looked out over the valley, to an outcrop of rock warmed by the bright sun, and that would warm them, too. Shading his eyes, Lincoln knelt at the edge of the precipice to drink in the breathtaking view of the valley, and the bright blue sky that crowned it. In the distance lay a town, maybe Longacre—he was too tired to ask, and didn't think it mattered anyway—looking like a picture postcard.

The valley. It sprawled before them, wide, rolling countryside that, four hundred years ago, had greeted pilgrims, puritans and charlatans alike, all of them buried now beneath a blanket of snow and enough history to build a country. A country born on the filthy deck of a rickety ship lucky to find safe harbor. A worm-ridden boat, host to a handful of lost souls grateful to land their feet on this frozen terrain in the dead of another winter, long gone. He thought they lingered in the crisp air, he was *sure* he felt them brush his brow. Lincoln laughed. Touched by ghosts! How fanciful! But he thought he'd never seen anything more beautiful, and he felt he was on sacred ground.

"You've been here before." It was a statement, not a question.

Valetta smiled as she opened her backpack and searched for the hot thermos. "Many times."

"With Mellie?"

"Many times."

"With Jack?"

Valetta's hand stilled.

"Yes, with Jack."

Lincoln said nothing as he gazed out across the valley, but he was keenly aware of the missing man, aware that he was standing in Jack's stead. The idea was disturbing, although the whole day was beginning to unsettle him. He was having thoughts he was unaccustomed to having. Unable to share what he was thinking, he looked to the child to distract him.

"Mellie, your mother is serving some wonderful cocoa over here. Do you want some, or can I have your share?"

They lingered at the plateau for a half hour, sharing stories, telling jokes, watching Mangy Yellow burrow in the snow for no better reason than he could.

"My family moved to Arizona when I was very young, about your age," he explained to Mellie when she asked why he never learned to ski. "My dad was sick, some sort of lung ailment, so he needed the dry air. It wasn't much help, our moving, I mean. He died within a year."

Valetta was all ears. She knew next to nothing about Lincoln's past.

"Where is your momma?" she heard her daughter ask, sitting cross-legged at his side.

"My mom died, too. When I was in college, in a car accident."

Mellie found that terribly sad. "That makes you an orphan, just like Anne Shirley."

"Anne Shirley?"

"From the book, *Anne of Green Gables,* silly. Didn't you ever read it? It's my absolute favorite!"

"I never thought about myself that way," Lincoln mused, "but yes, I suppose I am an orphan."

"Nobody wanted Anne because she was a girl, but then they got to love her because she was so smart. And she talked a lot. My mom says we have a lot in common. Lincoln, where do you go for Christmas?"

Valetta gasped and would have liked to call a halt to Mellie's questions but Lincoln shook his head. "It's all right, Valetta, let her ask, I don't mind. The truth is, Mellie, I don't care that much about Christmas."

"You don't care?" Mellie was shocked. "Don't you like to get presents?"

Lincoln smiled. "My employees give me scarves and stuff. No, it's not the same, is it?" he said, reading the distress on Mellie's face. "Mellie, honey, I can buy myself anything I want so it's really not a big issue."

"What about Thanksgiving?"

"I don't have to wait for Thanksgiving. My cook makes me turkey whenever I ask."

Mellie wasn't satisfied. "Do you celebrate *any* holidays?"

Lincoln shrugged. "I guess not. But I take great vacations, and I don't have to wait for a holiday to take them."

"It doesn't sound like the same, though," she said dubiously.

"I suppose not, but that's the way it is. It's not something I get too upset about, though, so don't you sound so sad, young lady. Truthfully, I don't even think about the holidays, except about being short-staffed at the office," he said with a laugh.

The walk back to the car was much quieter than the morning's exciting beginning. Lincoln dropped the Faradays off at their house. "I think I'll catch a quick nap back at Patty's. If I return around six, will that leave enough time to drive to the Hartwells' for dinner? I'd definitely get lost if I tried to find their cabin by myself."

Valetta saw the strain around his eyes and made him an offer he didn't refuse. "We do have the guest bedroom…"

Having brought some extra clothes, Lincoln went off to change into dry things and was asleep soon after. Mother and daughter changed out of their own wet clothes and went down to the kitchen, having decided on the drive home to bake Ellen a cake. Over the mixing bowl, Mellie decided she wanted to talk. About Mr. Cameron. Valetta had a feeling she didn't want to have the conversation Mellie was about to force on her. She didn't want Lincoln in her life, or Mellie's, but apparently Mellie did, and Valetta had to respect that. But she had to wonder, too, why Mellie had taken such a strong liking to a perfect stranger, wonder why her daughter had decided to champion this knight errant.

"It's so sad about his having no mother or father, don't you think?"

"I suppose," Valetta agreed, as she handed Mellie two eggs.

"Mom, have you known Mr. Cameron for a long time?"

"Um, he's worked for my sister, your Aunt Alexis, for about twenty years, give or take a few."

"What does he do?"

Valetta stifled a sigh as she buttered a cake pan. "Mellie, honey, you know what he does. He's the editor in chief of the biggest newspaper in the country."

"But I thought Aunt Alexis was in charge."

Valetta's radar screen went on alert. The conversation was heading in a direction she had been dreading for years. In her own way, Mellie was asking about her family. Valetta just hadn't expected it this soon, but Linc's visit had apparently brought things to the forefront. She cautioned herself to tread carefully lest she find herself in a quagmire. She did not want to lie to Mellie, just buy the little girl a few more years of childhood before the burden of the Keane inheritance bore down on her. And it *would* be a burden, Valetta knew all too well. Look what it had done to her sister.

"Alexis is called the publisher," she said cautiously, "but she doesn't bother with the day-to-day running of the paper. She's too busy doing other things, so she pays an editor to do that, and her editor is Mr. Cameron. You've heard the expression *the buck stops here?* Good. Well, in the case of the *Connection,* it stops at Mr. Cameron's desk. Nothing is printed without his say-so. Of course, that can be dangerous. If he gets his information wrong, he also gets in trouble. To tell the truth, though, I've never heard that happen to Lincoln but maybe once."

The wise little girl perked up immediately. "How do you know? Do you read his newspaper?"

Valetta blushed at her little slip. "I read a lot of things online. It's my job, too, to keep up with the news."

Mellie was impressed. "You mean you have the same job as Lincoln?"

Valetta chuckled. "I never thought about it quite that way, but yes, I suppose I do."

"So, if he moved to Longacre, he could work for *you*."

Valetta's heart stilled. Her daughter had no idea of the arrow she had just shot, that pierced her mother's heart. But as quickly as it cut, Valetta dismissed the images it conjured up. There was no room in her heart for Lincoln Cameron, and Linc certainly had no room for her. He had made it more than clear that he was the messenger, not the beneficiary. He was just passing through, and she would not tease herself with unattainable dreams. But Mellie was not made of such stern stuff.

"I think Mr. Cameron would make a perfect father," the little girl said with a sigh as she carefully broke the eggs into the mixing bowl.

"Mellie!" Valetta laughed, taken by surprise.

"Well, I do! And I think he needs a little girl to take care of. It's very sad that he has no family, not even a sister or brother! Everyone should have someone!"

"But what about me?"

"You're my *mom*. I need a dad, too, to help me do the things you can't. I'll bet Mr. Cameron knows math real good. He could help me with my math homework.

Play The *Lucky Hearts* Game

and get...

FREE BOOKS & a FREE GIFT... YOURS to KEEP!

Yes! I have scratched off the silver card. Please send me my **FREE BOOKS** and **FREE MYSTERY GIFT**. I understand that I am under no obligation to purchase any books as explained on the back of this card. I am over 18 years of age.

Scratch Here!
then look below to see
what you can claim...

E8II8

Mrs/Miss/Ms/Mr _____ Initials _____

BLOCK CAPITALS PLEASE

Surname _____

Address _____

_____

Postcode _____

Twenty-one gets you
4 FREE BOOKS and a
MYSTERY GIFT!

Twenty gets you
1 FREE BOOK and a
MYSTERY GIFT!

Nineteen gets you
1 FREE BOOK!

TRY AGAIN!

The Mills & Boon® Book Club™ — Here's how it works:

Accepting your free books places you under no obligation to buy anything. You may keep the books and gift and return the despatch note marked "cancel." If we do not hear from you, about a month later we'll send you 6 brand new books and invoice you just £3.15* each. That's the complete price — there is no extra charge for postage and packing. You may cancel at any time, otherwise every month we'll send you 6 more books, which you may either purchase or return to us — the choice is yours.

*Terms and prices subject to change without notice.

NO STAMP NEEDED!

THE MILLS & BOON® BOOK CLUB™
FREE BOOK OFFER
FREEPOST CN81
CROYDON
CR9 3WZ

NO STAMP
NECESSARY
IF POSTED IN
THE U.K. OR N.I.

You're not so good at math, you know. We got three answers wrong last time. I didn't want to tell you and make you feel bad, but we did."

Valetta looked at Mellie as if her daughter had sprung a second head and was maybe working on a third. She was grateful for the silence they shared over the next few minutes as they finished mixing the cake. But when the cake was in the oven and Valetta was wiping down the counter, it was clear the subject wasn't closed.

"Why don't you marry Mr. Cameron?" Mellie asked as she licked the bowl clean. "Then I would have a dad. He likes you, I can tell."

"Now, how can you possibly know that, silly goose?"

"Because he's always looking at you. And you could use a husband, too, Mom. Mr. Cameron is so strong he could carry in all the groceries at once, and he could mow the grass in the summer, and fix the chimney so we could have a real fire, and shovel the snow so your back wouldn't hurt. And he could give Yellow a bath sometimes so he doesn't look so...mangy."

Her eyes filming with tears, Valetta drew her daughter into her arms and kissed the top of her head. "Mellie, people don't marry for those reasons. Rico can do those kinds of things for hire."

"But you have to pay Rico. If you married Mr. Cameron you wouldn't have to pay him. Gosh, Mom, don't you like Mr. Cameron?"

"Of course I like Mr. Cameron."

"Do you think he's too old? I know he has gray hair like Jerome, but he doesn't have that much."

"No, Mellie!" Valetta laughed. "*Not quite* as much as Jerome."

"And I know he's younger than Jerome, but if you wait too long he'll get old, too, and then you won't want to marry him."

Valetta was taken aback by the worry in Mellie's voice. "Honey, getting married has nothing to do with age. People fall in love for all sorts of reasons and age has nothing to do with it."

I could marry you, Lincoln thought, his hand gripping the door frame as he stood on the other side of the kitchen door. His heart beating fast as he shamelessly eavesdropped, he suddenly knew that to be the truth. This could be *his* family, this could be *his* daughter talking to *his* wife.

"I want a father!" he heard Mellie complain. "Almost everyone in school has a father and I want one, too!"

What he could not see was the searching look Valetta sent her daughter. "Have you been discussing this in school?"

"Just a little, but Hannah and I tell each other everything. She doesn't have a daddy, either."

"Yes, I know that."

"We made a secret pact," Mellie revealed. "We both think that Mr. Cameron is perfect for you. Even Hannah's mom said so, and she needs a husband, too. She said that if you don't take him, she might, but that you had first dibs."

"Did Christie say that?" Valetta gasped and Lincoln had to bite his lips from laughing. "Ohmygosh, is the whole town talking about my love life?"

"What's the matter, Mom? Isn't Christie your friend?"

"Mellie Faraday, nine years old is old enough to know *not* to discuss this sort of thing with the whole town!"

"It wasn't the whole town!" Mellie said indignantly, but before she could further defend herself, Lincoln sauntered into the kitchen. He almost laughed the way they hushed so abruptly, taken off guard by his sudden appearance. He could almost see Valetta's mind churning, wondering if he had overheard their conversation. Even from a distance, he could see her cheeks redden, and it pleased him to know she was affected by his presence.

"Good evening, ladies. Thanks for letting me sleep. Hey, Mellie, ready for another hike?"

Mellie giggled. "But it's dark outside!"

Lincoln glanced past the kitchen window. "Why, so it is," he said, pretending to be surprised. "Wow, does that cake smell good! I could eat a cow, I'm so hungry. So, what are we up to here? Are we ready to head up to the Hartwells' or was I interrupting something? I thought I heard voices." It pleased him to tease Valetta a little, she was so beautifully uncomfortable.

"We were just talking," Mellie began.

Terrified of what her daughter might say, Valetta quickly cut her off, dropping the gooey cake pan. Batter dotted the floor. "Ooh, what a klutz I am. Mellie, honey, come help me clean up this mess."

"Allow me," Lincoln offered, and before Valetta could stop him, Lincoln knelt down to help her to wipe up the spill.

"Thank you," Valetta murmured, overwhelmed by his sudden nearness.

"My pleasure," Linc said with a smile. "Wait, Vallie, you've got batter on your cheek."

"How could I possibly?" Valetta spluttered.

"Here, allow me," Linc insisted, ignoring her protests.

Kneeling beside her, Lincoln clasped Valetta's chin and slowly wiped away the batter. The soft brush of his fingers on her skin sent her heart hammering, a tantalizing array of emotions threatening her composure. The intoxicating musk of his body...the sight of the fine black hair that peppered his knuckles...his sweet breath fanning her face... This was far more potent than a kiss. His eyes locked on hers; she knew that he knew.

"Lincoln, stop," she cried softly, helpless in his arms.

His look wickedly audacious, Lincoln dropped his hands and scrambled to his feet. "Come on, Vallie." Smiling, he held out his hand to help her rise. "Don't look so alarmed, honey. It's only cake batter, after all."

Chapter Nine

The entire drive up the mountain to the Hartwell house, Valetta wondered how long Lincoln had been standing by the kitchen door and what he had heard. His behavior in the kitchen had been so confusing, she couldn't figure it out except to notice he was in unusually high spirits. The man she used to know had never been one to show emotion, but here he was laughing at Mellie's *knock-knock* jokes as if she were the best thing in stand-up comedy. Now *that* was suspicious. The surreptitious looks she managed found nothing amiss, but she knew Lincoln Cameron was fully capable of dissembling. Fully capable!

Standing just inside his doorway, Davey Hartwell welcomed them warmly. They were welcomed, too, by the gruff bark of a huge, floppy sheepdog. Lincoln was introduced to Pansy, mother to three pups born two weeks before.

"It's been a long time since I've been greeted by a dog so enthusiastically. Actually, about an hour," Lincoln said with a wink to Mellie as they followed their host into the living room. The air was redolent with the promise of a home-cooked meal, while two huge logs blazed in an open stone hearth bathing the room in a golden glow, its piney scent appealing.

"This is quite a layout you have here," he said, admiring the log cabin as Davey took his coat.

"He built it himself," Ellen said proudly, her hand extended in greeting. "How do you do, Mr. Cameron?"

Lincoln clasped Ellen's hand in his. She met his eyes so accurately it was hard to believe she was blind. If he had not remembered their meeting at *The Spectator,* he might not have known.

"Mrs. Hartwell, we meet again," he said, cradling her small hand in his to deliver a gallant, Old-World kiss.

Ellen's gentle laughter was a warm ring around Lincoln's heart. It was impossible to believe that Davey had had to be dragged to the altar to marry this lovely woman. He must have been exaggerating.

"Such gallantry! Watch out, Davey," she laughed. "Mr. Cameron is out to break hearts, I can tell. May I call you Lincoln? I wish *you* would call me Ellen."

"Thank you, Mrs. Hartwell…Ellen… Nothing would give me greater pleasure."

"Thank *you,* Lincoln," Ellen returned with a radiant smile. "Just try not to charm me overmuch. Valetta warned me you were a smooth talker."

Valetta laughed as Davey handed her a glass of sherry. "Did I say that? Yeah, I guess maybe I did, but Lincoln's real talents lie elsewhere. If you feed him, he might tell you his life story."

"Lincoln's *always* hungry," Mellie piped up. Hunkered down beside the basket of puppies, she had been almost forgotten.

"Mellie Faraday!"

"But, Mom, he said so in the car!"

Davey grinned as he handed Lincoln a glass of Scotch. "Don't worry, Cameron, Ellen has cooked enough food to feed half the town."

"And me and Mom baked a chocolate cake!"

Handing his wife a glass of wine, Davey chuckled. "Then I guess I'd better pace myself. Ellen, I think what Mellie meant to say was that Lincoln here is a big man, about six foot three, if I'm any judge." Which he was, being six-three himself.

"And he looks like a pirate," Mellie added, as she cuddled one of the pups. "He always does! It's his beard. He always looks like he needs a shave, even in the morning. I think he's been re-in-car-i-nationed!"

"You mean *reincarnated*. My goodness, Mellie Faraday, what's got into you tonight? The things you say, I don't know!" her mother exclaimed with a shake of her head.

Laughing, Lincoln rubbed his stubbly chin. "Oh, let her be, Valetta. It's true. Trust me, Ellen, I get told that all the time. I have the world's heaviest five o'clock shadow. I just have to hope the pirate Mellie is talking about is that handsome movie star from that buccaneer movie! Huh, Mellie? Do I look like a movie star?" he teased.

"You look like a pirate!" she insisted.

The two women chatted for a few minutes more, sipping their wine, catching up on the town news while Lincoln and Davey sat back quietly and took stock of each other.

Entertaining… Friends… The civilizing arts were new to Davey. Disfigured in a childhood car accident, the scars on his face had reached to his soul. As a result, he had been content to roam the Adirondack Mountains in lonely isolation, taking on the job of a forest ranger, which allowed him to hide his face from view. Then Ellen Chandler had come into his life, thrust upon him by something as corny and stale as fate. His father's ward, the responsibility of her well-being had fallen to him when his father died unexpectedly. But how he had resisted! He could hardly bear to recall what a brute he had been to her. But Ellen's patience had known no bounds. Blind though she was, with problems of her own, the tiny termagant had taken him on at every step. Battling for his love, she taught him to love life more than his scars. Now, every night that he took her in his arms, he thanked the gods for sending her to him. It was an ongoing struggle to break free of his shell, but with her help, he had turned the corner.

Lincoln, on the other hand, had no friends. Acquaintances, yes, but no real friends. Davey's gut told him it was so. He recognized the signs as ones he knew well, knew it the instant he laid eyes on Lincoln, although Lincoln, with his sophisticated West Coast veneer, was more adept at hiding the fact than he, Davey, had ever been. But it *was* a fact. The way Lincoln sat so stiffly, the way he toyed with his Scotch—restless, vaguely uncomfortable—Davey could tell he was a duck out of water, more used to the impersonal friendliness of Southern California than the intimacy of a log cabin in the woods. He could see it in the way Lincoln's eyes darted to Valetta with such alarming frequency. Davey wondered if she noticed, and he had to suppose she did, if *he* had picked up on it.

Davey was right, and Davey was wrong.

Lincoln was uncomfortable, and yet at the same time, he relished every moment of the evening. Nursing his Scotch, watching Mellie play with the puppies, listening to the low sweet murmurs of the women, he knew he was at a crossroads in his life. When he looked around the inviting living room with its cheerful red curtains and soft gray carpet, stared absently into the crackling fire, felt the Hartwell hospitality envelop him…

Comparing it to his own life, he came up empty. For instance, Davey's devotion to his wife…the way Ellen felt for Davey's hand. If nothing else about the evening touched him, it was their obvious deep and abiding love. Empty words he'd heard every so often, in a book or a movie, suddenly took on new meaning as he looked at Davey and Ellen. Watching the newlyweds, he thought he might have a glimmer of understanding of the phrase *true love.*

Although Davey was inclined to tell funny, affectionate stories of Ellen's culinary mishaps, it was obvious that Ellen Chandler Hartwell had mastered the basics of cooking, notwithstanding her blindness. The roast chicken, stuffed with lemons, was excellent; the kale, seasoned with sesame seeds, was steamed to perfection and the potatoes, sprinkled with balsamic vinegar, were crisp. The company was as good as the food and Lincoln could not think when he'd had a better time. But much of his pleasure was due to the pull of Valetta. Her gray eyes drew him in, the elegant grace of her figure, her mismatched clothes, her unguarded glances that made him restless.

Exhausted from their morning hike, Mellie fell

asleep on the rug, warmed by Pansy and her pups. They laughed at the sight, but were careful not to wake her as they lingered over their coffee. Davey made a fresh pot while Ellen told Longacre stories, amused Lincoln with the story of her courtship with Davey, and confided stories of Montana, where she had grown up, that even Valetta had not heard. Hating to end the evening, they all talked late into the night, but when a yawn from Ellen could no longer be stifled, they finally roused themselves.

Mellie slept the whole trip home, curled up on the backseat. Mangy Yellow knew better than to bark at one in the morning, so Lincoln was able to carry Mellie up the stairs without her waking. She had a pretty room, girly, filled with lacy pink pillows and dolls, her shelves filled with board games and mementos, her computer surrounded by a pile of books. Gently, Lincoln put her down and tiptoed out so Valetta could put her daughter to bed. But ten minutes later, when Valetta went to check the locks, she was surprised to find Lincoln sitting on the sofa. Sensing that something was bothering him deeply, Valetta knelt before him and rested her hands on his knees.

"Lincoln, what's wrong?"

"Nothing. Everything."

It was no use pretending. The evening held him hostage to feelings he was unfamiliar with. Everything around him was a message he was unable to sort.

And her mouth was so tempting.

"Valetta, what's happening?"

Smiling gently, Valetta ran her thumb across his rough, shadowed jaw as she cradled his face between her hands. "Poor Lincoln. Mellie's right," she teased gently. "There *is* pirate blood in you."

"Some pirate I am," he snorted, "sitting in the middle of a dark living room on the top of a snow-covered mountain, and not a ship in sight!"

"Nope. No ship. Nothing to escape with. Just you, me and Yellow."

He took a deep breath. "Valetta, why did you really leave home? Alexis alone couldn't drive you away. It was such a drastic thing to do, leaving the way you did, running away in the middle of the night."

Why did he always return to that night? It was so long ago, she almost felt as if it happened to someone else. In a way, it had. She had just turned eighteen, hardly an adult, mostly a child. Now, she was thirty, a grown woman, a widow, a mother. She hardly ever thought about her past anymore, except maybe around the holidays, or like now, when it was forced on her.

She had a hunch she was about to learn the reason Linc had come east. Something told her she didn't want to know, that a situation was about to be thrust upon her, a moral imperative she might not be allowed to refuse.

"You're right, it wasn't only Alexis," she said, rising to her feet, "although she was the main reason. She was my sister, but she was trying to be my mother, as well. She couldn't be both, and wasn't too good at either. I guess we both got tangled in the mess."

"What went wrong, do you think?"

"Oh, that's the easy part. She didn't want to be either sister *or* mother. You see who she is. That's all she ever wanted to be, a newspaper woman! It was just her bad luck to have our parents die unexpectedly and be left with a baby sister. And I *was* a baby, eleven, not much older than Mellie is now."

Valetta touched her hair, turned white with the grief

of Jack's death. "God, how I cried when my parents died. Buckets and buckets. Alexis was good, the first few years. She tried to comfort me, she really tried to do her duty. But that was part of the problem, kids shouldn't be a duty," Valetta said thoughtfully. "And they know when they are. I wasn't a difficult kid. It was the teenager I became that got to her. I can laugh now, but boy, did she hate having an adolescent around. Pimples, raging hormones and a bad attitude are a deadly combination for anyone. For Alexis, it spelled *nightmare.* Talk about clueless, she had no idea what to do. When I turned sixteen, she tried to send me to boarding school but I absolutely refused to go. So, there I was, a moody, high-strung teenager—normal in every sense—and she goes and hires a nanny!"

"I vaguely remember," Lincoln said. "Her name was Samantha, wasn't it?"

"You remember Sammie? I'm impressed. Poor woman, how I hated her! Alexis used to leave her *nanny notes* as she called them, on the kitchen counter. Pink notes told Sammie what I should eat for breakfast—to improve my skin!—and what I should wear to school. Yellow sheets covered my schedule: dance lessons on Monday, pottery class on Tuesday, violin every other Thursday. Doctor visits were written in blue, dental appointments in green. If I had a cold and simply wanted to stay home, tough luck. Sammie was too terrified of Alexis to ignore a single note. And as for friends…I had no friends. Thus did Alexis fill my every waking hour and try to pass it off as parenting. Half the time I was overscheduled, most of the time I was exhausted. Meanwhile, she hid across town in that ivory tower you call the *L.A. Connection.* I can't say that I blame her.

She didn't want kids of her own, so why should she want me?"

"Come on, Valetta, you were her sister."

Valetta shrugged. If he didn't want to listen… "It wasn't all bad," she said, with a twinkle. "Once in a while she would invite *you* to dinner. I would be in raptures all day, and standing by the door at seven waiting for you to arrive. Lincoln Cameron was coming to dinner! My big brother! That's how I thought of you."

"Which I tried to be."

"And which I pretended you were! If I never told you, I want you to know now that I adored you, Lincoln. When you came to visit, it was as if something wonderful was going to happen, and it did. You! The world-famous reporter of the most famous newspaper in the world was dining at our table *en famille,* making us laugh, entertaining us with the most wonderful stories. *How special was that?* I was in heaven."

"I don't remember making Alexis laugh."

"That's all right. You made *me* laugh. In all those years, you were the only guest we ever had, the only one! Don't you think that's weird?"

"Alexis's social skills are not finely honed. Oh, she's an amazing CEO, but she doesn't like to get too friendly. Even her office staff—and some people have been with her for years—is kept at a distance. But do you remember why those dinners ended, Vallie? I seem to recall there was an abrupt change just before you left."

"Sure. You got too close, so she stopped inviting you."

"She did not!"

"She did, too! Think back, Linc, think back."

Valetta watched as Lincoln paced the room, trying to rework the past.

"Don't drive yourself crazy looking for a reason because it wasn't anything you did. The simple fact is, Alexis found my diary. Remember, I was developing… You know the sort of thing I mean. Boys channel that growth spurt into sports and video games, but diaries are a common way for some girls to handle that energy, and it's every bit as healthy as a soccer game. Even Mellie has one. It's a rite of passage for girls, like their first lipstick. Another thing Alexis was ignorant of. And I paid dearly for her ignorance."

Lincoln was miserable but wanted to know everything, and Valetta was relieved to get her story off her chest. But having had the advantage of the healing power of time, she was able to view it less emotionally.

"Heaven forgive me," she laughed, "but I was beginning to be interested in the *B* word."

"The *B* word?" Lincoln frowned.

"*Boys!* You know, those awkward creatures little girls like to boss around. Well, at a certain age, girls don't want to *only* boss them around. They begin to be objects of intense curiosity. And when *you,* the only male of the species I was acquainted with up close and personal, when *you* began to look a bit different to me… Less like a brother, if you get my drift," she teased. "You've *always* had an air of mystery, an aura of glamour you couldn't help. You can imagine how confused I suddenly was, and with no one to explain the birds and the bees to me…" Valetta smiled ruefully. "Every night, in the privacy of my bedroom, I confided my trembling heart to the pages of my diary. And it was all about *you*. Every smile you sent me, every joke you told, every slight—real or imagined—was immortalized on those sticky pages. In purple ink, no less! The silly scribbling of a love-struck teenager in the throes of her first infatuation."

"Oh, Vallie, I am so sorry!"

"Sorry for what?" Valetta frowned comically. "It was a perfectly normal schoolgirl crush. And why wouldn't it be about you? We lived in Beverly Hills, didn't we? You looked just like all those movie stars I saw on Hollywood and Vine, tall, dark and *so* incredibly handsome." She sighed dramatically. "Someone I could never have. And nothing personal, Lincoln, but like any teenaged girl in the middle of her first crush, I didn't want to *have you,* I just wanted to look at you and moon over you and create horribly embarrassing fantasies about you. Jeez, Linc, I would have had a nervous breakdown if you'd ever made me any overtures. Which I knew you would not, your being blessedly unaware of my existence in that way."

"Amen to that!" Lincoln said with mock severity. "I never saw so many pimples in my life."

"See." Valetta grinned. "You fit *perfectly* all the parameters of an adolescent fantasy. It was absolutely innocent…and Alexis went berserk. She was clueless, and having no idea how to handle things, she decided to simply cut you off."

"Hey, is that why?"

"See, you *do* remember," Valetta said. "Alexis thought I was *really* falling in love with you! That's what our last fight was about. *You!*"

"No!"

"Yes, *you!* The only semblance of family I had after our parents died, a smiling face across the table during the occasional Friday night dinner, but she turned my adoration into something else. She found my diary, and worse, she read it. After that, it was all over. She said terrible things, humiliated me, made my life miserable. You would have thought I'd stolen her boyfriend, the way she carried on. One particular night, she went too far."

Lincoln shook his head in disbelief. "I must have been as clueless as Alexis not to be aware of this!"

"Oh, she wasn't going to say a word to *you*. If she confronted you, she would lose the best editor she'd ever had, and there was no way she was going to chance *that*. Besides, she knew it wasn't your fault. To be honest, Lincoln, it wasn't so much my fight with Alexis that upset me as the privacy issue. After she found my diary, she had the servants tear apart my room. Who knows what she was looking for, but that was the last straw, that's what flipped me over the edge. A few days later, she was stuck in bed with a head cold…it was the servants' night off… Sammie had left early… The timing was right. I slipped downstairs, shut the house alarm, climbed out my bedroom window—this took all of two minutes, mind you—and grabbed the backpack I had stowed away in the boathouse. I knew I had an aunt living in a small town in upstate New York, my mother's sister, so I bought a one-way train ticket east."

His face a mask of unhappiness, Lincoln was grief-stricken. "I am so sorry, Valetta. If I had known, I would have stopped her, I swear it."

Valetta met his eyes frankly. "No, Linc, you would not have. You *could* not have. You had no right to interfere, no power to change things. When it came down to it, you were just a family friend." Valetta smiled sadly. "Although Alexis and I, we really weren't much of a family, were we? I found my true family once I left home and my aunt Phyla took me in. Finally, I had a mother, even if it didn't last too long. I should have sought her out years before, but things happen the way they happen."

"And where did Jack Faraday fit in?"

Valetta smiled softly. "He was a good man. You would have liked him. Everyone did."

"No doubt I would have, but I wish I had known what happened to you. Why didn't you write me? Not a single word in ten years."

"Suffering from a full-blown case of teenage angst? I don't think so! I never even mentioned your name to my aunt, and *she* was the one who put me back on track. That wonderful woman hugged me to death, told me how great I was, and I believed her. The two years we spent together saved my life."

Lincoln started toward her, but Valetta waved him away. "Please, I would like to finish, I want you to know everything."

Lincoln backed away. The way he ran his fingers though his hair, a picture of despair, Valetta almost felt sorry for him.

"We were a pair, here in town, Phyla and I, inseparable. I blossomed, and it was all her doing. The day she was diagnosed with cancer was the worst day of our lives, and you know she took the news better than I did. Now it was my turn to save *her* life—and I was helpless. The tumor was virulent. Thankfully, the end was brief, although her pain… I never left her side and I didn't want to. Jack Faraday was her doctor—that's how we met—and he swept me off my feet. When Aunt Phyla asked to see us married before she died, it was no hardship to please her, we were madly in love."

"Vallie—"

"Life has a way of intruding, you know, Linc? You let something pass, momentum takes over—whatever—and it's gone. The way you should be!" Valetta gasped, jumping to her feet when she noticed the time. "It's almost three! Go home, Lincoln. Go home to California! It's really for the best."

"I can't. I haven't told you yet why I've come."

"It doesn't matter. I don't want to hear it," she said firmly as she handed him his coat.

"Perhaps you don't," he said, as he stepped out into the cold night air, "but I didn't come across the country just to tell you stories, or hear them. I know we're both tired, we've said a lot of things tonight...." Bending low, Lincoln pressed a kiss to Valetta's forehead. He was surprised when she raised her head.

On impulse, her fingers curled around his arms, felt the tremor of his surprise, heard his sharp intake of breath.

"Valetta?"

Lincoln's question became an answer. Gathering her into his arms, he enveloped her in his coat and molded her to his body. His mouth hovering on hers, their warm breath mingled together. Whatever unspoken history lay between them exploded into the open.

"Can I kiss you, Valetta? Can I kiss you?"

It had been years since a man had touched her but Valetta's hesitation was momentary. Shyly she parted her lips. If she found Lincoln's mouth hard, even a tiny bit bruising, her senses were awakened and she wanted more.

Rimming her mouth, Linc's tongue glanced off the tip of hers, a slow dance to assure himself he was invited. Oh, he was! He thought he'd die with want for her, shivered when he felt her tongue timidly seek his. Weak and confused, he almost laughed. Shouldn't it be the woman who felt that way? Hadn't he got it backward? Backward, sideways, upside-down, it didn't matter. He never wanted to let her go.

Intoxicated, Valetta tasted the faint remnants of coffee, almonds and something else—the sweet taste of Linc's reined-in passion. It had been so many years, she had forgotten the simple pleasure of a man's kiss. But the biggest surprise was Lincoln's willingness to meet her. She'd felt selfish throwing herself at him, and not a little embarrassed, but she had acted on impulse. Now, she was glad. He seemed to want this just as much as she.

And what to do?

And how soon?

And when?

How soon before they saw each other again and discovered whether this new pose was real? If that curious and odd light mirrored in each other's eyes—that flash of unexpected excitement—really existed. How pleasant it was for them to wonder whether that slight quivering they *just knew* they had felt, that heightened sense of anticipation, was in reaction to more than the cold night air.

In another lifetime, things might have happened this way.

But not this one.

Chapter Ten

Sundays in Longacre almost everyone slept late. When Lincoln finally made it down to breakfast, way past noon, there was a note from Patty propped against the toaster.

I had to leave early. Please help yourself. Chuck will lend a hand.
Patty

"That part about *Chuck lending a hand,* I'm sure she didn't mean it," Chuck said from behind his Sunday paper. "I'm not known for my culinary skills. But the coffee's fresh, the bread's in the bread box, and the eggs are in the fridge—that is, if you have the energy."

Lincoln succumbed to the lure of the percolator. "God, I need a shower, but that coffee smelled so great, I couldn't resist. Need a fill-up?"

"No, thanks, I'm fine, which is more than I can say for you," Chuck observed as he lowered his paper.

Scratching his beard, Lincoln refused to be baited. "Look here, bright eyes, I might have been up past my bedtime, but I started yesterday with the hike from hell."

"Is that a comment on the company?"

"On the contrary. But my poor feet! My God, that Mellie Faraday is amazing. I always thought if you had short legs, you couldn't move fast, but good Lord, I think we must have walked a hundred miles and she never complained, not once! In four inches of snow, no less!"

Lincoln sipped his coffee, grateful it was strong. "Then that crazy drive in the pitch dark up a mountain road covered with ice to have dinner with the Hartwells. A great meal, sure, but you'd be exhausted, too."

"Say, you ever do any winter fishing?" Chuck asked, unmoved. "Davey and I are heading out for an hour or so. If you're interested, we'll wait."

"You hear anything I just said?"

Chuck grinned. "I knew you'd want to come with us, that's why we waited. Don't worry, I'll lend you a rod. I have extras."

Lincoln gave up with a laugh. "Okay, give me twenty minutes. I really do need that shower." Coffee in hand, he was headed for the stairs when a thought struck him. "Tell me something, Chuck. Does this town ever do anything indoors, like, where it's heated? Bowling, for instance."

"Sure thing, *California*," Chuck said, straight-faced. "But only when it snows, and then it has to be a blizzard."

"Glad to know it. This snow-bunny stuff is exhausting. It's a good thing I'm in shape…sort of," he muttered as he shuffled down the hall.

An hour later, the three men made their way to a pond so well hidden that only a mountain man like Davey or a local like Chuck would ever know of its existence. They carried rods, an assortment of tackle, a couple of thermoses of coffee, some beverages, and some snacks. Lincoln followed them, scrambling across the snowdrifts awkwardly like the city boy he was. Pulling his wool cap low, he blessed Patty Carmichael for insisting he buy the heavier gloves.

The other two men marched ahead, gloveless, their heads uncovered. The cold didn't seem to affect them, but Lincoln told himself their blood was probably thicker. After spending most of his life in Los Angeles, he figured his blood was the consistency of Perrier.

"Got my hopes on catching some pike." Chuck's words drifted back to Lincoln on the winter air. "But I promised Patty some white crappie for dinner."

"Can you eat crappies…um…that fish?" Lincoln shouted as he clapped his hands to keep warm. "I mean, maybe there's no point to this, what do you think? Lobster, it isn't," he grumbled. "Not even shrimp."

Davey Hartwell turned to him with a lopsided grin.

"Hey, just asking," Lincoln muttered.

"A little salt and pepper, and lots of butter, you'll think you died and went to heaven," Davey promised, as he resumed his walk.

"Shoot, I think I did that already." Lincoln swore under his breath, although the smile he sent them was wide. But a few minutes later, when they rounded a bend, he was treated to the vista of a frozen lake so lovely, he couldn't speak. Nestled in the midst of the mountains, the lake must have been a half a mile wide, and Davey promised it ran north at least twice that. It was lined on either side by evergreens and browned-out deciduous trees. The low brush of winter was gone, but Chuck told him that when it returned in early spring, it painted the lake an emerald green. Lincoln couldn't imagine it more beautiful than this moment, but Chuck assured him it was. Slowly, the men ventured out to the middle of the lake.

"Talk about walking on thin ice." Lincoln shivered as he reluctantly followed their lead. Having never ice fished before, he was leery about standing in the middle of a fifty-foot-deep lake, much less cutting a hole in the center. And the more Chuck and Davey laughed, the more he frowned.

"Don't worry, Cameron, I was out here last Thursday to measure the thickness. The ice was seventeen inches, and it has to be more by now since it snowed. The temperature's been down to a nice even five degrees these past few nights, so we don't have to worry about any cracks," Davey promised.

Oh, great! What a relief!

"Believe me, Lincoln, we bring the girls out here, so we're very, very careful. But hey, look," Chuck grinned, "if it makes you feel any better, should something happen, do you have any messages you want me to deliver? You were out so late last night, I thought…"

"One and one doesn't always make two," Lincoln warned Chuck.

"Ah, but more often than not, it does, my friend!"

"Let him be, Carmichael," Davey admonished Chuck. "I don't know when you ever claimed to be a math genius, anyway."

"Too true," Chuck admitted. "Okay, here we go, Lincoln. Let's get this hole finished and we'll set you up with a rod. It's a bit late, being Sunday and all, but maybe we can still find some dinner. I sneak over here almost every weekend in the summer to swim and do some fishing, so I know it's pretty well stocked."

"Mostly you nap, though." Davey laughed.

Lincoln listened, charmed by their childlike banter. They seemed to relish unwinding away from their wives, and as they set up shop, it was clear they knew their business. When they handed him a five-foot rod, the name-dropping began. Twister tails…four pound test… short shank jobbies…slab crappies…slip bobbers…

What the hell were they talking about?

"Gently…gently…" they warned him as he stood half-frozen on the edge of an ice slick, a million miles from nowhere. But when they handed him a flask of *the beverage,* whatever it was, Lincoln began to feel warmer. Much warmer. It wasn't coffee, but it sure took the chill away. To hell with the fish!

"Got to get Cameron here a proper pair of boots, for next time," Chuck said with a laugh.

They stayed for three hours, until *the beverage* was finished, the coffee gone and not a crumb left to eat. And not a single fish between them! Since Davey hardly partook of the flask, he did the driving home. Lincoln sat in the middle of the pickup, his frozen hands pressed against the heat vent. Did this mean Lincoln wasn't going to attend the derby?

"The Kentucky Derby?"

"Just listen to him!" Chuck roared. "For heaven's sake, man, do you see any magnolia trees? I'm talking about the Annual Crappie Derby!"

"The Annual Crappie Derby?"

"As annual as possible," Davey chuckled. "Global warming will do that!"

"They've had a few misses, is all," Chuck explained. "The ice thawed a couple of years back so they had to cancel. But for the most part, it does take place. And they must be doing something right because the purse keeps getting bigger every year, though most of it goes to the kids."

"But some goes to restock the lake," Davey added. "It's a beautiful lagoon, a lovely sight. We'll take you sometime."

"That would be great," Lincoln murmured, wondering how they came to move a lagoon from Puerto Viejo to upstate New York. Marvelous, the things they could do these days, he thought, as he fell asleep in a warm haze of *the beverage*.

When Lincoln arrived at Valetta's office Monday morning, his rip-roaring hangover was subdued by about a thousand aspirin. He was even less pleased when Ellen told him that Valetta had gone up to Utica for a few days, on business. A conference. Hadn't she mentioned it?

No.

Ellen was distressed. Maybe Valetta forgot, it had been booked quite a while ago. She had left the running of the paper to Andrew and Ben, but unfortunately they, too, were out at the moment. Was there anything she could do for him?

No.

Ellen looked so uncomfortable, Lincoln regretted having stopped by. Not wishing to cause her worry, he hid his disappointment, explaining that he really only wanted to remind Ben and Andy that they were all set to go for this evening. The journalism class they had asked him to hold. To offer a few pointers. No big deal. Very off-the-cuff.

Oh, yes, she remembered. They would all be there, around seven.

All?

Of course. Oh, but since Mellie was staying with her and Davey for the week, would Lincoln mind if they brought her to class? She was such a well-behaved little girl, he would never notice her presence. She had given Ellen her word that she would sit quietly in a corner and do her homework.

That would be the day, Lincoln thought. "No trouble," Lincoln agreed, although he would rather have refused. Mellie was sure to tell her mama about the classes first thing when Valetta returned on Friday. No, she would probably tell Valetta over the phone that very night!

Having only a vague idea of how to conduct a journalism class, Lincoln drove over to Patty's dry goods store and picked up a ream of paper, packs of pens, markers, and the like. He even sprang for a small black-board and chalk.

He was so keyed up that Patty had to hide her smiles as she helped him set up a makeshift classroom in her living room later that evening. She had a hunch enthusiasm was an underutilized emotion for Lincoln Cameron. Her husband agreed, but she thought Chuck seemed as eager for the evening's event as Lincoln. It seemed to her that their houseguest was breathing new life into her husband. Although farming was Chuck's life, she sometimes wondered if he wasn't just a little bit bored. An avid reader—he always seemed to have his nose in an almanac or a farm manual—he was also interested in a host of subjects outside agriculture. Joke as he might about Lincoln's lamentable lack of fishing prowess, she wondered if Chuck wasn't glad to have him there to challenge his intellect.

When Lincoln opened the door that evening, he was surprised to watch the entire workforce of *The Spectator* troop in. Andy and Ben found seats as close to the chalkboard as possible, while Julie Berry, having long discovered who Lincoln Cameron was, pulled up a chair beside them. Recuperating from the flu, Flossie McGowan set her tissue box on the rug and waited patiently for things to begin. Kirin Red munched on a ham sandwich as he talked quietly with Patty, while Jay Logan, running late, tried to find an empty coat hook.

And true to her word, Ellen Hartwell brought Mellie Faraday, who hugged Lincoln's knees and settled smack-dab in the middle of the circle, her homework spread across the rug. Since Ellen was one of the attendees, it stood to reason that Davey would join her, and since he had to drive to town to pick up his wife, he decided to come a little early and sit in on the class. *If Lincoln didn't mind.*

Of course not, Lincoln said, wondering where the huge man would sit.

Mellie, having mentioned the class to her best friend, Hannah, Hannah naturally mentioned it to her mom, Christie, when she got home from work. Thus Christie showed up, too. *If Mr. Cameron didn't mind.* See, she was secretly writing this book…

Of course not. Lincoln smiled faintly as she found a seat.

Someone having mentioned the class to Jerome Crater that afternoon, no one was surprised to find the old man knocking on the door, shortly after seven.

"Kicked everybody out early," he growled as he handed Patty his coat. "Young Cameron...heard he was giving a lecture...interesting idea. Cheaper than the movies," the old man opined as he settled down in the lone rocking chair.

Rico Suarez was the last to show, having driven to town with his wife, Nancy, for a dish of pistachio ice cream. Seven months pregnant and subject to whims— you have no idea, Rico whispered to Lincoln, his eyes rolled to heaven—Nancy was upset to see the lights out at Jerome's restaurant. Reading the note pinned to the diner door, they hurried over to the Carmichael house. Since we were already in town, Rico said with a sheepish grin. It wasn't like there was a whole lot to do on a snowy Monday evening in Longacre, he explained. Nancy was fretting, she'd been stuck inside all day. *If Lincoln didn't mind.*

But this was a class on *journalism.*

You never knew, said Rico.

No, you never knew, Lincoln thought, as he watched Rico shepherd his wife to the sofa.

Lincoln began with an overview of the *L.A. Connection* and its history. Since it was established in 1927, just before the depression, there was a lot of ground to cover. He moved from a discussion of the periodical's original, simpler purpose to its evolution as a world-class paper. The similarity between its own roots and a small-town paper like *The Spectator* was inescapable.

He continued by examining his paper's parts, explaining how the huge daily was sectioned off to be optimally productive. How information was gathered, how responsibility was delegated. No one asked him about the redoubtable Alexis Keane, and he didn't volunteer to talk about the influence of the owner on the paper. He was amused that no one asked about *his* role until it occurred to him that they were probably being polite.

The class was such a rousing success that it ran an hour later than expected. Around ten, Lincoln had to finally insist everyone leave, reminding them that not only did Patty and Chuck have to go to bed, but they did, too! Well, that was of no account, Chuck assured Lincoln, but they did all have to go to work the next day. But if they liked, and if Mr. Cameron didn't have anything better to do, they were all welcome to return the next evening.

You never knew, Lincoln thought with a smile to himself, as he nodded his agreement.

Tuesday, Lincoln spent the whole afternoon preparing an outline for the evening discussion. His students' eagerness was so impressive and so engaging, he felt it was the least he could do. When they filed in later that evening—and not a soul was late!—he was armed and ready. Even Rico's wife, Nancy, toddled in, shyly presenting the Carmichaels with a home-baked bundt, a sort of thank-you, she whispered to Patty. Pleased with the cake, Patty insisted on brewing a pot of coffee, so the class got off to a late start, but the enthusiasm of the group paid Lincoln back threefold. Before he knew it, his energy riding high, he had established a schedule for the rest of the month.

For the rest of the month? When he was alone in his room later that night, he was aghast at himself for having done such a foolish thing. How on earth had he committed to the next four weeks when he was supposed to return to L.A. by the end of this week?

Alexis was never going to understand, never!

And what was Valetta going to say when she got wind of this?

And when was he going to fulfill his obligation to Alexis? Time was of the essence. Alexis couldn't wait on his whim of being a small-town journalism professor. She was ill. Every day was precious. He must speak to Valetta as soon as possible.

Damned if the whole town hadn't seduced him! They should have a sign, he thought ruefully, out on Route 28, that said:

Welcome to Longacre...The Town that Never Says Goodbye

Or maybe:

Welcome to Longacre...We Rent By the Month

Or maybe even:

Welcome to Longacre...Gotcha!

Chapter Eleven

"**Y**ou come home on the next plane, Lincoln Cameron, *the very next flight!*" Alexis ordered him over the phone the next morning. "I'll have my secretary book it. Nonstop, Albany International to LAX," he heard her call to her secretary.

Lincoln took a deep breath as he juggled his cell phone. "Alexis, listen, I just can't up and leave. Valetta isn't even here. She drove out to Utica, some sort of business meeting. You know how they can crop up suddenly."

"When is she coming home?"

"I'm not sure," he lied. "It depended...on things. Monday, at the earliest, and I'm sort of involved here...helping to babysit Mellie...."

Well, it was sort of the truth, he told himself. "So you see, I can't possibly leave yet." Lincoln could almost hear her mind spinning, trying to sort through the lies and half truths.

"Did you speak to her about coming home?"

"Sort of." Lincoln took a deep breath. "Well, to be honest, not precisely."

Alexis's silence was louder criticism than any words she could have uttered.

"Alexis, I warned you it wouldn't be simple. Valetta is very involved here, for goodness' sake. She has a life, a child, good friends—really good friends—not acquaintances...like us." That last was hard to say, but he forced himself to say it, ignoring the shiver in his heart. "I'm telling you, Alexis, it won't be easy to pry her away. The fact is, I think the townspeople love her way too much to let her go without a fight. They have a way here of protecting their own, and she's part of their fabric, very much so.

"Mellie, too, maybe even more. Mellie is their future. It's not like in Los Angeles. Here, one person leaves, it impacts big-time on the entire town."

"What about *me?* I have obligations, too. For instance," she said with chilling emphasis, "the future of my paper? Remember that? What about all the people here in Los Angeles who depend on the Keanes for *their* livelihood? And not the least, what about *you?*"

"I know," Lincoln said with a sigh. "Believe me, I've been giving it a great deal of thought. But I want you to know, if you don't already, that I'm in constant contact with my desk editors. We e-mail each other twice daily, and my secretary calls me almost hourly with updates. The paper is under my complete control. There is no crisis I cannot handle, even from this distance. But you know all this. You have nothing to worry about, as far as that is concerned."

"Do I have *anything* to worry about, Cameron?"

Unsure how to answer, Lincoln backed down. "Look, Alexis, give me a few more days. I haven't spoken to Valetta yet. She may surprise us and decide to return to California."

"Surprise us? You must *insist* that she return to California. You must tell her that, first thing, when she gets back. It's long overdue for her to come home!"

Lady, are you ever missing the point. She *is* home, and that's the problem in a nutshell.

"…she's had her fun…"

Her fun?

"…but she has responsibilities she can no longer ignore. And I have to be honest, Cameron. No matter how many pills my doctor prescribes, my health is not as good as it could be."

Lincoln squirmed uncomfortably. "I'll talk to her, first thing, Alexis. I promise."

"Lincoln, you sound dreadfully strange…different. Are you all right?"

"It's the connection, Alexis. You sound different, too." Far away. A stranger, Lincoln thought as he shut his cell phone.

Was it because he had become a stranger to himself? Aside from the depressing conversation, he couldn't remember the last time he had felt so energized. He was actually curious about things that had nothing to do with newspapers or stories or deadlines. Why, just last night he had actually volunteered—*volunteered!*—to drive Jerome to the doctor. And as soon as she came home from school this afternoon, he was going to tutor

Mellie in math because she had a big test on Friday that—her words—she just had to pass with flying colors! And on Saturday—at 4:00 a.m. for heaven's sake!—he was going hunting with Chuck and Davey. Not that he was going to shoot anything! Not that any of them would, Chuck had promised, but it was that rare opportunity for the guys to get away. Not that they didn't love their wives, not at all! But it was fun to climb a blind, hunker down with a hot thermos of coffee and tell wild stories of great untruth.

No, Lincoln didn't know, but he was damned if he couldn't wait to find out!

Lincoln shook his head. He *was* a stranger.

Valetta smiled as she opened the door Friday evening to see Lincoln holding two huge, brown bags. "Is that Chinese food?" She sniffed with unconcealed delight.

"How can you tell?" he asked with a grin. "I just happened to be in Albany. You and Mellie haven't eaten dinner yet, I hope?"

"No, we didn't eat. But no one *happens* to be in Albany, Lincoln. It's over two hours away. Here, let me get those bags while you take off your boots. Oh, this smells wonderful."

"I took Jerome to Albany this morning for a checkup," Linc explained as he unlaced his boots. "His legs were bothering him."

"Why, that was very nice of you, Lincoln!"

"It was only what anyone else would have done."

"Perhaps, but why you? Rico usually drives Jerome if I'm not available."

"Rico was nervous about leaving Nancy—her due date is approaching, so I volunteered. It was really no trouble. We actually had a great time. We went to lunch after his appointment, I took him to a fancy inn, and I think he enjoyed himself even if he complained nonstop."

But Lincoln had no time to finish his story. Mellie was bounding down the stairs, shouting his name. "Lincoln! Lincoln! You're back! And I smell Chinese food, just like you promised!"

Just like you promised?

"Got it in one, sugar baby!"

Sugar baby? Valetta looked from her daughter to Lincoln, surprised by their new dimension of friendship.

"Did you get an extra wonton soup?"

"Wonton soup and egg rolls, spareribs and egg foo young, fried rice and shrimp in lobster sauce!"

"And fortune cookies?"

"Enough to set up a business, sweetums!"

Sweetums?

Valetta had had enough. "Mellie, take these bags into the kitchen and set the table. I'll wait while Lincoln takes off his boots. Yellow will keep you company."

When she was sure Mellie was out of hearing, Valetta turned to Linc and crossed her arms.

"Well?"

"Well, *what?*" Linc asked innocently, his nose buried in leather and shoelace.

"What's going on, *sweetums?* Worrying about Nancy's due date, taking Jerome to the doctor, coming back with Chinese food…"

"You know, Vallie, sarcasm doesn't become you."

"And subterfuge does not become *you!* I thought you'd be gone when I got back."

"Is that why you left? That *was* a pretty impromptu business meeting, if you ask me."

"No one asked you. What I did not expect was to come home to find you delivering Chinese food to my daughter—"

"And you."

Hands on her hips, Valetta faced him with a narrow squint. "What's going on, Lincoln? Why are you still here? Don't you have a job to go back to?"

Lincoln scratched his five o'clock shadow, a cautious smile on his lips. "Of course I have a job, and it's nearing time for me to leave. But does that mean I shouldn't be civilized? Or would you rather I didn't help Jerome out, and Rico and Nancy, in the bargain? And since I was in Albany, it was no trouble to pick up some takeout. When Mellie told me she loved Chinese food the other day, when I was tutoring her—"

"When you were *what?*"

"Hush, Valetta. The child might hear you and it would spoil her dinner. She's weak in math, you know."

With a backward glance at the kitchen door, Valetta pressed a pointy finger to Linc's chest. "Make no mistake, Mr. Cameron. We are going to have a long talk. *Tonight.* Do you hear?"

There was nothing Lincoln could say to that ultimatum except, "Yes, ma'am," as he followed her down the hall. A mother and daughter reunion, he thought as he padded into the warm kitchen and the warmth of the Faraday women. "I guess I overbought. I wasn't sure who liked what."

"So you bought one of everything?" Valetta asked, bewildered by the mass of white containers covering the table.

"Almost." He grinned as he sat down. "Don't worry. I'll finish whatever you two don't eat."

"Well, no question, this was very generous of you, Lincoln," she admitted while she watched Mellie gather the fortune cookies into a small pile. "Hey, slow down, miss. How about some soup before you open all those cookies?"

"I was only making sure they didn't get lost," Mellie protested as she pulled her dinner plate closer.

"Sure, sure. Here, let me pour you some soup. It smells wonderful, doesn't it?"

It only took a few minutes before they had finished their soup and were filling their plates with other delicacies. Watching Mellie serve herself some fried rice, Valetta was reminded of something her daughter had told her earlier on. "Mellie's been filling me in on some sort of group you've been running over at the Carmichael's," she said as she reached for the bag of spareribs.

"Oh, that!" Carefully, Lincoln played the whole thing down. "Ben and Andy corralled me, wanting my advice about the publishing industry. Star power," he said sheepishly. "It was nothing. We got together and it turned out to be fun. When the group…um…expanded a little, Miss Mellie here came along with the package. Did you learn anything, Mellie?" he asked, trying for light and airy.

Her mouth too full to speak, Mellie nodded avidly. Her mother filled in for her. "She made it sound so interesting, I'm sorry I missed it."

"Oh, but you can go on Monday, Mom," Mellie said, reaching for another sparerib. "Right, Mr. Cameron?"

"Monday?" Valetta repeated, turning to Lincoln. "I was under the impression that this was a one-time thing."

"Oh, no, Mom! Mr. Cameron said he's going to do it for the rest of the month!" Mellie said brightly. "He has a blackboard and chalk and everything, just like a real teacher."

"Oh, really?"

When Valetta put down her fork Lincoln knew it was not a good sign. "It's not anything formal. I just figured since I was here… I warned them I wasn't sure how long I'd be staying." Lincoln's voice trailed off when he saw Valetta's brow rise.

"Gee, Linc, I would love to hear more."

"But Mom, we rented a movie, remember?"

"Well, then, Mr. Cameron and I will talk after you go to bed," Valetta said ominously.

The way she said that, Lincoln would have liked to skip the movie, but Mellie wouldn't hear of it. So he sat with them in the living room, searching for suitable answers to the questions he knew were coming, while some weird-looking green ogre lumbered across the television screen.

By nine o'clock, Mellie was nodding off in Valetta's arms. Ready for bed, she asked Lincoln to carry her. She was such a tiny thing, it was no effort, and she was deposited on her bed with a gleeful plop.

"Good night, Lincoln," she giggled, and gave him a smack on the cheek that he felt right to his teeth.

"Whoa, Miss Mellie," he said, a teasing light in his eyes as he rubbed his jaw. "You sure do know how to say good night. I think I may have to see a dentist now!"

"Will you take me ice skating tomorrow?" she begged while Valetta scrounged around for her daughter's pajamas. It seemed that everything lived beneath Mellie's bed except her nightgown.

"That depends on your mom," he said, spotting the warning glance in Valetta's eyes. "We'll see. She may have plans."

"Good night, Lincoln!" Mellie's cry followed him all the way down the stairs, her muffled giggles reaching his ear while he sat in the living room.

Lincoln was so involved in watching the news that he didn't hear Valetta's footsteps as she came down the stairs. It gave her a rare moment to study him. He was easy on the eye, that was for sure. But more importantly, Lincoln appeared more relaxed than when he'd first arrived, less stiff. He even wore his hair in a longer, carefree style. The way it fell across his brow, her hand itched to brush it back.

Such thoughts!

"Lincoln," she called sharply, annoyed with herself for getting carried away.

Lincoln jumped. "Sorry. I don't know why I'm so tired. Must be the egg rolls." His eyes sleepy, he watched Valetta settle down at the other end of the sofa. "Did you have a good trip up to Utica?"

"Too much snow."

"But mission accomplished?"

"Business," she said noncommittally. "You know how it goes."

"Too true. Well, then," he said, rising abruptly. "Perhaps I should get going. You must be tired, and I've got an early start in the morning."

"Going back to California?" she asked, half-hoping, half-afraid.

"Is that what you want?" Lincoln asked.

Valetta thought for a moment, then shook her head.

"Good, because it's more like a hunting trip with Chuck and Davey."

"Well, you do make friends easily. But I wish you'd stay for just a moment longer so we can talk. So you can tell me why you came to Longacre, a long-overdue conversation, I know, and my fault, I'm sure. But don't you think it's time for you to tell me your secret? Or rather, Alexis's secret. Out with it, Cameron," she said when she saw Lincoln hesitate. "Say it quickly. I'm sure it won't bite me."

Oh, sweetheart, you should be careful what you wish for. The truth no longer negotiable, Lincoln took a deep breath. *Looks like you get your wish, too, Alexis.* "Your sister…she has…she's seriously ill. Alexis has been diagnosed with breast cancer."

Valetta blanched. "But how? I mean… When? Oh dear, oh dear. Poor Alexis!" *What news!* Tears filling her eyes, Valetta shook her head sadly. "Is she…?"

Lincoln knew exactly what she meant. "No, no, they caught it very early, thank goodness. It showed up at her yearly checkup, barely visible on her mammogram. She has a great radiologist, and she's going to be fine, Vallie, I would never lie about such a thing. It's just that, what with the chemo treatments, the meds, the doctor visits, and all…they're taking their toll. She's very tired, of course, although I must say, she's handling it very well."

"She was never one to feel sorry for herself."

"No, complaining is not her style."

"I assume she's getting the best care possible?"

"Naturally. She's going to the Beverly Hills Women's Center for treatment. But the bottom line is, she wants you to come home and take over the running of the paper. And the family holdings, as well. The whole kit and caboodle. It's yours for the taking."

"What?" Valetta gasped.

Shocked, she buried her face in her hands, which distressed Lincoln, no end. "Vallie, please don't shut me out. I want to help you. I want to help you both."

Valetta's grief for her sister made it difficult to think, but her eyes, fastened on Lincoln's, grew wide. Poor Lincoln, to be the bearer of such news. Alexis was the one who should have called instead of asking him to deliver this gloomy message. Why he had agreed, Valetta could not guess. As he hunkered down before her, holding her hands between his, she tried to find the reason in his eyes, but his beautiful brown eyes, thick-lashed and piercing, were carefully camouflaged. Valetta held his gaze, forcing herself not to panic. After all, she had known from the first that Lincoln's visit wasn't a pleasure trip. But bad news was bad news.

"Help me?" she repeated numbly. "Shouldn't you be in California helping Alexis? You may be the only friend she has."

"The help Alexis wants me to provide is to bring you home. That's the only thing she wants from me. I've known her twenty years and this is as personal as it gets. Not that I ever wanted more from your sister, if you want to know the truth."

It was you I wanted. I know that, now. But he didn't dare say that. The realization had come to him late, and he was still adjusting to the idea.

"And what do you think?"

"Oh, she'll be—"

"No, I mean about my taking over the paper?"

Lincoln shrugged. "This is a family matter."

"But I haven't ever had anything to do with it, and now, this… It really belongs to you. She should be giving it to you."

They sat a moment, each absorbed in their own thoughts. For Valetta, the present was so hampered by the past, it clouded the possibilities. "I don't know what to say. I don't know what to do."

"Well, I've been here long enough to know that no decision you make is going to be easy."

"Oh, Lincoln, I will *never* return to California! If you delivered that message, *that* would be helpful!"

"If your decision is to not return home, you'll have to tell Alexis yourself, face-to-face."

"Some help you are!" she said tightly. "You'll deliver *her* dreadful message, but not mine?"

"Yours is different."

"I don't think you're listening, Lincoln. This is my home!"

"Sorry, Vallie, I didn't mean it that way. Believe me, I told Alexis exactly that."

"What did she say?"

"She doesn't want to hear that stuff. But look, Vallie, no one is going to force you to do anything you don't want to do."

"But she'll try!" Valetta cried, unpleasant images flashing through her mind. "Don't you see? Using you as her messenger is only the beginning."

"Come on, Valetta, I don't have that kind of power, and neither does she. You're a grown woman, educated and smart, but you have to understand, Alexis doesn't see that, she still thinks of you as a child. She lives in a time warp. She hasn't seen you in years, and as for Mellie—no offense, but Mellie is just a photograph and the occasional birthday card."

"Are you saying that none of this has ever jelled with her?"

"That's *exactly* what I'm saying!" Lincoln sighed. "Sometimes I think that woman lives on another planet! Why do you think she's never come East? If she did, she would have to deal with all this. Your leaving was more traumatic than she'd ever admit, but it was mitigated because you had your aunt Phyla on your side. How could Alexis fight her own aunt? And if I'm not mistaken, Phyla had shares of stock in the paper, right? Alexis wasn't going to dare mess with that!"

"She left them to Mellie in her will."

"There you are. And think about this, too. Your living with Phyla made Alexis's life easier. I've given this a lot of thought, as you see, and the way I figure it, when Alexis was finally ready to take you back—when Phyla died, and when you had finished growing up—surprise! surprise!—along came Jack Faraday! Hell's bells, Vallie, she didn't dare take on Jack, not your husband! Not *Doctor* Jack Faraday! From everything I've heard about him, it would not have been an easy task."

"No, he would not have made it easy, and I would never have gone without him, even if I had wanted to return to California."

"Lucky man. And I'm doubly sure that when he died, it passed through her mind to try to tempt you back again. But you were probably in no shape to think straight. And you were also having a baby."

"Not exactly her forte," Valetta murmured.

"Not exactly her forte," Lincoln echoed softly. "By the time you were back on your feet, too much time had passed. Isn't that how it works, Val? Didn't you say that just the other day? Suddenly, it's too late. I'm sure she regrets waiting. Now, though, she needs you, or at least she thinks she does."

Valetta pressed her hands over her eyes, weary and confused. Lincoln had said a mouthful, and it all *sounded* logical, but Valetta wasn't sure of his motives. Was he was playing both ends? It was possible. He had been in Longacre for weeks, but was only now getting around to telling her the sad news about her sister. Why the delay? Given his standing at the paper, surely he stood to lose a great deal if things didn't go Alexis Keane's way. No doubt he could find other work, but very few papers carried the prestige of the *Connection,* and the Lincoln Cameron she used to know cared very much about that sort of thing.

"Hey, there, Vallie, don't look so sad," she heard him say.

His voice was soothing, yes, and comforting, but could she trust him? Searching for answers, she saw compassion in his eyes, but she couldn't be certain what else she saw. The rug had been pulled from beneath her in one short hour and when the dust cleared, she wanted to still be standing on her feet. And she wanted to be very certain where Lincoln Cameron stood. Something told her there was a good deal at stake.

So she listened hard to his next words.

"These things, they're just family squabbles, when you come right down to it, but they always seem to work out, one way or another."

No, Lincoln, things weren't always so simple, she thought glumly. "Wishful thinking, Mr. Cameron. My sister and I have hardly said a civil word to each other in ten years. A lousy track record, don't you think?"

"Well, one can hope."

"Hope for what?" she asked impatiently. "A reconciliation would be miraculous."

She was tired, getting grouchy, Lincoln heard it in her voice. Scratching his bristly chin, he rose to his feet, trying to keep things light, not wanting to be a target. "Well, I'm hoping at least *we* can be friends?"

"Friends?" Valetta laughed, sounding brittle even to her own ears.

Frustrated, and not a little embarrassed, Lincoln stiffened. "You know, Valetta, you could take me a bit more seriously. I am doing my best to help you. To help you both."

"Perhaps. No, you're right. I'm sorry. You've been more than generous to my family. You always have been, and we owe you big-time. But this news is very upsetting. Shocking. I need time to think, and quite frankly, I'm too tired to do that right now."

"Okay, I'm out of here. I know when I'm getting shown the door." He smiled. "I suppose, in a way, I'm ahead of the game."

"Ahead of the game? What game?"

What game? Lincoln didn't answer. Let her figure it out, he thought as he walked to his car. If these Keane sisters knew how to play hardball, so did he.

Chapter Twelve

Lincoln gave Valetta a great deal to think about for the rest of the weekend. The biggest decision was whether to contact Alexis, or rather, how to handle their contact, because Valetta knew she couldn't ignore her sister's plight. But developing a plan proved impossible. In the end, she found herself with some downtime, late Saturday afternoon, while Mellie was doing her homework. Dialing her sister's private number was a cinch, but thinking of the right words to say proved difficult.

"Alexis?" was all she could muster.

"Valetta? Valetta, is that you?"

Valetta flinched at the sound of her sister's voice. It sounded gruffer than she remembered, but since the phone line seemed okay, she thought it might be a result of Alexis's illness. "Hello, Alexis. It's been a long time."

Valetta listened to Alexis breathe heavily across the

continental divide—a good term, she thought drily. Alexis always did practice the art of the long silence, often using it as a weapon, like right now. Valetta took a deep breath, recalling Lincoln's warning of her sister's skewed views to help her through the moment. Determined not to lock horns, she schooled herself to stay on track and keep to the facts. "Lincoln told me you were ill."

She heard Alexis study the moment. "Yes, well, he took a long time telling you. He's been there two weeks, or very nearly. Or was it *you* that took such a long time to call?"

Valetta spoke softly, trying for gentle. "Does it make a difference, since I'm calling now?"

"It could," Alexis said tersely.

Valetta schooled herself to be patient. After all, Alexis was seriously ill. "Well, you sound like yourself, and since I got you on your office line, can I hazard a guess that you're holding your own?"

"I suppose you could say that," Alexis said grudgingly.

"Lincoln says that you're receiving excellent care."

"Of course. We have hospitals, here. Good ones, too. New York is not the hub of the medical world."

"No, no, of course not. I never said… That's not what I meant." Valetta did her best, although flapping in the wind was not her favorite exercise. "Is there anything I can do to help? Lincoln was vague."

"Lincoln *vague?* How odd. We had an in-depth conversation as to his errand."

Valetta was glad that blushes didn't transmit over telephone lines, else her white lie would have seemed a great transgression. Still, she didn't want Lincoln to suffer any adverse effect. "He did mention that you wanted me to visit."

"Well, he got *that* part right," Alexis snapped.

The way she said it, Valetta was suddenly visited by a horrifying thought that sent a cold shiver down her spine. "Alexis, is Lincoln's future contingent on my... visit?" she asked fearfully.

"Oh, for goodness sake, Valetta! I am not in the habit of letting my private life influence my business. And Lincoln Cameron is *all* business, no matter what he says. He was born with printer's ink in his veins. His heart is with the newspaper. We're only talking *partnership,* the only marriage that's ever interested him, if you ask me."

"He must have forgotten to mention it," Valetta whispered but Alexis seemed not to hear.

"On the other hand, I could have chosen someone else to meet with you. I chose Lincoln for *your* sake. What you do with him is your decision."

"What I *do* with him?" Valetta repeated, so nervous she could hardly think straight. "You've lost me, Alexis."

"Come, come, Valetta. Cameron is an attractive man, and very available. A playboy, if you will. But he's getting too old for that nonsense. It's time he settled down, raised a family. It would set a good example for the staff. If you came back to California in his company, I would have no objection."

Valetta gasped, unsure if she had heard right. "Do you mean as a couple?"

"As his wife."

Valetta was staggered by the outrageous suggestion. Given how angered Alexis had been by Valetta's high-school crush on Lincoln, it didn't make sense. She had thought her sister capable of a good many things, but never using a man's life as a bargaining chip.

"Tell me, Alexis, have you run this scenario by Lincoln?"

"Of course not!" Valetta heard her sister's scorn. "What has *he* to say about the matter? He's pushing forty, you know. If he ever really wanted to marry, don't you think he would have already done so? Like I just said, he's married to the paper. *This* arrangement is between you and me. I thought you would understand that, when I sent him to you."

"You *sent* him to me?"

Alexis sighed loudly. "Why do you keep repeating everything I say?"

"Why do I feel like I'm your puppet?"

"That's ridiculous! You have options, I am seeing to that. But can we please not waste time talking about Lincoln Cameron? Surely we have more important matters to discuss."

A masterful evasion Valetta was reluctant to allow, but she reminded herself of the bigger picture. "All right, then. Do you want to tell me about your illness?"

"There's nothing to discuss. I have breast cancer," Alexis said brusquely, "and I'm dealing with it. The state of my health was not the message I wanted Lincoln to deliver, not directly. I want you to come home."

If only she would *ask,* Valetta thought sadly. If only once she would say, Val, could you come home, please? I need you.

"Alexis, surely you must know that I can't just pick up and leave New York. I have a full life here. And it's not just me. Mellie has ties here, also, to her school, her friends, her soccer team."

Alexis was unimpressed. "Mellie is only a child. Her *soccer career*—" Valetta winced at her sister's irony "—can be continued here, I am sure of it. And as for picking up and leaving, you did it once, you can do it again. Your roots here go deep. You're an heiress, or have you forgotten? And we have vast holdings besides the paper. The cattle ranch in Texas, that silly copper mine in Venezuela, the orchid farm in Connecticut. There's a host of other things besides the paper."

"I haven't forgotten," Valetta said slowly.

"Good. Because for the last decade, I've been doing all the work, and you've been reaping the benefits."

"Not true! I haven't touched a dime of Keane money since I left!"

"No, but it's been accruing, and earning interest, too, I might add. Even if you don't want it, Mellie may decide differently, someday. You may not have realized this, but she stands to inherit my share of the estate. I've made her my chief beneficiary."

"She doesn't even know who the Keanes are."

"Knowing you, I don't expect she does. That's partly why I sent Lincoln. To remind you of that. I know she's only eight—"

"Nine!"

"Nine, then. Fine. At her age it doesn't matter all that much, but mark my words, Valetta, someday Mellie will figure it all out, and what will you say then, Valetta? What happens if someday she takes a journalism class and her professor happens to mention my name? Or she takes a film class, and they get to watching that ridiculous Willie Hearst movie, and remark its resemblance *to that other California publishing house?* Do you really think Mellie won't be able to add one and one,

Valetta? What are you going to say to her then, sister? *Sorry, Mellie, I kept meaning to tell you, but yes, that's your Aunt Alexis they're talking about!*"

Valetta was shaking. "What's your point, Alexis? What do you want?"

"I want you to come home! I want you to take over the Keane holdings."

Valetta covered her mouth. Think! Stay calm. She's trying to manipulate you. There's a way to deal with this.

"Valetta?" Alexis's sharp voice stabbed the air.

"I have to think," Valetta whispered. "I have to think."

"Yes, you do! And then you have to come home! I may not be dying, but I'm sick, and to be honest, Valetta, I'm tired. That's why I want to turn things over to you."

"I'm not equipped for this!"

"Don't be ridiculous, you can buy all the help you need. Lincoln would be there for you. He told me so."

"He told you so? What are you saying, Alexis?"

"Come to Los Angeles and I'll tell you. I'll tell you *many* things. But don't take too long, Valetta! And Lincoln's return is long overdue. Tell him that I—"

"Tell him what?" It was strange to hear hesitation in her sister's voice.

"Just tell him to hurry." Then the phone went dead.

Valetta's hand shook as she put down the phone. As usual, Alexis had met her every dreaded expectation. They might speak infrequently, but every time they did, Valetta hung up thinking it was enough to last a lifetime. And now it looked as if she would have to go to California, at least temporarily. But to leave

Longacre *permanently?* Could she, *really,* if it came down to that? The idea was painful. She was happy here. Alexis had never understood that happiness was a fair exchange for the money. And no question, it was *all* about money. Tons of it.

Lincoln. She would talk to Lincoln, he would know what to do.

Or would he? Alexis had implied he had hopes. A partnership, she had said although it was hard to imagine Alexis giving up control of the paper. Lincoln hadn't mentioned it, a glaring omission, if there ever was one, and he had certainly had the opportunity to tell her last night. But maybe, just to be fair, Alexis was way ahead of herself, maybe it was just talk. Would Lincoln tell her? Would he be honest? Would she be able to tell if he were not?

On the following Monday, after overhearing her staff discuss Lincoln's journalism class, Valetta immediately changed her evening plans. Closing the office early, she picked Mellie up after school, hurried home to eat a hasty dinner and quickly drove back into town. When she crossed the Carmichael's threshold, she was shocked to see practically the whole town there. This wasn't a class, this was a town meeting! What was Lincoln thinking?

Lincoln must have picked up on Valetta's grim mood because, watching her settle down, Mellie sprawled at her feet, he could almost see the steam coming from her ears. Well, what did she expect? he thought, as he passed around some copies of notes. This class wasn't even his idea in the first place, but since he had decided to cooperate, the least she could do was be happy about it. Everyone else was thrilled. Besides, what was so wrong with adding a little excitement to a country town buried knee-deep in snow for another two months?

"A whole darned lot," she argued, when he posed the question the next day over lunch. Unable to speak privately at Patty's, they had arranged to meet at Jerome's Diner, but Valetta could hardly bring herself to touch her soup. Lincoln, on the other hand, was doing real justice to a turkey club, offered by Jerome in a generous moment, concerned that Linc was losing weight. She tried not to watch.

"Don't you see? These people think you care about them!" she whispered, afraid to be overheard.

"But I do!" Lincoln protested, munching on a potato chip.

"Not like they care about you. They care as in wanting you to stay. I saw it in their eyes last night. They were interested and excited, and they were depending on you to feed that excitement. But what happens next month, when the crocuses come up, Linc? You'll be gone, that's what," she said grabbing the mayo from his hand and slamming it on the table.

"Oh, come, Val, you're overdramatizing. They know I'm just visiting. I've made that very clear from the onset."

"Lincoln, they haven't the faintest idea why you're here, but the way you've insinuated yourself into their lives, I'm sure they think you're more than visiting, at this point. I know these people. They like you, don't you understand? And what's more, they think you like them."

"I *do* like them!"

"Sure you do. You like lattes, too."

"My dear Valetta," Lincoln said, "you give me absolutely no credit for having any feelings. You're making me out to be a cad. It isn't true and it isn't fair. I may not be big on personal commitment, but that doesn't make me irresponsible. I've been working for Alexis for close to twenty years, so I do have *some* sense of duty."

"I don't doubt it, Lincoln, but you just said it yourself, you travel light. When you check out of the Hotel Carmichael—just look how Patty and Chuck took you in when they're normally closed, no questions asked—and return to the West Coast, Longacre will be a fond memory. But Longacre will remember *you,* and it will be more than a passing fancy. They have hopes, you see. They have dreams. They'll be collecting their pens and pencils, arranging for babysitters, and suddenly remember, *oh, right, no class tonight, Mr. Cameron went back to California.*"

"Valetta, you have a streak in you that is positively Shakespearian."

"And what about Mellie? She adores you! She doesn't understand about people like you, people who are just *passing through.* The only person who ever left her was her father, and he died!"

"Watch it, Vallie, you're beginning to make me angry!"

Valetta's brow furrowed. "Is that a threat, Lincoln? Because if it is, I don't know why you think I would be afraid to make you angry. I would have to be afraid of losing something, and you haven't offered me anything."

Lincoln put aside his sandwich, his appetite gone. "*Nothing,* Valetta?"

"Are you talking about a few stolen kisses? Oh, please, Linc, we might as well have been in the backseat of a Pontiac." Well, that wasn't entirely true, but Valetta would die before she let him know the effect his kisses had.

"Wow, you are one cold woman!"

Valetta squirmed. "I didn't say I didn't enjoy them, but let's face it, there wasn't a whole lot of emotional investment there."

"Now, how would you know?"

Valetta shrugged, ignoring his dark, angry scowl. "You've been here—what?—two, three weeks? Are you going to spin me some nonsense about love at first sight? Look, let's not argue, it's not important. We shared a few kisses, fine, great. That's not the issue. We're talking about roots. I am, in any case. Why do you think I stayed here after Jack died? You of all people know I could have returned to L.A. and lived like a queen. Believe me, I'm not all that crazy about shoveling snow! I stayed because I wanted to make a home for Mellie that had more meaning than that horrid mansion I grew up in. I wanted her school to be a place where she knew everyone and they knew her, not that dreadful high school Alexis sent me to that had four thousand students. We talked, by the way."

"You and Alexis?" Lincoln was caught by surprise. "Really? Well, well, well, will wonders never cease. How did it go?"

"It was awful, exactly like I thought it would be."

Lincoln's mouth twitched. "It sounds like Alexis is feeling better."

"She sounded awful."

"She does have cancer," Lincoln reminded her.

Giving up on her meal, Valetta twisted her napkin into a violent knot. "She was very mysterious, too. She said she would explain things when I came home. She said she would explain *all sorts of things,*" Valetta said, searching his carefully schooled face. Another failed opportunity for him to tell her his plans. "She also said to tell you to come home."

"And would you come home with me?" he asked, his voice casual.

Surprised by the question, Valetta tried to read him, but his eyes were carefully hooded. "Oh, hell, forget I said that," he growled. "It was just an idle question."

Yeah, right. The day Lincoln Cameron asked an idle question...

But suddenly it was all too much for her. Lincoln would have to figure things out for himself. She had enough on her plate.

"I was toying with flying out for a few days. Patty said she would watch Mellie, but I've been leaving Mellie with my friends so much lately, I'm not sure what to do. I know they don't mind and I know Mellie treats it like one big sleepover, but I don't like it. On the other hand, I don't want Mellie around if there's going to be the slightest chance of a confrontation between me and Alexis."

"If you brought her to L.A., I would watch her. I would fly back with you, if you like. I could take her to Disneyland."

Valetta laughed. "The grand sacrifice, huh?"

Lincoln smiled. "I *would* prefer the Getty Museum, but she would probably object."

"Without question. Well, thanks, but I don't need your help with Mellie," she said brusquely. "And anyway, it would be best if I saw Alexis alone. But right now, I have to get back to work. Jerome," she called, "we're leaving."

Jerome waved. "Will you be back for dinner?"

"Not tonight. Mellie has too much homework—a big project is due in a few weeks—and soccer practice started up again. And Mr. Crater," she said, pointing an admonishing finger at Jerome, "don't forget I'm taking you to pick up your new glasses tomorrow."

"Now, Valetta—"

"Tomorrow! At ten!" she said crisply. "No excuses. Then, maybe next time you make chili, you won't add so much chili powder like you did last week. You nearly took down half the town! Mamie Blanche said her pharmacy never sold so much antacid in her life."

"People liked it that way!" Jerome protested.

"Two people did, Chuck and Davey. Hey! Is *that* why you sold so much beer that night? Did you plan it that way?"

"*That* you'll never know, missy." Jerome grinned wickedly. "But you're making a big mistake not coming in tonight. I'm serving a *sauce piquant* over broiled chicken, and they don't call it *piquant* for nothing!"

Giving the old man a kiss on his leathery brown cheek, Valetta slung her bag over her shoulder. "Tomorrow at ten!" she warned him one more time as she walked out into the bright sunlight.

"You know we haven't finished talking." Lincoln watched as Valetta draped her red wool scarf about her slender neck, letting it trail delicately over her shoulder. Today, her hat was a lavender wool, but oddly enough, it went with her purple leggings. She would never want for color in her wardrobe, he thought, and it was all very flattering, in his opinion.

"Well, it will have to wait until the weekend. Mellie isn't the only one with a deadline. And by Saturday,

I'll also know what I want to do about flying out to see Alexis."

That woman had too much attitude, Linc thought irritably, as he watched Valetta head back to work, leaving him the lone soul on the deserted sidewalk. But she was wrong about him. Dead wrong. Lincoln was perfectly able to make a commitment. It was just that *that* wasn't the primary reason he was there. He was on a mission, and he was never one to lose sight of the goal. If a body lost focus, all manner of things could go haywire. Wasn't that why he was the man he was today?

Impatient with the world, he slid behind the wheel of his rental and let the car idle while he thought about putting a hex on the Keane sisters. But he abandoned the idea when he realized that he didn't know any witches for hire.

So then, how to fill his time, otherwise? He could return to his room and prepare for his classes, but the next one wasn't until Thursday, and that was two full days away. Besides, he wasn't in the mood. The sky was too blue, the crisp winter air too appealing. It was a day to be outdoors, just the thing he needed to waylay his sudden spurt of temper. Flipping open the glove compartment, he pulled out a map. The Erie Canal. He'd always wanted to travel the Erie.

Lincoln was driving 87 South in minutes. The road signs for schools pointed every which way. Buffalo… Syracuse…Binghamton…Cornell… This must be the most educated state in the union, he mused. Pulling into a gas station to fill up, he was told by a grease-smudged attendant that if he kept driving south, he would find himself in Waterford where the Hudson and Mohawk Rivers met. There he would discover the eastern entrance to the Erie Canal. Of course, it still being winter, the tourists were gone and so were the tour boats, but he might be able to hop a working tug. No, the attendant laughed in response to Lincoln's amused query. The mules and barges were long gone.

Sooner than he expected, he was exiting the highway, driving a county road, in no rush to do anything but admire the scenery. For the first time in years, he had no direction and no appointments to keep. It was a soothing drive that worked wonders on his bad humor. The road meandered through the mountainside, across flat land, up and down sloped valleys, past towns that were more like villages, and villages that were really small hamlets. It was a picture-perfect, snow-covered parade, and Lincoln was sure many a postcard had been sent as a result, and many a picture taken of the frosty fields and ice-capped trees. He could tell precisely when school let out because a little after three, the low hills were suddenly dotted with children, sleds and dogs. He was surprised to discover how much he missed Mellie. He even gave a passing thought to Mangy Yellow.

Lincoln easily found Waterford, and the Old Champlain Canal that was still rambling through the center of town after two hundred years. Glad of a walk, he quit his Jeep, and strolled along the waterfront, discovering Lock Two Park in the twilight. With an hour of light still remaining, he was able to explore the canal and check out some of the amazing tugboats berthed along the floating docks. Talking to one of the deck hands, he was steered to the *Cheyenne,* where he was able to convince the captain to take him on board the next day. They weren't going anywhere special, the captain warned, just doing some local shipping, but Lincoln promised that was more than enough for him. He just wanted to ride the canal, if Captain Ron didn't mind. The captain was more than happy to accommodate the stranger, especially when he heard who Lincoln was and where he worked. The possibility of free publicity was a tempting sugarplum.

Walking back across the park in the twilight, Lincoln headed for Broad Street where he found a small inn and rented a room for the night. The hot shower was a treat, and the down bedcovers tempting, but he was, as usual, hungry, so he headed back down to the lobby for some dinner suggestions from the elderly innkeeper.

There was only one place to eat at that hour, his hostess told him firmly, a fish house known for its fresh catch from the Mohawk River, even this time of year. An apprentice ice fisher, he believed her. Famished, he eagerly walked the three short blocks she mapped out. In ten minutes, he found himself standing in front of an old brick warehouse that had been converted to a minimill, restaurant and gift shop. The restaurant's evening specialty was haddock and salt potatoes, and he later swore to the beaming owner that he hadn't tasted—with apologies to Jerome—a better meal in months. The owner was so pleased with Lincoln's compliment that he had the waitress bring them a bottle of cognac to polish off the dinner.

The bottle warming comfortably between them, the two men talked quietly until past eleven. Lincoln learned a great deal about Waterford and the outlying area. It was such a close-knit community he wasn't surprised to hear that the owner knew all about Jerome Crater and his culinary skills. Lincoln promptly invited his new friend to visit Longacre. Shaking hands good night, Lincoln promised to return in the not-too-distant future, and to bring a guest or two. Valetta would love this place, he was sure.

Bring Valetta? Linc mused as he strolled back to his hotel. Now what on earth had made him say that? He knew darned well he could do no such thing, that he had no intention of staying long enough to do that. Hadn't he made that clear to Val this very day, when she ripped in to him for being *uncommitted?*

Not to mention her opinion of his kisses! Her *very low* opinion of his kisses!

Although he told himself it was the cognac, his face turned five heated shades of red just thinking about it. No one in his entire adult life had ever disparaged his skills in the romance department! Worse yet, the stolen kisses he'd shared with Vallie had left him seriously moved. He had thought she'd been moved, as well.

Can I kiss you, Val?

He remembered quite clearly the look in her eyes when he'd asked her permission—and who on earth did *that,* these days! The way she had said *yes.* Shyly, too, but she had managed to kiss him back quite eagerly.

Come to think of it, her enthusiasm had been un-mistakable.

The realization stopped Linc in his tracks. Was it possible… Had she not been *quite truthful,* he wondered as he threw back his head to watch the winter sky. Had she been more touched by his embrace than she liked to admit? Was she really concerned only for the townsfolk, when she worried at his lack of commit-ment, or was she protecting herself as much as them?

Shivering against the cold, Lincoln hurried back to

the inn to slip beneath the covers and mull over this new perspective. But he was waylaid by a heavenly feather-bed and the pleasant surprise of a log burning low on the hearth. The events of the long day won out. He was asleep in minutes.

Already warned by Captain Ron that the *Cheyenne* got an early start, Lincoln left the inn long before everyone else was up, although something told him he was the only guest. Eager to get a glimpse of canal history, he retraced his footsteps back to Lock Two Park where he was greeted by Captain Ron, and invited to go below deck for coffee. He was chatting with the cook when he felt the sway of the small tug and quickly returned upstairs, eager to watch their departure.

The lock was narrow, maybe fifty feet wide and three hundred feet long, but Captain Ron was careful nonetheless to steer wide of the lock's walls. It wasn't long before they were navigating the Mohawk River, stopping to pick up a load of brick destined for a small upstream town, then turning around to drop off some heavy construction equipment.

Much of the day followed this pattern, Captain Ron steering the sturdy tug to scheduled pickups, deliver-ing supplies to waterside towns, shooting the breeze with the locals who paused to say hello whenever they docked, lunching with the crew. Most often, though, Lincoln just stood leaning on the rail, mesmerized by the river's ebb and flow. He had always had an affinity for water. Most of his vacations over the years had been to beach resorts and the like. One summer, he had even taken a trip up the French canal, loving the gentle sway of the barge he rode, the hushed lapping of water against its hull, the peace of the countryside they passed along the way so in contrast to his everyday life. He thought that, under different circumstances, this might have been an honest way for him to earn a living. Now, he had commitments.

But as he watched the wintry, black river disappear beneath the tug, staring at the huge chunks of green ice floating by while he tallied up the towns and villages they passed, he came to wonder what they were, his commitments.

And which way was home?

Valetta's slim figure loomed large in his mind. And if it wasn't for her sake, why on earth was he standing there hugging the rail of a raggedy tugboat? Why was he wondering about job opportunities in a town as far from civilization—as he knew it—as could be when he was already king of the mountain? *No,* he told himself, it could not be because he had been feeling vaguely restless all this past winter. *No,* it could not be because his step had grown heavier as he approached forty. No, it could not be because he was falling in love! The very idea made him smile.

Chapter Thirteen

Lincoln was hungry as a bear when he got back to the Carmichael house late Thursday, an hour shy of his class. Since the house was empty, he helped himself to whatever he found in the refrigerator, a liberty he had taken early on. A quick shower, a change of clothes, and he was ready for his *visitors*. He couldn't bring himself to call them students, not after his conversation with Valetta, but when they started filing in that evening, he saw them in a new light. Valetta had altered his vision; now he wondered what *they* wondered.

He was glad when Valetta didn't show up, but he didn't know, until he saw Patty tuck Mellie into bed later that night, that Valetta had taken an early-morning flight to Los Angeles. Patty didn't explain why, but he didn't have to ask. Still, he was annoyed that she had left without a word. It was definitely a message to him to stay out of her business. Didn't she trust that he could have helped?

He could not have helped.

Although Valetta knew Lincoln would not be happy at the abrupt way she had left New York, she hadn't wanted his company. Although she and her sister had exchanged the obligatory holiday cards, it had been ten years since they had seen each other and her sense, in talking to Lincoln, was that Alexis had never revealed how estranged the sisters were.

And then, the way she and Lincoln had parted the last time they had been together… She'd never look at turkey again without remembering that lunch. Remembering that he had *not* taken the opportunity to tell her about his plans for the future—the partnership Alexis had alluded to. Apparently, the rolling stone he claimed to be really didn't gather moss. If she was disappointed, who was to blame? Did she honestly think that a few kisses constituted a marriage vow?

Good grief, Valetta, how lame can you get?

Oh, pretty lame, she answered herself honestly.

Putting Lincoln Cameron from her mind, she exited the plane and stood on the sidewalk outside LAX, searching for a cab. But goodness, she *had* missed the weather! The balmy breeze was a delight after the long winter of snow back east, the gentle, warm wind riffling her hair. If Alexis played her cards right, Valetta might actually consider returning home. The East Coast had many things, but it didn't have palm trees.

On the other hand, the traffic was horrendous. It slowed her cabby's progress north on the Pacific Coast

Highway, but her driver was philosophical—and glad of the lucrative fare—and Valetta was even happier for the leisurely trip up the coast. It gave her time to acclimate and prepare herself to meet Alexis. But it also gave her time to enjoy the Pacific, to smell the salt air. She had forgotten how beautiful California was, how much she had missed it. This *was* her first home, after all, where her roots were, even if she had adopted New York. Suddenly, she wished Mellie were there. They had been to the Atlantic Ocean, even visited Marconi Beach on Cape Cod, and Marconi was impressive, but the Pacific… It was one of a kind. If Mellie were there, they would rent a car and drive to—

"Just got in, huh?" The cab driver's voice cut through her thoughts.

"Yes, I did, from New York."

"Yeah, I could tell by the way you've been looking out the window, and your accent. First trip?"

"It's been a few years," she admitted.

"Staying long?"

"The question of the century," she murmured. Thankfully, he took the hint and left her to her thoughts.

The cab driver's eyes almost popped when he heard the address Valetta gave him. It was a house that everyone knew, a landmark that tourists made a point of passing, marveling that anyone could be so lucky as to inhabit such a palace. And it *was* a palace, a palace nestled in the clouds, the blue California sky an exquisite backdrop to a lavish display of brick and mortar. Privacy was insured by the huge wrought-iron gates that surrounded the estate, but the guard on duty in the roundhouse didn't bat an eyelash at Valetta's arrival. He knew who she was the minute he set eyes on her. Hadn't he chased her back to the house a hundred times when she was little more than a baby? Hadn't his wife tended many a scratched knee and soothed Valetta's tears with a cookie? Doffing his cap, the wink he sent her said it all.

"Miss Valetta?"

"Oh, Henry, is that really you?" Valetta cried, stepping from the taxi when she recognized his wide, toothy grin.

"How good it is to see you again," he said, returning her hug. "Look at you now, all grown-up and looking mighty fine, if I may say so! Wait till I tell my wife you're home. She'll be thrilled."

"Thank you, Henry. Tell her I'd like to stop by and see her, if it isn't too much trouble."

"Oh, Miss Valetta, you know she'll make time for you. She'll probably whip up a fresh batch of shortbread when she hears you're back."

Swinging wide the gates, Henry flagged the cab up the long, winding driveway. The house was situated on the top of a bluff, and nothing held a candle to the stone building that always seemed a magical revelation when it first appeared. Its famous twin towers were often featured in conversations about great houses of the nineteenth century. Wide stone stairs led to the huge castle entry, and the rare guest always seemed disappointed not to find a moat. Mullioned windows covered the entire front facade, while the second-story balcony promised an unimpeded view of the ocean. It was the jewel that outshone every other house in the crown that rimmed the Pacific bluffs.

Alerted by Henry, the housekeeper was waiting on

the steps when Valetta's cab pulled up. The butler stood beside her, and they were both excited beyond words.

"Miss Valetta!" the housekeeper cried, her heavy arms ready to embrace her favorite. "*Madre de dios,* it's so good to see you!"

"Rosie, Rosie! It's so good to see *you* again," Valetta said, as she returned the elderly woman's hug.

"Just look at you, little miss," Rosalina wept. "My baby is all grown-up, all grown-up. But where is *your* baby?" she clucked, squinting at the taxi.

"I'm sorry, Rosalina, not this time," Valetta apologized. "My daughter couldn't miss school."

"Ah, Miss Valetta." The butler smiled. "Welcome home!"

"Johnson!" Valetta cried, giving him a hug. "Do you never change? You look exactly the same as the day I left."

"Thank you, miss. I certainly can't say the same for you, though!" Johnson grinned. "You've grown into a lovely young woman and it's good to see you again."

Rosalina sniffed regretfully. "She's grown up so much, I don't even know her. And the baby, don't we ever get to see her?"

"That *baby,* as you call her, would be so mad if she heard you call her that!" Valetta said with a laugh. "Maybe next time, Rosie." But the housekeeper looked doubtful as she led the way inside the house.

Stepping through the threshold was like stepping into wonderland. The grand foyer Valetta crossed was bigger than most people's homes, a splendid display of Carrara marble, mahogany wainscoting and ornate plasterwork. The marble floors glowed, the huge urns of flowers were as fresh as the hothouse could manage, and the sweet smell of beeswax lingered in the air. A delicate refectory table displayed the day's mail, while a golden bowl of lilacs perfumed the air. If Valetta was not mistaken, that Picasso was on the wall the day she left, but that new statue tucked away in the corner could be a Rodin. Reminded that this was the world Lincoln inhabited, it made her wonder how provincial they must appear to him back in Longacre, and it made her understand a little better his hesitation to embrace change. Who, after all, would not mind being greeted by a Rodin every time he walked through the front door, instead of a pair of roller skates? Or a servant on hand to take his coat and inquire what to serve for dinner? Not mac and cheese, that was for sure!

"Just like you left it," Rosalina said proudly, as she opened the door to Valetta's old bedroom. "Freshly dusted, the sheets scented. I always knew you'd come back, so I keep it clean. There isn't much to do around here, anyway, there being only Miss Alexis to look after. I wouldn't mind another little girl to care for," she said bluntly. "I fixed for your Miss Mellie, too, a pretty room right next to yours, with lots of pink pillows. Miss Alexis once told me that maybe one day Miss Mellie would come and we should be ready. I bought lots and lots of pink, you bet!" Rosalina laughed. "Your little girl likes pink, no?"

"Mellie loves pink, Rosie, and I will tell her what you did. You're right, she's getting older, maybe she should see all this. Maybe this summer," Valetta said thoughtfully.

"You mean that, Miss Val?"

"I'll think about it." Valetta smiled. "Right now, though, I promised myself a nap. Oh, and Rosalina, Alexis doesn't know I'm here."

"Should I call the office?"

"No, please don't. I don't want to interrupt her day. Tell her when she comes home, okay? I really need a nap."

After calling home to let Mellie know she had arrived safely, Valetta took her nap. She was still sleeping when Alexis came home. When Rosalina told her that Miss Valetta was upstairs in her room, sleeping off jet lag, Alexis didn't bat an eyelash, but Rosalina could tell she was pleased. How could she not be?

Alexis took her dinner in the small dining room, as she did every night, and Rosalina served her, as she did every night, making small talk as her mistress dined. Alexis ate very lightly, her appetite fallen since her chemotherapy had begun, but Rosalina went to great lengths to tempt her mistress. An excellent cook, she succeeded for the most part.

A creature of habit, Alexis followed dinner with a hot bath. She had a theory that if she adhered strictly to her schedule, her cancer would proceed more slowly. It was based on nothing, but still, it seemed to be working. A few days ago, well into treatment, her doctor had given her the results of the latest batch of blood tests. Happily, they showed no evidence of new cell growth. Valetta's presence notwithstanding, Alexis crawled into bed as she did every night, sometimes with a book, sometimes with a folder from the office, occasionally with a report from her attorney or her estate agent. She spared no time for pleasure—but then, she never had—and rarely succumbed to the frivolity of television.

Fantasy was not a part of her construct. She didn't even read fiction, unless it was pertinent to the paper.

Valetta slept through dinner, and then some. When she awoke, her groggy state left her so off balance she was unsure where she was. But as the pale moonlight filtered in, it only took a moment to compute that the gorgeous bedroom was real and not something out of a dream. She luxuriated in the satin bedding rustling against her bare legs, admired the rich furnishings she once took for granted. Shaking free of her languor, she decided to treat herself to a leisurely bath. Rosalina had been as good as her word. The gleaming white bathroom was still stocked with a myriad of colorful bath salts, exotic oils in glass-stoppered bottles and a shelf of costly shampoos. Plush towels hung on warming rods while a thick chenille robe dangled from a silver hook.

A rush of memories met Valetta as she slid beneath the steaming water. As she soaked and her mind wandered, she could almost hear her mother's light voice and her father's heavy footstep echo down the hall. Where had the time gone? One day it had all been so comfortable and safe, the next day, her world exploded. And how had it all gone so wrong between her and Alexis? Her eyes misting, Valetta shook her head against the sadness that threatened to bring her low. Rising quickly, she grabbed the fluffy robe. Becoming depressed would serve no purpose.

Valetta tried not to make any noise as she tiptoed down to the kitchen, not wanting to wake the staff. If Rosalina knew she was up, she would insist on cooking Valetta a proper meal, and nothing Valetta could say would stop her. And Rosalina did *not* believe in peanut butter sandwiches! Fortunately, though, Rosie did believe in cheese, so Valetta was able to raid the well-stocked refrigerator and fill a plate with peppered goat cheese, a slice of brie, crackers and fresh strawberries. A glass of orange juice completed her meal.

"Bring your tray to my room," she heard a disembodied voice order her crisply as she padded softly back to her bedroom.

Startled, Valetta jumped at the unexpected sound. Searching the shadows, she found Alexis standing at the head of the dimly lit stairs, wrapped in a blue silk kimono.

"Alexis, um, is that you? It is you, of course it is! Um…hi…it's good to see you… Long time, no see… Jeez, Alexis, you scared me half to death!"

Catching her breath, Valetta climbed the stairs until she was face-to-face with her sister. "Hello, Alexis."

Nodding faintly, Alexis's eyes fastened on Valetta's white hair, its corn silk texture a far cry from the thick, red curls she'd known. Her hand almost moved, but she managed to stifle the impulse. No words escaped her pursed mouth, either. Turning lightly, she vanished down the hall.

Hello to you, too. Valetta sighed as she followed the shadow of her wraithlike sister.

Alexis's bedroom had changed little since Valetta had last seen it, but as ever, it was a symphony of design. The elegant cherrywood furniture was still in place, although the white carpet was new, as were the blue silk curtains that shimmered uncertainly in the midnight air. Valetta perched on a boudoir chair and made space for her plate on a delicate accent table. She watched as Alexis made slow progress back to her imposing bed, a queenlike structure draped with floral chintz that billowed from its majestic canopy.

If Alexis were after the regal look, she had certainly achieved it, Valetta thought wryly. Oh, well. Reaching for a strawberry, she hesitated. That rug was awfully white.

"Why are you smiling?" Alexis asked, as she slid back beneath her bedcovers.

"Hmm, nothing, just a passing thought." Valetta smiled as she eyed the plump strawberry.

"Tell me."

Valetta nodded in the direction of the thick, white shag. "The strawberries…so red…"

"Valetta, we have servants for things like that."

We? "Um, sure," she said agreeably as she opted for a cracker.

But Alexis was no longer interested in strawberries. "It's been a long time, sister."

Then why does it feel like yesterday? Valetta wondered. Another subject she would not touch. "Yes, well… You're looking good, Alexis, thinner, but not… I thought you would look…oh, I don't know…"

"On death's doorstep?" Alexis's stab at humor didn't reach her eyes.

"Something like that," Valetta agreed with a clipped laugh.

"Forget about BOTOX, chemo is the way to go. It does wonders for your skin, among other things. Brings out the roses. If the doctors put that in their brochure, I can't imagine the increase in sales it would effect," she said with a grim laugh. "But you're looking well, also. To what do I owe this unexpected visit?"

"Come, come, Alexis, you sent your commander in chief to get me!"

"I sent Lincoln Cameron to bring you *home*—which

he obviously has failed to do, given the absence of your daughter."

Valetta took a deep breath and schooled herself to speak quietly. "I never said I would return home *on a permanent basis*. Don't confuse your wish with reality."

"Well, then, where *is* Mellie? And where is Cameron?"

"Which one first?" Valetta asked lightly.

"Mellie, of course. She's blood."

"But Lincoln is family, too, isn't he?"

"Family, perhaps, but not by blood. There's a difference."

"I'm not sure Lincoln would appreciate the distinction, but in any case, I left them both in New York, in excellent health. I think Lincoln is in shock from all our snow, although Mellie took him sledding and he actually survived the experience. It's beginning to melt, of course, but I'll bet he misses this. The ocean," she explained when Alexis sent her a puzzled look. Walking to the window, she thrust aside the gauzy curtains and gazed out across the palisades. Tiny shards of light anchored the ocean. "The boats...the salt air...it's the one thing I miss."

"If you came back..."

Valetta kept a steadfast hold of her temper. "Alexis, not now, I just got home. Let's not quarrel so soon."

"Are you so sure we will?"

"Alexis, stop!"

Valetta's voice was so sharp, Alexis was caught by surprise, but the face Valetta showed her was composed. "Look, I know you're busy, and I'll understand if you have plans, but do you think you could take tomorrow off? It would be great if we could spend some time together."

"I think I could rearrange my schedule," Alexis said gravely. "I am the boss, after all."

Even with the best of intentions, Valetta slept past noon. Searching out her sister, she was chagrined to find Alexis waiting for her in one of her many greenhouses, tending to her plants.

"I am so sorry," she apologized, as she followed Alexis down the narrow aisles of the splendid greenhouse. "Thanks for not giving up on me and going in to work."

Mesmerized, she watched as, armed with cutting shears, Alexis carefully trimmed a small plant. It looked liked a bonsai, but Valetta wasn't entirely sure. She could hardly keep her own garden in order. If she needed to plant flowers or bulbs, she hired Rico Suarez. Talk about bad feng shui, she couldn't even water bamboo without drowning it! But Alexis could—she *always* could—and the flourishing greenhouse was a testament to her gift. Valetta envied her the thick vines creeping toward the skylight, the dripping barks of orchids, terra-cotta pots overflowing with miniature roses and gardenias and paper lilies.

"You know, Alexis, you could start a business."

"Just what I need, another job," Alexis snorted.

"Well, you sure know what you're doing."

"It's a hobby," Alexis said dismissively. "And you, what's yours?"

"Me, a hobby?" Valetta laughed. "By the time Mellie is in bed, I have just enough energy to empty the dishwasher, take a shower and crawl into bed with a good murder mystery. My husband used to have a huge mystery collection, but I gave most of them to the local library when he died. Now, irony of ironies, I have to reserve the very books I donated. And if I'm late returning them, Mrs. Prentiss makes me pay the fine! There's poetic justice for you!"

Alexis was puzzled. "Why don't you just buy books?"

"*Buy a book?* A single mom can't afford to *buy* books!"

Alexis was visibly annoyed. "Valetta, you are an exceedingly wealthy woman."

"On paper, maybe, but not back home."

"Home." Alexis left the word dangling in the air.

"Alexis, have you ever thought of coming east?"

"With all that snow? Never!"

"Oh, come on!" Valetta laughed. "Even Lincoln is getting used to the cold. It's not as if it's Siberia. And New England is lovely in the spring. You especially would love the wildflowers. Daisies, larkspur, snapdragons, there's even one called a California poppy—no kidding! And the summers are hot and hazy, just like they're supposed to be, although the mountains where I live are quite cool in the evening, after the sun goes down. And Mellie would be thrilled."

"Thrilled to see me?"

"She asks questions about you all the time."

Alexis was noncommittal, and Valetta accepted that that was all she was going to get for the moment. "I asked Rosalina to serve tea in the conservatory. I always loved that room."

Alexis made a great show of putting away her tools, but the sisters soon made their way to the conservatory. Alexis settled into a sturdy wicker chair that was so plush Valetta thought she would never be able to rise without help. And she looked as if she might need lots of help. In the unforgiving light of day, Alexis looked fragile. Valetta would have liked to discuss the matter of her cancer, but Alexis would not hear of it. She insisted that their conversation be kept to the mundane, like how she took her tea.

"Cream, one sugar," Valetta said quickly.

Alexis smiled faintly. "You have a good memory."

"It's no great feat. I only have one sister," Valetta said with a smile as she lifted the china teapot. An heirloom from days gone by, she recognized the paper-thin porcelain as one of her mother's favorites. She guessed she was an honored guest, in Rosalina's book. Filling an equally delicate cup, Valetta felt Alexis study her white hair, always a surprise to strangers. Alexis was no stranger, but the last time she had seen her, Valetta had copper curls, so Valetta was ready for the inevitable question that would come.

"You never thought to dye your hair?"

"And become a slave to my hairdresser?" she said, giving the same answer she always did. "I don't have the time, or money. Besides, it's too caught up in a memory."

This was the closest they had ever come to talking about Jack's death, and Valetta did not encourage the subject. She knew—after the fact—that Alexis had called when Jack died, that she had wanted to fly out, and that Valetta's friends had discouraged the idea. Valetta had been hospitalized, they'd explained. She was in the last trimester of her pregnancy. The doctors were worried...the baby...the excitement...it might not be best. One of the few times in her life that Alexis allowed herself to be guided, and Valetta regretted her absence. Now they were strangers, and she had no idea how to breach the gap. Her attempts to make amends seemed to always fall flat. Even now she felt her words float on empty air.

"Alexis, did you ever consider that there's more to life than the paper? Perhaps you should be rethinking your priorities, not asking *me* to take your place. If you're asking me to take over the *L.A. Connection,* then anyone can." Desperate to know, Valetta dared herself to ask the question that gnawed at her insides. "If you're that sick, why don't you sell it to Lincoln? He would love to own it, I'm sure."

But Alexis missed the point. "Why do you resist taking over the *Connection?* Surely you've learned a great deal running *The Spectator.*"

Disappointed, Valetta had no choice but to move on. "Because I have no grand ambitions. *The Spectator* does fine for what it is, but it's a small-town rag with no pretense to anything else. Some weeks, I carry more want ads than news."

"That's not true."

Her head tilted, Valetta sent Alexis a curious look. "Now, how would you know that?"

Alexis shifted uncomfortably. "I'm a subscriber."

"*No kidding?* Live and learn."

"You didn't know?"

"I use a service, but hey, thanks. We need all the customers we can get. In any case, it's what I do to keep me and Mellie fed. But I don't think you understand, Alexis. I like my life as it is. I'm here to sign my shares of the paper over to you, not to replace you."

"You're here to dismantle the Keane domain," Alexis said, sinking farther into the cushions.

"Come on, Alexis, you talk as if this were the

Ottoman Empire. The *Connection* isn't that old. Grandfather started it, remember? Dad just took it over when he died, as you did when Dad died. Who knows what he would have done with it if he'd lived longer, and what you would have done with your own life if you hadn't decided to take his place? Or did you always intend for all *this* to be?" Valetta asked, her hand sweeping the conservatory, so lovely in the afternoon sun. *Such a civilized place to spend the day,* she thought. But it was a relic from a time long past. Did Alexis not know it?

"Did you never have other plans?"

"What does it matter?" Alexis asked, visibly irritated. "The past is the past."

"It matters to you, a great deal, it would seem. But if you're ill, now, Alexis, doesn't the paper become less important?"

"No! Maybe it becomes more important. Maybe it makes me worry more about its future."

"It seems so, doesn't it?" Valetta agreed softly. "Look, Alexis, I don't want to hurt you, I don't mean to be unhelpful, but I don't know if any choice I made would make you happy. Except maybe to move back to California."

"Which is not going to happen."

"Which is not going to happen. Try to understand, Alexis, my life is in New York, it's the path I chose, even if it chose me first! To get up and leave, just like that…I can't. Mellie and I have commitments, to people we love and who love us."

Valetta smiled. "Look, I have this friend, this old man, and if I didn't return to Longacre, I don't know how he would get to the doctor, next week. He can't drive, and even if he could, he likes me to hold his hand when he gets his shots. And Ellen Hartwell is expecting us for dinner next week, and Mellie is having a sleepover on Saturday and I promised we'd bake cupcakes—chocolate with sprinkles…. The list is endless, but Alexis, that list makes up the borders of my life."

"But *I* need you."

"Not in the way you think. I would return for you, Alexis—*for you*—but not for the sake of a newspaper."

Alexis was unconvinced—she would probably never be convinced—but the fight seemed suddenly to leave her.

"I'm sorry, Alexis," Valetta said, reaching for her sister's hand, "but that's what I came to tell you. And to tell you, too, that there's room for you in my home, if you want to consider coming back with me. There will *always* be a place for you. Not as fancy as this—" Valetta smiled ruefully "—but not that uncomfortable, either. And Mellie is worth the trip."

But Alexis would not be mollified. "I'm feeling tired," she said, rising to her feet. "I have to lie down. Will you join me later for dinner?"

"Of course," Valetta said lightly, her feelings hurt even if she hadn't really expected an answer. "I'll tell you funny Mellie stories. Maybe that will change your mind."

Her interest flagging, Alexis left the conservatory with a half smile. Valetta watched Alexis's small form grow even smaller until she was alone with only her thoughts for company. Bad company they were, too. In the main, she was already regretting her suggestion that Alexis sell the paper to Lincoln, if he could even afford to buy it. If Alexis did that, and if Lincoln accepted, then where would it leave *her*? Because, if she had to be honest, she was having fanciful imaginings of Lincoln settling down in Longacre. She knew it was a long shot, the very longest in light of their argument at Jerome's diner the other day, but she was hoping that when she returned home, she'd be able to persuade him to at least consider moving east. *To at least consider* extending his visit. To convince him of the contributions he was making to the town, to her life.

In fact, to have another argument with him, as many as necessary, until she won him over.

Chapter Fourteen

"There's my mom!" Mellie cried, when she and Lincoln picked up Valetta at Albany Airport on the following Sunday. Hugs all around, even for Lincoln, Valetta was so happy to be back. Mellie chattered all the way home about everything that had happened since Valetta had left. In turn, she wanted to know exactly what Valetta had brought her from California. And did she like baked ziti? Because Lincoln had made it from scratch from a recipe book and it was just waiting to be heated up and he didn't burn anything this time and did she mind that they'd brought Yellow because he'd started to cry when they left and looked so sad they just had to?

On and on Mellie went, telling stories from the backseat while Mangy Yellow sat beside her, panting wildly as he looked out the window, pleased with himself and the world. Mellie brought Valetta up-to-date on everything her mom had missed, while Valetta and Lincoln exchanged amused glances. At one point, Lincoln even pressed Valetta's hand, his pleasure at her return obvious.

The baked ziti was terrific, and it wasn't because Valetta was hungry. Apparently, Lincoln *could* read a cookbook. Ziti plus a salad and freshly toasted garlic bread made for a festive homecoming meal. Mellie was positively hyper, but conversely, Valetta thought she had never seen Lincoln so relaxed. When Mellie reappeared after dinner with her backpack and announced she was *ready,* Valetta understood why he'd declined a glass of wine. He was driving Mellie to Hannah's for a sleepover.

"You forgot it was her birthday!" Mellie accused her mother.

Valetta's hand flew to her mouth. "Oh, my goodness, Mellie, I did! Oh, honey, I'm so sorry. But tomorrow is Monday. Isn't there school?"

"It's a teacher's day to do the report cards, I think, so we're off. Did you forget that, too?"

"I did, I did, I forgot. I must still be on California time. But what about a present for Hannah? What are we going to do about a gift?"

"Don't worry, Mom, Lincoln took care of it," Mellie announced smugly, holding aloft a beautifully wrapped box. "He went to the mall and walked all over until he found exactly what Hannah wanted."

"I looked real cute buying a pink boa scarf," Lincoln said with a dopey grin, "but that's what Hannah said she *absolutely, positively* needed. I don't think the saleslady believed me when I told her that rose was not my color!"

Mellie giggled, and Valetta had to smile. This was a side of Lincoln she had never seen.

"So," he said, rising to his feet, "for just this once, Mrs. Faraday, you can sit back and not worry about driving, or doing the dishes, or even unpacking. I'll run Mellie over to Hannah's and be right back to clean up. You put your feet up, watch some TV while I'm gone and enjoy that chardonnay."

"You know, I think I'd rather take a ride with you guys. The wine has made me a bit sleepy and the drive will wake me up. Besides, I'm homesick for my baby. The ride will give me an extra few minutes with her."

"Oh, Mom, I'm not a baby!" Mellie protested, but Valetta noticed she didn't resist another hug.

The short drive to Hannah's house was a hodgepodge of giggles and more tales from the backseat. Mellie also asked a thousand questions about California and her aunt Alexis, and was shocked to hear that Valetta had not gone to Disneyland. But Valetta's lapse was forgotten the moment they arrived at Hannah's, when the front door swung wide and half a dozen girls crowded around Mellie, their loud screeches painful to Linc's untutored ears.

"Poor Christie," he groaned as they drove away. "All those little girls! All that noise!"

Half-asleep, Valetta only smiled. "Oh, I think she can handle it." Feeling the car stop, she opened her eyes. "Is anything wrong? Why are we stopping?"

"So I can do this." Before she could stop him, Lincoln leaned across the seat and planted a hungry kiss on her lips, his mouth a plainspoken message. Her lips, parted in willing response, were all that he could wish for. Searching her mouth with his tongue, he found the taste of her desire and need. It matched his own.

"I've been wanting to do that since Albany," he whispered, nibbling at her earlobe, his grasp tightening as he became more serious. His hand sliding beneath her coat to wrap around the soft curve of her waist, he pulled her closer to plant a kiss in the hollow of her neck. "So soft," he murmured, traveling her jawline to brush her brow with his lips. "So soft, so soft..."

Wanting to give, as well, Valetta tunneled her fingers through his thick hair, something she had yearned to do for the longest time, and drew his face down to hers. His stubbly beard against her skin was no deterrent, in fact, it was exciting, a sensuous feeling. Her emotions spinning, her breath coming lightly through her parted lips, she pressed her mouth to his. An electric shock scored her body. Then, as suddenly as it began, the long kiss was over and he had pulled back onto the road.

"If we don't stop right now," he said ruefully, "I won't be responsible... Well, for *anything*." He laughed.

Caught unaware, Valetta felt the cool night air wash over her. She didn't say a word the rest of the way home, but her head was whirling, and every enticing, sinful, giddy fantasy she had ever had about Lincoln Cameron was part of that delightful whirlpool. Surely that kiss was encouragement to make demands on him.... Okay, *not quite,* she warned herself. But minimally, her plan to ask him to stay on in Longacre, if only for a little while, was not coming from left field now. Kisses like that had *meaning*.

Didn't they?

When they arrived back at the house, Lincoln wouldn't hear of Valetta helping with the dishes, and after those soul-searing kisses, she appreciated a few minutes to gather her wits. Linc must have guessed, because he handed her a glass of wine and banished her to the living room.

"You haven't touched your wine," he remarked as he settled down beside her ten minutes later, his own glass in hand. "It's good stuff. I picked it up when I went shopping for Hannah's present. The one thing this town sure could use is a liquor store, not the boozy kind, mind, but the type that sells a decent bottle."

"It's a thought," Valetta smiled, "but then you'd have to teach people about the refinements of fine wine. It could be that you'd need to start up a wine-tasting class. Bet you'd get a good-sized crowd for that!"

"Yeah, I might have to start up a winery to handle that crowd. Either that, or send for my wine cellar."

"You could probably start a liquor store with what you have in your vault!"

Carefully putting down his glass, Lincoln inched closer to Valetta, and took her hands in his. "Sweetie, it's not Longacre I'm thinking about this minute, it's Longacre's favorite daughter," he said softly, kissing the tip of her nose. "I'm crazy about you, Vallie."

The fatigue Valetta had been feeling only moments before disappeared in the excitement of Linc's touch. His hands kneading her shoulders were a pleasant jolt.

"I guess you could say I've been thinking along those same lines lately, Mr. Cameron." Instinctively, she arched closer, her palms spread across his chest. The planes of his body were sketched beneath her hands, the thumping of his heart pronounced.

"That's good, that's good," Lincoln whispered, as he felt her hesitant touch cross the contours of his body. She might be shy, but she seemed willing. His eyes were deadly serious as he planted little kisses along her jaw. "Then I guess if I made love to you, there wouldn't be a whole lot of objection?"

"Not a whole lot," Valetta murmured, her eyes closing at the glorious sensation of his touch. What would she do if he stopped?

"Good," he whispered, his lips brushing hers, "because I haven't thought about anything else since you left."

"Is that true, Lincoln?" Valetta asked, raising her head. "Because you don't have to talk pretty just to get me to... Make me..."

Lincoln's eyes grew dark. "*Make you?* Would I have to *make you?* Because I don't want you, if I must."

Valetta cupped his cheek with her long fingers and studied him earnestly. "Oh, no, Lincoln!"

Lincoln's relief was a loud sigh. He drew Valetta close, his touch less restrained, pressed a soft kiss to her mouth, light and teasing. It made for one blouse button unbuttoned.

He pressed his mouth against the soft, pink swell. "Hmm, baby soft." Another button.

Her eyes pressed shut at the pure pleasure of his touch. Valetta could hardly speak. Hmm, wonderful...wonderful...

Lincoln swooped down, reclaiming her lips. She didn't object, either, when she felt another button pop. Oh, my, no, she had no objections.

Neither could say who spoke, or if anyone actually did. A fourth button, then a fifth, and Lincoln was sliding Valetta's blouse past her shoulders and down along her arms. He didn't know the damage a simple cotton bra could do to his heart. Slowly, he eased the lacy cup aside.

"Wait!"

"What?" Lincoln could hardly bear to stop for the sight of her bare, pink breast, the faint brown nipple peeking from her bra.

"I...I..."

If the room had been brighter, Lincoln knew he would see Valetta's cheeks for the burning, red slash they had become. "Am I going too fast?" he murmured as he captured her hand and began to kiss her fingers.

"No...no..." Embarrassed, Valetta tried to snatch back her hand.

"Good!" Lowering his head to her breast, he teased a swollen nipple with his moist mouth, first the one, then the other, until he felt her sink back into his arms. "Has it been that long?" he asked, reflecting on her hesitation.

"Hmm." Way too long.

"But you trust me?"

"Hmm." Valetta sighed, unable to speak for the pleasure he was giving her. He talked too much, she thought vaguely. But the way he nibbled on her earlobe, how could Valetta possibly object to such pleasure? Her body ached for a man's touch...no, *his* touch. Only *Linc* would do, or this would have happened long before, even in the small town of Longacre.

Unsnapping her bra, Lincoln threw it...somewhere. Unbuttoning her jeans, he ran his fingers over her belly. Finally, she was his! Slipping his hand beneath her waistband, he felt for her warmth, and felt her body tremble in response. Brushing her clitoris, he felt her dampened curls, her soft, urgent appeal for more. Feeling with his fingers, he found her pleasurably wet, and knew she was ready, but Lincoln steeled himself to slow down. He wasn't a kid, but damned if she wasn't the most entrancing woman he'd ever known.

He even begrudged the time it took to remove his own clothes, when he was unable to wait any longer. There was hardly any time left for exploring, if he didn't want to embarrass himself. Fumbling like a schoolboy, he managed to remove the rest of her clothes, too, then stretched out beside her. Her bouquet would never be erased from his memory. His hands circling her hips, he rolled over to cover her naked body with his and felt his chest abrade hers, but she didn't seem to mind. Her nipples pressed to his were their own seduction. Taking her hand, he guided it to himself.

"See what you do to me, Valetta? Touch me. Oh, hell, don't," he laughed. "Big mistake."

"No, let me, Linc," Valetta commanded as she pushed him down, suddenly taking the lead, her hands splayed across the crinkly brown mat of hair that covered his torso. "You are so beautiful that simply looking at you could almost be enough."

"I hope not," he muttered, trying not to move, although it was becoming difficult.

Valetta's mouth was a warm smile on his hot skin as she pressed a kiss to his belly and felt the tremors her little kisses caused. Straddling his hips, she leaned forward and kissed his mouth boldly until he sent her flying beneath him.

"No good..." he panted, "...can't wait... Spread your legs for me, my darling."

Her fingers harnessed to Lincoln's rippling muscles, Valetta did as he asked. Her legs wrapped around his buttocks, she felt him lift her hips and search for entry, wriggling against the moist juncture of her thighs as he propelled himself forward. Unable to contain her impatience, she welcomed him into her body, to meet him, thrust for thrust. Her dormant sexuality was fully awake. On a tide of passion, urged on by his patient loving, Valetta found her satisfaction. She felt him follow close on, with a loud shout that seemed to drain him with a deep shudder. They fell to earth together in splendid defeat.

Valetta woke first, embraced in Lincoln's arms, his heavy legs wrapped about her thighs. It was the first time she had lain with a man since Jack, and the sensation of his warm body on hers was alien. She even forgot for a moment what had happened. But only for a moment. And she really did like the way his hold tensed when she stirred, even if his eyes were shut and his breathing steady. Relaxing, she allowed herself some liberties. The liberty to enjoy her cheek pressed against his shoulder, run her hands along his muscular forearms, delight in the pleasure of his hair as it tickled her cheek. For the first time in years, feeling a man's arms about her waist, she felt safe and at peace, something she hadn't felt in years. Closing her eyes, she burrowed closer. She knew how she felt and she liked it. She liked it even more when he returned her hug. And was only slightly disappointed at his love talk.

"Are you hungry?" he whispered.

So much for romance, she thought, smiling to herself as she hugged him closer. "You're always hungry."

"Why do I think you're not going to make me some eggs?" he said, his lips pressed to her temple.

"I don't know," she murmured, as her hand began to explore his warm skin. "I mean, I would, if I had to," she said, pressing her mouth to his flat, brown nipple, "but somehow I don't think that's what you want this very moment. Do you?" she asked sweetly, feeling him grow large in her palm.

"Vallie," Lincoln groaned, "if you keep doing that…"

"Yes?"

"Yes!"

It was well past midnight when they put on a pot of coffee, but they both agreed the wait was worth it. Sated, feeling a bit wobbly, Valetta made it to the shower, hoping to steam herself back to one piece.

"Don't worry, I couldn't," he said, grinning at her look of dismay when he pulled aside the shower curtain. "Three times in one night, hey, I'm not as young as I used to be, lady. I can just manage to soap up your back."

"Good. Do that and I might be able to manage to break some eggs."

Waking the next morning to the sound of a robin parked outside her window, Valetta marveled at her sense of well-being. When she opened her eyes and saw Lincoln gazing down at her, his tousled head propped on his hand, she knew why.

"How long have you been up?" she asked with a sleepy smile.

"A little while," Lincoln admitted, returning her smile with a kiss. "Watching you sleep was a nice way to spend my time."

"Quality time?" Valetta murmured as she slid back beneath the covers.

"Um," Linc agreed as he followed her down, his hand searching out her warmth.

Thirty minutes later, fresh from another shower, Lincoln's feet were still bare but they were headed to the kitchen in search of the coffeepot. Smiling at the evidence of their midnight snack, he threw away the old coffee grinds and washed the dirty pot. Staring idly past the kitchen window, he caught a glimpse of the garden, just beginning to bud. He discovered, too, that whatever Valetta might brag about, it would never be her gardening skills. Truthfully, calling it a *garden* was generous. Clay pots stacked every which way, a rake rusting in a corner, two shovels left to corrode, it bordered on unkempt. Maybe he should take a few minutes to putter around out there, get some exercise, later that afternoon, just to clean it up a bit. Spring *was* in the air, after all. Lincoln caught himself up. *What the hell was he thinking?*

"My goodness, those must be deep thoughts," Valetta said with mock severity as she plopped down on a kitchen chair.

Lincoln softened his expression. "Not at all. I was checking out your garden. It needs work," he said lightly.

Valetta followed his glance. "Yes, well." Her shrug was equally light. "Who has time? And the results never seem to justify my efforts." She sighed. "So, is that coffee you promised ready?"

"Coffee and a kiss," Lincoln said as he passed her both. "And toast," he added as he set down a plate.

"How domestic we are this morning," she observed as she reached for a piece. "Not even burned."

Lincoln shook his head. "I don't know why you think I'm incapable of cooking."

"Might have something to do with those pots you burned last month." She groaned as she lifted her mug. *"You think?"*

"Oh, Lincoln, I'm just teasing! It just seems out of

character—the idea of the famous Mr. Cameron toiling away in a country kitchen."

"Does that give me clay feet?"

"No, it's just out of character—although this coffee is *terrific*. You do seem to have mastered the important stuff," she said, smiling. "But you may be right. I don't know you all that well, do I? There are areas of your life that you seem to avoid discussing, so how can I say?"

"Uh-oh." Lincoln grinned over his own steaming cup. "Is this going to be one of those *morning after* conversations?"

Blushing seven ways to Sunday, Valetta tugged her robe closer, unconsciously defensive. "Did I sound like that?"

"A little," Lincoln teased. "But if you have questions, ask away. After all, I did just partake of your luscious body," he added with a wicked smile, "so I suppose I can spare you a few answers."

"Keep talking like that and you may have to justify more than your cooking," Valetta retorted. "But I *have* been meaning to talk to you about some things. Nothing serious," she reassured him, noticing the unease that flashed in his eyes. "Just a few things beyond *what have you been doing for the last ten years.*"

"For instance?"

"Something I was thinking about while I was in California." Valetta took a deep breath, then rushed ahead. "I was hoping that you would consider remaining in Longacre a little longer. Wait," she said, raising her hands quickly. "Hear me out, Linc. I'm just asking you to think about it. This has nothing to do with me. Spending last week in Los Angeles made me think about things. In particular, what you share with Alexis. I know she's sick, Linc, but it's beyond that. She was always such a joyless woman, so dour, and since my visit, I've discovered sadly enough that she hasn't changed at all. And since you work for her—you *are* around her a great deal—the way I figure, it has to have an effect on you."

Valetta looked at him earnestly. "Lincoln, you seem so happy here, and you've made so many people here the happier for your visit."

"That's very kind of you to say."

"I'm not trying to be *kind*. And I'm not the only one who wants you to stay, not by a long shot. Where this— *we*—went last night is second to any other consideration. If you remember, we did talk about some of this before last night happened. Remember that conversation we had at the diner, before I left? Look, I'm not saying I don't want *us* to go somewhere. After last night, I think we have. I just want to be clear that if I'm asking you to think about remaining in Longacre it's not because of this new side to our relationship."

"You mean the sex?" Lincoln teased.

Valetta blushed. "Yes, the…sex."

"The wonderful sex," Linc emphasized, enjoying how the heat rose in her face.

"The *wonderful sex*," Valetta allowed with a small smile. "But it wasn't just sex, was it, Linc?"

"No, it wasn't," he admitted. "And I won't say I don't like being here. I'll even go as far as to say you may be right about how I feel about California and working for Alexis. Quite frankly I *have* been feeling restless lately, long before I came east. It's partly why I agreed to come here in the first place."

"Partly?"

"*You* were most of the reason, sweetheart. I was curious to see you. The moment Alexis asked me to come here, she had me hooked. But I do have commitments that reach beyond Alexis."

Valetta held her breath, waiting to see if he would confirm Alexis's offer of a partnership.

"Like I said, I've been a bit restive, lately. But that's not necessarily a reason to move three thousand miles. And if I did move here, it would be as much about you as anything else. Come on, Vallie, how could it not be? I'm crazy about you. And how often do you think I have wonderful nights like the one we shared last night?"

Disappointed that he didn't confide in her, Valetta was still grateful for what he gave her. "Thank *you* for saying *that*. And I know all about obligations. The difference is in the fact that I love my life here, and my obligations are things I enjoy. I wish I could believe that yours were, also. I won't say that I know all that much about you. It's been years since we've seen each other, and I wasn't too experienced back then, but I know enough *now* to put that on the table. Tell me true, Lincoln, are you all that happy in L.A.?"

Linc didn't want to answer; he was beginning to find the conversation too nerve-racking. No matter what Valetta said, it *was* a *morning after* conversation. Silk ropes were sliding round his neck—not tight, but weighty—the weight of *what came next,* words like *obligation, relationship, commitment* hovering in the air, threatening to be voiced, words he had spent his life avoiding.

I have to go back, he murmured to himself, and

then more loudly. "I have to go back. I need time to figure this out."

Valetta fought the fear rising in her chest. If Lincoln returned to California, he would never come back.

"Can't I help you?" she asked, her hand resting on his shoulder. But she knew he would say no. She watched him force a hapless grin.

"Valetta, I could no more up and leave L.A. on a moment's notice than you could leave Longacre. If you want the truth, part of me *does* want to stay here and never go back, but even so, I have responsibilities. People depend on me. They're waiting for my return. I'm supposed to be reorganizing the Denver newsroom. I'm booked to fly to Belgium. And although I may be an editor, I still like to keep my reporter's notebook open, so I committed to cover the World Health Conference in Mozambique next August...." Lincoln left off, unsure what else to say. *I've loved you forever, but the idea scares the bejesus out of me?*

His head bowed, Lincoln pressed his cheek to Valetta's. "Vallie, I know we have something going here, but I've never... This is new to me. I need time to catch my breath. Please trust me, Vallie. Can you do that for a little while? Can you give me some time...a month?"

Blinking hard, Valetta smiled. "I suppose I can do that. I love you enough to do that."

"You love me?" he asked with a tender smile.

Valetta cupped his cheeks with her long fingers. "You know I do. I never would have slept with you if I didn't."

Lincoln kissed her gently. "Well, I sort of guessed, but didn't dare presume. And I guess you know I would never have asked you if I didn't care deeply about you."

"What a pair we are." Valetta smiled sadly. "Declaring our deepest feelings in the face of cold coffee."

"Well, I can fix one of those problems," Linc said as he reached for her. "Coffee will take a little more work."

Chapter Fifteen

"So, Mellie, what do you think?"

"About what?" Mellie asked absently as she chewed at her pencil, her face buried in a huge textbook.

Valetta knew she wasn't listening. Fondly, she ruffled Mellie's mop of curls. "Never mind. I'm just thinking out loud."

Mellie took a moment to glance out the window but immediately returned to her books. "I have *so* much homework! That Mrs. Gerard, she doesn't care about *anything* except giving us tons of homework and reports and spelling tests. If Lincoln was here, he would help me with my math, I just know it."

"Oh, honey, I'll help you."

"Sorry, Mom, but you're not so hot in math."

Chagrined, Valetta offered to make cocoa instead. It was Saturday morning, she had a million things to do, and no incentive to do any of them. Where was Lincoln? It had been over a month, it was the end of May and he said he would return in spring. He had promised.

"Those little purple flowers are up," she said vaguely as she glanced out the window. Her sigh was so pronounced that Mellie looked up.

"You miss Lincoln," she declared.

"What makes you say that?" Valetta asked, as she placed a frothy mug in front of her daughter.

"Because I do. And besides, you kept saying all week that you had a gazillion things to do this weekend so not to make any plans or ask you to drive me anywhere, and now you're just hanging around the kitchen and not doing anything except talking about those dumb old flowers and everyone knows how much you hate flowers!"

"I do not hate flowers! On the contrary, I kind of like those little purpley things," Valetta protested. "I can't grow them is all."

"They are not *things*, Mom, they're flowers, and they're called crocuses! See what I mean? You can't even remember their name, because you hate them!"

"They're just not high on my list is all," Valetta said meekly.

"You miss Lincoln!"

Valetta sat down opposite her daughter and sighed. "I miss him terribly."

"So why don't you go to California and bring him home?"

"Because this is not his home."

"Yes, it is. I know it is, because he was happy here. And he wasn't happy in California."

"And how do you know that, Miss Know-It-All?"

Mellie looked at her mother as if she was crazy. "Because he *told* me, that's why!"

"He did? When?"

"Remember when you went to see Aunt Alexis and I stayed with Patty and Chuck? Well, Linc used to help me with my homework. One night, when Patty was making us dinner, Linc said that the way Patty cooked reminded him of when he was a kid and his parents weren't killed and his mom used to make dinner every night while they waited for his dad to come home, and he would do his homework, just like we were. And Patty said, then why didn't he come live in Longacre, if he was so happy here? And Linc said that he would love to, but Aunt Alexis wouldn't like it. So Patty said, what difference did it make what Aunt Alexis liked? And Linc said he owed her big-time, so Patty said, well, *what* did he owe her? And Lincoln said it didn't matter, and Patty got mad and said he owed things to some other people she could name, and then Linc said—"

"Whoa there, Mellie Faraday! Did they know you were eavesdropping, because you were, you know."

"No, I wasn't," Mellie said, unmoved by the accusation. "It's not my fault if grown-ups don't pay attention to kids, especially if they're being quiet and trying to do their homework."

"Mellie, I think that's called splitting hairs."

Unconvinced, Mellie sipped her cocoa thoughtfully. "Mom, can I ask you something?"

"Sure, sweetie."

"Do men cry?"

"Mellie! Why...I...I... Yes, of course they do. What a strange question. Why do you ask?"

"Well, that night, while I was sitting there and they were arguing, Lincoln's eyes got all shiny, but then Chuck came home and Linc jumped up and was smiling and stuff, so I couldn't be sure." Mellie shrugged. "Linc would never cry, would he, Mom? He's a man. I don't think men cry, except in movies."

Bending her head, Mellie returned to her homework. Ten minutes later, though, deep in thought, Valetta jumped at the sound of her daughter's voice. "So, are you going to go get him?"

"I don't know."

"I wish you would, and soon. I miss him a lot, and I'll just bet he misses us. He can't be happy without us, can he? Not if he was happy here, and he's not here."

Valetta smiled wanly. "There's logic in that, I suppose."

"*I* think you should go to California tomorrow and make him come back. Just tell Aunt Alexis that she has to share him, that it's our turn to have Lincoln. Phone calls aren't enough."

"It's that simple, huh?"

"He'll listen to you, I know it."

"And how do you know that? Do you have a crystal ball?"

"I just know," Mellie declared with the assured wisdom of a nine-year-old.

Valetta sat deep in thought as she watched her daughter work diligently on her math. She never knew whether it was her love for Lincoln, or Mellie's long sighs over her sums, but next thing she knew she was calling Patty Carmichael to see if she was available to watch Mellie. Winter break was coming up, so Patty wouldn't have to chauffeur Mellie anywhere.

Her errand wouldn't take any longer than a round-trip ticket to L.A.

Valetta landed in Los Angeles late in the evening, but this time she booked a hotel room. It would have been tactless to stay at the Keane mansion when she was trying to steal Lincoln away from her sister. Besides, she had been a Faraday for years, and wanted it to be as a Faraday when she stormed the offices of the *L.A. Connection,* which she was planning to do the very next day.

Waking the next morning, she went for an early jog, then returned to take a leisurely shower and order a hearty breakfast from room service. Ready to take on the world—or at least Lincoln Cameron—she rode down Hollywood Boulevard feeling as if she had half a chance to win him over. The problem was Alexis. Hopefully, they wouldn't cross paths.

What was she thinking? Even if Alexis hadn't had her own built-in radar, the security at the *L.A. Connection* was state-of-the-art. When Valetta arrived at the paper, she was immediately stopped in the lobby and had to show her ID. Without an appointment, she wasn't going upstairs, either, so she forced the security guard to call Ms. Keane. Disbelief written all over his face, the guard called Alexis's secretary, but he was smiling when he hung up the phone. He had been ordered by Miss Keane *personally* to escort *her sister* up to the eighteenth floor. Apparently, Alexis was taking no chances. The return of the prodigal daughter would definitely make headlines. No doubt she wanted to be sure they were standing at the elevator bank when Valetta got off so that Alexis was the first thing she saw, meeting her head-on, exactly as Valetta hoped she would not. At least surprise favored her, Valetta thought, if the annoyed look on Alexis's face was any measure. "What are you doing here?"

Quick and to the point! "Well, Alexis, you're looking better than the last time I saw you."

Alexis was no fool. "Come into my office and I'll have him paged."

Valetta followed her sister down the carpeted hall, surprised to see the walls lined with the same paintings their father purchased years before. She knew this because, as a child, he had often invited her to come by after school and play on the rug in his office. He knew she had liked doing that far better than visiting her friends. And every time he bought a new painting for the office, he would hold it up and ask her what she thought. She never thought *anything*. She was far too young to have an opinion of Degas, far more interested in playing with the teddy bears at her feet. Her father never seemed to mind. He would just laugh and set the painting aside for the carpenter coming to hang it. She wondered if her sister had such memories, and was about to ask, when they passed Alexis's secretary. Quietly, Alexis requested that Mr. Cameron be summoned, then beckoned Valetta into her office, the very one Valetta played in as a child. How could Valetta have thought otherwise? It was only logical that Alexis take over their father's office.

"He won't go."

"*Who* won't go *where?*" Valetta asked Alexis, startled from her reverie.

"Lincoln, of course. He loves his work," Alexis

asserted. "He just interviewed the Brazilian president yesterday. It was quite a coup. And he's off to Belgium any minute now, to cover the Olympic games. All those healthy young girls." She smiled unpleasantly. "I didn't ask him to go, you understand, he volunteered months ago. To be honest, I was surprised—you know how he hates traveling—but he was always one for a pretty face."

"I know what you're trying to do, Alexis, and it won't work. Besides, I have no intention of begging Lincoln to come back. I'm just bearing a message...from Mellie."

"You've come a long way for something that could have been said in a letter," Alexis snapped.

"You sent *him* a long way to deliver me a message that would have come better from *you!*"

Wherever their argument was going, it was lost in the moment as Lincoln strode into the room. His appearance was a shock to Valetta. Expensively attired, his hair freshly cut, his shoes a glossy shine, he was an intimidating sight. *An important man.* Her confidence wavered. She had been right to worry; he seemed to have slid right back to his previous lifestyle, as if Longacre had never happened.

"Valetta? What a surprise."

"Is she?" Alexis asked with false cheer as Valetta scrambled to her feet.

Lincoln frowned. "Of course she is. Is everything all right, Vallie? Is Mellie all right? Nothing's wrong, is there?"

"Mellie's fine," Valetta assured him. "Everyone is fine."

"Well, that's good. But then, why are you here?"

"The crocuses are up." Suddenly unsure of what to say, she faltered.

Lincoln glanced past her shoulder to where Alexis sat, watching their every move. He wished she would give them some privacy, but he knew she wouldn't. And there was Valetta, tugging at his sleeve.

"Mellie sent you a message, Linc," Valetta said, gaining courage. "She said to tell you how much she misses you."

Lincoln smiled. "I miss her a lot, too, but I told her when I left that I wasn't sure when I could return."

"It doesn't matter what you said. Kids don't have the same frame of reference we do. She thought…we all thought…" Valetta sighed. "I warned you that the town had expectations. Well, I'm their emissary. They sent me to remind you of your…obligations."

"Remind me of my *what?*" Darting a quick glance at Alexis, he laughed, but it was a hollow sound even to his own ears. "I have none, and they know it."

Valetta looked at him curiously, unable to understand why he was acting so distant. She could understand he might be ill at ease having this conversation in front of Alexis, but the part of her that was a Keane was also a force to be reckoned with.

"Is there somewhere private we can talk?" she asked, annoyed by her sister's unconcealed interest. Surely he wouldn't deny her a few minutes' privacy after she had flown three thousand miles to see him.

"A good idea. My office is down the hall."

"I'll expect you both for lunch," they heard Alexis call after them. But Lincoln was already out the door, taking the hall in long strides. Following close behind, Valetta thought that he looked gaunt, that he must have lost weight since the last time she saw him.

Skirting the nest of cubicles that housed the desk editors, she tried to avoid the inquiring eyes that followed their hurried march. Lincoln's office was magnificent, a wood-paneled suite that competed with Alexis's, although it didn't quite win. A huge picture window took up most of the far wall, the panorama of Los Angeles just beyond. The rest of the office was an unmistakable study in power and wealth, a clever display of oil paintings, plaques and awards, a private bar, an Aubusson rug. That and the inevitable bank of televisions tuned to various news channels, telephones and computers. The only discord was the stack of newspapers and magazines strewn across the sofa— the competition, no doubt. She must have interrupted his breakfast because a coffee mug still sat on the coffee table, a half-eaten roll beside it. In fact, Linc offered her a fresh cup but she motioned him away. She hadn't come to drink coffee. Sweeping her hair away from her eyes, she plunged in, determined not to mince words.

"First of all, Mellie wants me to say that if she doesn't get help with her math project, she is *definitely* going to fail."

"Valetta, I wish you hadn't come."

Ignoring his blunt words, Valetta plowed on. "Let's see, now…" Valetta began to tick off messages on her outstretched fingers. "Patty said to tell you that she bought some folding chairs at a garage sale if you want to continue the class. Chuck says he needs your help enlarging the hunting blind. Davey and Ellen said you promised to help cook Easter dinner, and since you missed it, you can do the Fourth of July. Oh, and Andy wants you to know that he enrolled in a journalism course at Binghamton University, and he doesn't understand a word of it and when can you tutor him? Rico said to tell you that he and his wife had a baby boy—they named him Clay, and they're both doing well—and that he's waiting for class to start up again, and can Nancy bring the baby? And Jerome... Well, Jerome just heaped curses on your head, but I won't quote him *exactly,*" she said with a faint smile.

"Valetta, don't."

But Valetta wouldn't stop. "They love you, Lincoln Cameron, and they want you to come home."

"That's very kind of them, I'm sure."

"Kind of them?" Valetta repeated, her brow furrowed. "When have I heard you say that before? And since when did you become so condescending?"

"I didn't mean it that way."

"How then did you mean it?"

"I told you I needed time to think."

"Oh, yes, right. You said you needed a month and you've had your month, so what have you decided?"

"I—"

"I knew it!" Valetta interrupted him impatiently. "I just knew that if you came back here, it would be the biggest mistake of my life."

Lincoln had to smile. "Of *your* life? I thought this was *my* life we were talking about."

Valetta's eyes softened. "I was hoping you would rethink that, too."

"I am."

"No," she said sadly, glancing at the cluttered couch. "I'll bet you didn't think about me at all. I wasn't asking you to marry me, if that's what you were worried about. I just wanted to be part of the picture."

"You are, Vallie, it's just that I found I couldn't just up and leave. I warned you about that. It could take me a year."

"A year! You said a month!"

"There were things I forgot about."

"And what about me? Am I supposed to wait a whole year until you decide if you're coming back? Don't you understand, Linc? I love you! And it's more, you know, than just loving you. It's *you* loving *me*."

"I never said that!"

"Oh, you cruel man!" she gasped. "You said it every time you kissed me…. The night I let you touch my body… You said it with your eyes. You said it in the morning, when you woke beside me."

Provoked by Valetta's love song, Lincoln pounced. "Well, what if I did? Do you honestly think that love is enough?" he said with scorn. "Let me tell you something, Mrs. Faraday. People get old and stale, and so does love, but this…" Lincoln swept his arm across the room, the trophies and pictures and plaques a testament to the empire he had helped to build, *his* trophies, pictures and plaques. *"This is for always!"*

"Oh, Lincoln, trust me. Nothing is for *always*," Valetta said sadly. "But wouldn't you rather grow old in Longacre with your *friends*, than sitting alone in this big, cold office?" Valetta shivered, rubbing her hands together for warmth. "All the carpets in Turkey couldn't warm this place, Linc."

"Yesterday I interviewed the Brazilian president. Can you top that?" he challenged her.

Valetta was unimpressed. "The Brazilian president delivers a speech filled with hollow words, and everyone applauds politely and drinks a toast to his health. But do you know what he does when he's done speech-ifying, Lincoln? He flies back home, to Rio, *to his family,* Lincoln! That's what's missing from your pretty wall displays—a picture of your wife and kids!"

Valetta could see she had touched a nerve, and he was growing angrier and angrier, but she figured this was her last chance to persuade him. She would not make this trip again.

"Every night, when I put Mellie to bed, I drag myself to bed, and you come to mind. But my bed is empty. Every morning, when I wake, I want you there. I reach for you, a silly thing to do, I know. I spend days picking on my staff, who have no idea what's wrong with me— or else they're too diplomatic to say so—except for Patty, of course. She put it to me quite succinctly the other day, but then, she's my friend."

"What did Patty say?"

"She said, *get on the next damned plane and bring your man home!*"

His guard down, Lincoln laughed. "Yes, that defi-nitely sounds like Patty."

Valetta shook her head. "This is Alexis's doing, isn't it? It is! I can tell by the way you're behaving. What did she offer you, Linc? The keys to the kingdom? She hinted something about offering you a partnership, but you never said, one way or the other." Her eyes wide, Valetta stepped back when she saw Lincoln turn to face the window. His stiff posture was her answer.

"She did, didn't she? *She's offered you the paper!* Oh, how could I be so stupid? It's what you've waited for all your life."

Lincoln turned back, his eyes clouded. "Listen, Valetta, you have to understand…"

But Valetta was unmoved. "Oh, Lincoln, why didn't you say so when I first walked in? Why didn't you stop me? Do you think this stuff is easy to say? You think it was easy to make this trip, to set aside my pride and come begging?"

"And you," he said with a sigh, his voice filled with anguish, "do you think it was easy to come back here? You're damned right I've been waiting all my life to take over the paper, so what did you expect?"

"I don't know," Valetta said, her eyes filling with tears. "I don't know what to believe. Maybe it *was* easier for you to choose the paper. Taking risks is risky business, isn't it? Giving up the memory of Jack for you was pretty damn hard, let me tell you! *I loved him!* And it was safe to love the memory of him, too. No risk to love a dead man. But then I thought, hey, *I love Lincoln, too,* and wasn't that a pretty great thing to happen, loving two fine men in one lifetime?"

Looking to Lincoln for some sort of reaction, and finding none, Valetta slung her bag over her shoulder and headed for the door. "I'm on the ten-thirty flight, tomorrow morning for Albany. I took the liberty of booking the seat next to mine. Whether you use it is for you to decide. We can always send for your damned wine collection."

Having failed to claim Lincoln, Valetta found herself with more free time than she'd expected. Refusing to dwell on the unhappy impasse, she strolled down Hollywood Boulevard and bought Mellie every conceivable Mickey Mouse doll she could find. Her arms loaded with Disney paraphernalia, she returned to her hotel.

Her courage ebbing, she called Spago and ordered the best dinner they could deliver. Feeling wicked, she charged it to Alexis Keane. That brought them scrambling! The pasta with vanilla lobster sauce delivered an hour later was still piping hot, and the chocolate truffle cake was as light and airy as she remembered. But it was all a fond memory when she took her seat the next morning, on the plane. Anxiously, she kept a lookout for a familiar face, her hopes still high even when the stewardess closed the door. Undeterred, she fantasized that they would turn the plane around just as it headed down the runway. Sorry, folks…a late arrival…a life-and-death situation. The doors would fly open and Lincoln would suddenly appear. Slowly, she would rise… He would take the seat beside her…

The seat next to Valetta remained empty throughout takeoff, and remained so the entire flight back to New York. Her stomach was still churning as they landed in Albany. What would she say to Mellie? Valetta had warned her that the mission was a very iffy task, but she knew that, like her mother, Mellie had harbored hopes. But her smart little girl made no comment when Valetta picked her up—*alone*—at Patty's, later that afternoon.

"No more trips, Mom, okay?" The hugs they shared were comfort enough.

Longacre drifted from late spring to early summer the week Mellie turned ten. Her June birthday heralded summer, and together she and Valetta planned the party of the century. Valetta always made sure it was a loud and colorful affair that forced everyone to dig in their closets for their bathing suits. This year was no different. The early-summer sun blazed hot, the sprinkler ran wild at the bottom of the garden, kids screeched, and a hundred pink balloons invited everyone in town to stop by for a cold glass of pink lemonade. And if that weren't enough, pink streamers fluttered from every low-lying tree branch, to remind anyone who missed the message that Mellie Faraday was having a birthday.

Every birthday Mellie celebrated was tinged with regret for Valetta. Her baby was growing up and Jack wasn't there to see it. Now, neither was Lincoln.

"What's the matter, Val?" Patty asked, looking doubtfully at the gooey mess Valetta had made of her piece of birthday cake, as they stood watching the kids tumble on the grass. "You can't fool Aunty Patty. Like the song says, *you've got troubles.*"

"What song?" Valetta asked, forcing a smile.

"Just about every song I know!" Patty snickered.

Valetta's shoulders fell. There was no sense in trying to fool Patty. "Don't mind me. I get a little teary this time of year."

"You miss Jack."

"Terribly," Valetta admitted, her cake beginning to resemble mousse. "And then, Mellie getting older, leaving for sleep-away camp next week. I know, I know, it's only for two weeks, but still…"

"Val, you know what I think? I think you need another kid."

"You think so?" Valetta's mouth curved sardonically.

"I wouldn't waste my breath saying so if I didn't," her friend retorted.

"Well, let me know when there's a good candidate for daddyhood. There is *that* aspect, remember?"

"I do. And as a matter of fact, I think there's a really terrific candidate right outside your front door."

Patty's smile grew as she set Valetta's plate aside and steered her to the front porch. There, taking up most of the driveway, was a limousine, its shiny black doors swung wide. A familiar lanky figure was barking orders to a young beleaguered driver who was trying to extricate a huge, wooden crate from the backseat.

"Look here, young man, do be careful with those bottles! Some of that wine is a hundred years old! Here, allow me! Gently. I said *gently!*"

Panic-stricken, the driver turned his head so abruptly he banged it on the door. His curse words were amazing, but not nearly as amazing as the amount of luggage strewn across the lawn, two steamer trunks and half a dozen cardboard boxes. And in the middle of all the excitement, Mangy Yellow danced wildly about Lincoln's heels, barking deliriously.

With a familiar shiver of awareness, Valetta hurried to his side. "Need some help?"

Lincoln looked down at Valetta and suddenly the wine no longer mattered. His own happiness magnified a thousand times in her sparkling eyes, he swept her into his arms. "God, how I missed you!"

Crushing his mouth to hers, Lincoln's hungry kiss was a search for the past. Raising his mouth from hers, he saw the promise of their future in her smile. "I will never, ever leave you again, and that's a promise!"

"A promise?" she said with a smile.

"*A vow,* which I mean to exchange with you—if you'll have me."

"I think I already do," she said softly. "You always had *me*."

"I think I always knew that. And it scared me to death. It made me run, in the wrong direction, unfortunately. I knew it the minute I landed in California. It just took me a while to own up to it."

Valetta studied him tenderly. "But you found your way home."

"The next time I get on an airplane, you'll be in the seat beside me. As my wife."

The warm glow that filled Valetta enveloped Lincoln, too. They stood in the sunlight like two teenagers discovering love, until a rustling in the background brought them to their senses.

"It seems we have an audience," she whispered shyly.

Lincoln looked up to find a small crowd had gathered on the porch. "The whole town, it seems," he said wryly as he set her back on her feet. "What's going on?"

"It's Mellie's birthday."

"No kidding? Talk about good timing."

"She'll be absolutely thrilled when she hears that you're here. But what's in all those boxes? Your famous wine collection?"

"My choicest bottles. I'm having most of my collection shipped, but there were a few bottles I didn't want to trust to the airlines. But with this heat, God knows what condition they're in," he said sadly. "We really do have to do something about a wine cellar. Good grief!" he shouted as the hapless driver let slide a crate. "For heaven's sake, that's a small fortune you're about to destroy! Oh, be still my heart, I can't bear to watch!"

Valetta had to bite her lip to keep from laughing, but Lincoln read her correctly.

"Believe me, sweetheart," he growled. "He's getting very well paid for this day's work."

Valetta didn't doubt it, and was glad for his sake that the crowd on the porch began marching down the steps to help.

"Hey, buddy," Chuck greeted him, clasping his shoulder as if Lincoln had never left. "There's a sale on fishing rods happening next week, down in Kingston. It's going to be a long summer, and the fish are really biting this year." Smiling, he lifted a box in the air and headed back to the house.

Dressed in his ranger uniform, Davey swept by to help unload the car. "Don't worry. I'm off duty. Ellen told me she'd make my life miserable if I didn't stop by."

Rico challenged Lincoln with a friendly shoulder punch. "Yo, dude, ready to start summer school? I have some ideas I'd like to run by you. Oh, and by the way, Nancy and I are looking for a godfather." So saying, he relieved the grateful driver of a huge box labeled chardonnay and headed back to the house.

"Hey there, young feller," Jerome Crater called to Lincoln from the safety of the shaded porch. "You coming in, or you gonna stand there all day? I got a barbecue burning up the coals out back. And bring that young feller with you. Poor kid looks like he could use a good meal."

"I sure will, old man. You just set us up a plate," Lincoln shouted back. "When did he begin to use the walker?" he asked Valetta softly.

"The end of May," she said. "We think he might have had a mild stroke, but the X-rays didn't show much."

"I was wrong, you know," he said, staring after Jerome thoughtfully. "It was never a question of loving you, Vallie."

"I never thought it was," she said, taking his hand.

"You were right. Alexis had partnership papers drawn up while I was away. They were waiting on my desk when I returned. She sprang a tender trap, and I fell right into it. But the oddest thing was that every time I asked her when we were signing, she had an excuse to delay it."

"Are you saying she lied?"

Lincoln grimaced. "I don't want to use that word. When I finally pressed the issue, she told me that since the chemo treatments were over and she was feeling so much better, did I mind if she stayed on? *Keep her hand in,* were her exact words. I felt like a first-class fool. Your showing up unexpectedly scared her to death. The day after you left, Alexis told me she was ready to sign. She shouldn't have stalled. I was no longer sure what *I* wanted."

"Hush, Lincoln, you don't have to say this stuff."

"No, sweetheart. I do," he said. "I owe you an apology, big-time. Your visit reminded me how much I had wanted out long before I arrived in Longacre, and of many other things I should not have so easily forgotten."

But before he could explain further, Mellie was shrieking and running down the path to throw herself in Lincoln's outstretched arms.

"Oh, Lincoln, you came back, you came back!" she said over and over, sobbing happily as she wound her arms around his neck. "Does this mean you're staying?"

"It does, if you don't choke me to death," he said as he hugged Mellie tightly.

"And you're going to marry my mom?" she whispered loudly.

"I will if she'll have me," Lincoln whispered back.

"Oh, I think she will! Then that means I get to call you *Dad!*"

"I would be honored," he said softly.

"Good," Mellie giggled, "because I told Hannah that you were coming to the Fourth of July picnic and—"

"Mellie, you didn't!" Valetta cried.

"Oh, Mom! I only said I was *hoping* he would come, but here he *is,* isn't he? So, anyway, then she started crying and saying where was *she* going to get a father so I said I'd share you and—"

Glancing past Mellie's shoulder, Lincoln smiled crookedly at Valetta. Her beautiful platinum hair a halo in the midday sun, her own wide smile filled with promise, her hand tucked in his a guarantee of their future.

A wife, a kid, a dog, friends... Must be my lucky day, Lincoln thought as he hoisted Mellie onto his shoulders and followed Valetta up the path.

And Mangy Yellow sat on the porch, his tail waving wildly as he waited for his family to join him.

* * * * *

Mills & Boon® Special Edition
brings you a sneak preview of Marie Ferrarella's
Capturing the Millionaire…

*It was a dark and stormy night…when lawyer
Alain Dulac crashed his BMW into a tree, and
local vet Kayla McKenna came to his aid. Used
to rescuing dogs and cats, Kayla didn't know
what to make of this stranger…but his
magnetism was undeniable…*

Don't miss the fantastic third story in
THE SONS OF LILY MOREAU *series,
available next month, October 2008, in
Mills & Boon® Special Edition!*

Capturing the Millionaire
by
Marie Ferrarella

The first thing Alain became aware of as he slowly pried his eyes opened, was the weight of the anvil currently residing on his forehead. It felt as if it weighed a thousand pounds, and a gaggle of devils danced along its surface, each taking a swing with his hammer as he passed.

The second thing he became aware of was the feel of the sheets against his skin. Against almost *all* of his skin. He was naked beneath the blue-and-white down comforter. Or close to it. He definitely felt linen beneath his shoulders.

Blinking, he tried very hard to focus his eyes.

Where the hell was he?

He had absolutely no idea how he had gotten here—or what he was doing here to begin with.

Or, for that matter, who that woman with the shapely hips was.

Alain blinked again. He wasn't imagining it. There was a woman with her back to him, a woman with sumptuous hips, bending over a fireplace. The glow from the hearth, and a handful of candles scattered throughout the large, rustic-looking room provided the only light to be had.

Why? Where was the electricity? Had he crossed some time warp?

Nothing was making any sense. Alain tried to raise his head, and instantly regretted it. The pounding intensified twofold.

His hand automatically flew to his forehead and came in contact with a sea of gauze. He slowly moved his fingertips along it.

What had happened?

Curious, he raised the comforter and sheet and saw he still had on his briefs. There were more bandages, these wrapped tightly around his chest. He was beginning to feel like some sort of cartoon character.

Alain opened his mouth to get the woman's attention, but nothing came out. He cleared his throat before making another attempt, and she heard him.

She turned around—as did the pack of dogs that were gathered around her. Alain realized that she'd been putting food into their bowls.

Good, at least they weren't going to eat him.

Yet, he amended warily.

"You're awake," she said, looking pleased as she crossed over to him. The light from the fireplace caught in the swirls of red hair that framed her face. She moved fluidly, with grace. Like someone who was comfortable within her own skin. And why not? The woman was beautiful.

Again, he wondered if he was dreaming.

"And naked," he added.

A rueful smile slipped across her lips. He couldn't tell if it was light from the fire or if a pink hue had just crept up her cheeks. In any event, it was alluring.

"Sorry about that."

"Why, did you have your way with me?" he asked, a hint of amusement winning out over his confusion.

"You're not naked," she pointed out. "And I prefer my men to be conscious." Then she became serious. "Your clothes were all muddy and wet. I managed to wash them before the power went out completely." She gestured about the room, toward the many candles set on half the flat surfaces. "They're hanging in my garage right now, but they're not going to be dry until morning," she said apologetically. "If then."

He was familiar with power outages; they usually lasted only a few minutes. "Unless the power comes back on."

The redhead shook her head, her hair moving about her face like an airy cloud. "Highly doubtful. When we lose power around here, it's hardly ever a short-term thing. If we're lucky, we'll get power back by midafternoon tomorrow."

Alain glanced down at the coverlet spread over his body. Even that slight movement hurt his neck. "Well, as intriguing as the whole idea might be, I really can't stay naked all that time. Can I borrow some clothes from your husband until mine are ready?"

Was that amusement in her eyes, or something else? "That might not be so easy," she told him.

"Why?"

"Because I don't have one."

He'd thought he'd seen someone in a hooded rain slicker earlier. "Significant other?" he suggested. When she made no response, he continued, "Brother? Father?"

She shook her head at each suggestion. "None of the above."

"You're alone?" he questioned incredulously.

"I currently have seven dogs," she told him, amusement playing along her lips. "Never, at any time of the night or day, am I alone."

He didn't understand. If there was no other person in the house—

"Then how did you get me in here? You sure as hell don't look strong enough to have carried me all the way by yourself."

She pointed toward the oilcloth she'd left spread out and drying before the fireplace. "I put you in that and dragged you in."

He had to admit he was impressed. None of the women he'd ever met would have even attempted to do anything like that. They would likely have left him out in the rain until he was capable of moving on his own power. Or drowned.

"Resourceful."

"I like to think so." And, being resourceful, her mind was never still. It now attacked the problem of the all-but-naked man in her living room. "You know, I think there might be a pair of my dad's old coveralls in the attic." As she talked, Kayla started to make her way toward the stairs, and then stopped. A skeptical expression entered her bright-green eyes as they swept over the man on the sofa.

Alain saw the look and couldn't help wondering what she was thinking. Why was there a doubtful frown on her face? "What?"

"Well..." Kayla hesitated, searching for a delicate way to phrase this, even though her father had been gone for some five years now. "My dad was a pretty big man."

Alain still didn't see what the problem was. "I'm six-two."

She smiled, and despite the situation, he found himself being drawn in as surely as if someone had thrown a rope over him and begun to pull him closer.

"No, not big—" Kayla held her hand up to indicate height "—big." This time, she moved her hand in front of her, about chest level, to denote a man whose build had been once compared to that of an overgrown grizzly bear.

"I'll take my chances," Alain assured her. "It's either that or wear something of yours, and I don't think either one of us wants to go that route."

It suddenly occurred to him that he was having a conversation with a woman whose name he didn't know and who didn't know his. While that was not an entirely unusual situation for him, an introduction was definitely due.

"By the way, I'm Alain Dulac."

Her smile, he thought, seemed to light up the room far better than the candles did.

"Kayla," she told him. "Kayla McKenna."

* * * * *

Don't forget **Capturing the Millionaire** *is available in October 2008.*

From the Number One *New York Times* bestselling author NORA ROBERTS

Stars
Containing the classic novels
Hidden Star **and** *Captive Star*
Available 5th September 2008

Treasures
Containing *Secret Star*, **the exciting final part in** *The Stars of Mirtha* **trilogy, plus a special bonus novel,** *Treasures Lost, Treasures Found*
Available 7th November 2008

Don't miss these two sparkling treasures!

FREE!

4 Books
and a surprise gift!

We would like to take this opportunity to thank you for reading this Mills & Boon® book by offering you the chance to take FOUR more specially selected titles from the Special Edition series absolutely FREE! We're also making this offer to introduce you to the benefits of the Mills & Boon® Book Club—

- ★ **FREE home delivery**
- ★ **FREE gifts and competitions**
- ★ **FREE monthly Newsletter**
- ★ **Exclusive Mills & Boon Book Club offers**
- ★ **Books available before they're in the shops**

Accepting these FREE books and gift places you under no obligation to buy. you may cancel at any time. even after receiving your free shipment. Simply complete your details below and return the entire page to the address below. You don't even need a stamp!

YES! Please send me 4 free Special Edition books and a surprise gift. I understand that unless you hear from me. I will receive 6 superb new titles every month for just £3.15 each. postage and packing free. I am under no obligation to purchase any books and may cancel my subscription at any time. The free books and gift will be mine to keep in any case. E8ZEF

Ms/Mrs/Miss/Mr ....Initials............................

BLOCK CAPITALS PLEASE

Surname ....

Address..

....

....Postcode ....

Send this whole page to:
UK: FREEPOST CN81, Croydon, CR9 3WZ